I0597807

FIREBIRD SERIES – BOOK THREE

THE GIRL WITH A DRAGON'S HEART

DAWN FORD

Published by Expanse Books,
an imprint of Scrivenings Press LLC
15 Lucky Lane
Morrilton, Arkansas 72110
https://ScriveningsPress.com

Printed in the United States of America

Paperback ISBN 978-1-64917-383-6

eBook ISBN 978-1-64917-384-3

Editors: Erin R. Howard and Linda Fulkerson

Cover design by Linda Fulkerson - www.bookmarketinggraphics.com

To Lori. God knew writing was in my destiny. You took me along for the ride and opened my eyes to the possibilities. What a precious gift and friend you are.

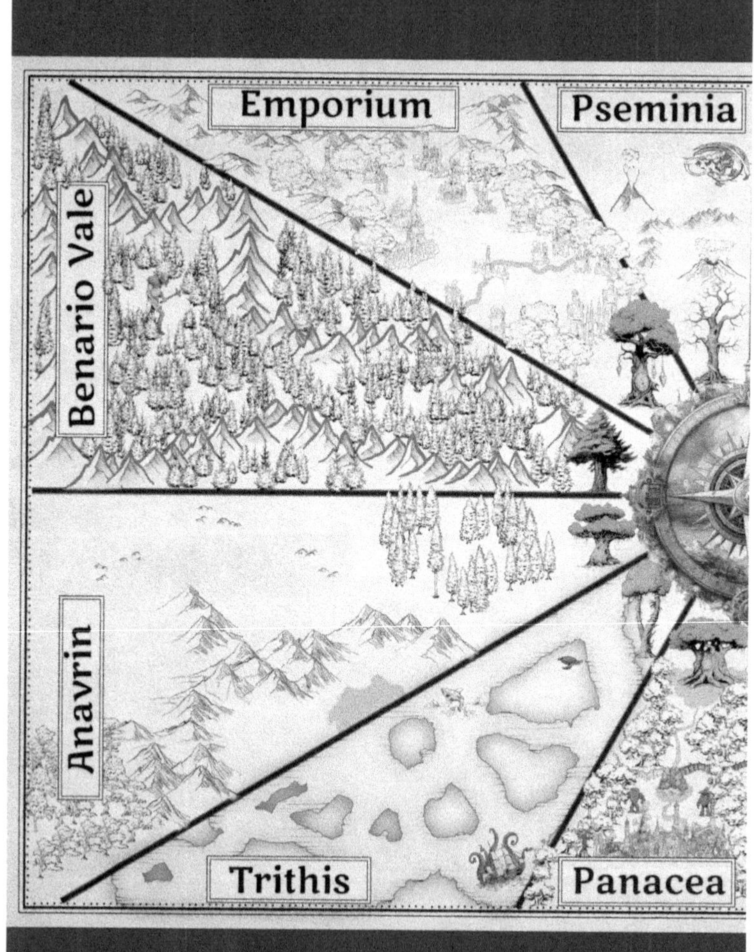

Emporium
Pseminia
Benario Vale
Anavrin
Trithis
Panacea

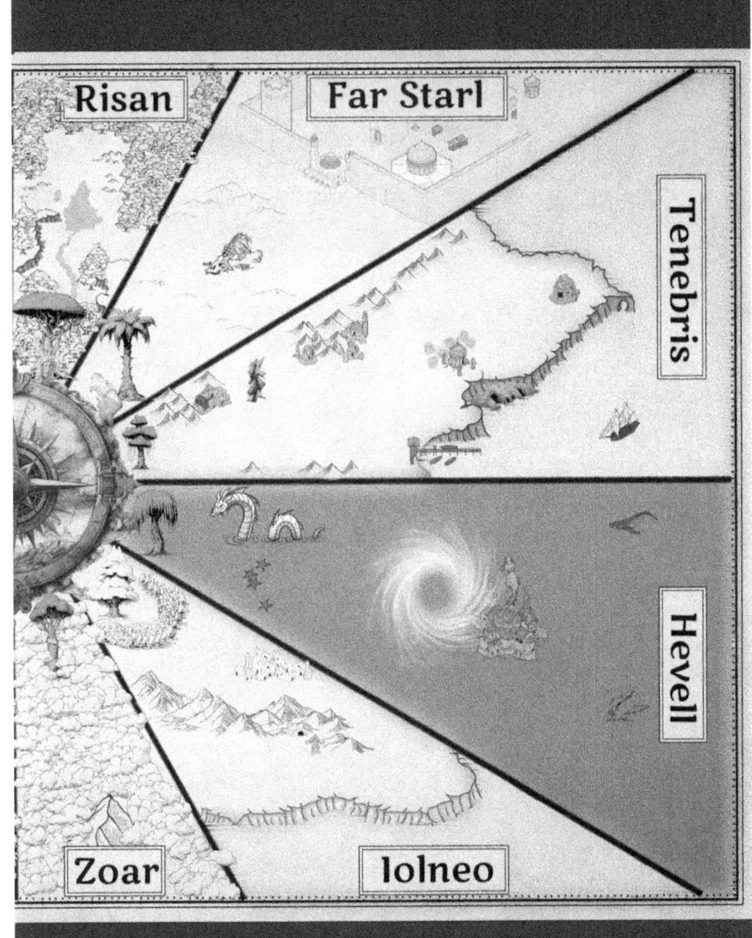

Risan
Far Starl
Tenebris
Hevell
Zoar
Iolneo

ACKNOWLEDGMENTS

As a writer, I must thank God first and foremost for gifting me with this story and then trusting me to play it all out. It was He who placed the characters and their story in my heart. I was immersed in this twisted fairy tale from the beginning and each time after as I worked with Tambrynn to bring her story to life.

For my readers, it has been a wild ride with many ups and downs. For those of you who sent me comments about how much you enjoyed The Firebird series so far, you lift me up higher than I thought possible. You make my journey worthwhile. I am humbled by your words of encouragement. I hope The Girl With the Dragon's Heart, takes you on a deeper journey with Tambrynn and Lucas, along with Bennett, Audhild, and Rekspire. I pray it's worth the time you spend with them. As always, if the story manages to pull you in for the ride, my job as an author is successful.

For Jennifer Rupprecht, thank you for your editing expertise. You rock! Thank you also to Drew Torres for the maps you've made for this series. They are incredible.

And to Linda Fulkerson and all the staff of Expanse and Scrivening's Press, I am humbled by your belief in me and this story. It is a part of my heart and soul, something I trust to very few. You all are amazing, and I'm so glad to be on this journey with you.

Part One

1

I gasp at the sight before me.

The Bloodthorn Forest's trees obliterate the horizon with trunks as big around as houses. They stretch-up into an endless blue sky, and an urge to fly into the branches which reach into clouds almost overtakes me.

"It's magnificent, isn't it, Tambrynn, Lucas?" A grin splits Grandfather's face.

My grip on Lucas's arm tightens as I glance up, up, up. I almost tip over backward as I take it in. Though we'd seen these trees from afar as we traveled here, standing beneath one makes me seem as small as an ant in the dirt.

A wave of dizziness hits me. I almost fall over taking in the astounding height of the trees. Or is it because of my injury—the actual reason we are in this forest? Though I'm over my fear of water since the flood, the injury I suffered when my father's cursed talisman broke remains. It worsens with each day that passes. The only consolation I have is the cure the Guardian Theocles gave me.

That cure centers on a specific ingredient found only in this forest. I pray silently, not for the first time, that Theocles was right, and it will work.

"Wow, Bennett." Lucas glances at my grandfather, awe clear in his wide-eyed gaze. His enthusiasm is catching, and I smile at them. "You said the trees reached to the heavens, but I didn't realize you meant it so literally."

"How is it possible for anything to be this massive?" I let go of Lucas and step around the trunk, which would take four or five people to reach around the base. Or three dragons. I'm stunned by the beauty, and I almost forget the pain from my injury.

Wrinkles that grandfather gained from our last adventure ease, and his body visibly relaxes. "Each kingdom has wonders to it. This is one of Anavrin's greatest marvels." He takes a deep breath and lets it out. "I love the smell of this forest. Madrigal used to rub a lotion made with oil from these leaves on her skin. It was better than any perfume ever produced."

My heart pricks at the wistful tone in his voice. He proved how much he loved his late wife, my grandmother, Madrigal. If only I could remember her, but I was only a babe when we left Anavrin all those years ago.

Rich loam mixes with a startlingly sweet cleanness that surprises me. It's less pungent than fir trees, but somehow more refreshing. We traveled several days to get here, and each step took us higher. We traveled farther above Grandfather and Audhild's keep. It's astonishing the ease I'm able to breathe here compared to the mountains.

"Why don't they use the lotion more often then?" I gaze at the spikes that cover the trunks. They're longer than the length of my hand and wide enough to grip and climb, though only if one was brave.

"Unlike you and Lucas, most people cannot fly up above the thorns to get to the leaves." He raises his hand and points with a clawed fingernail. "It's easily twenty-five feet before the first branch. Imagine an eldrin trying to climb that."

Lucas laughs. "Only a few djinn can get up there. Most of my kind aren't able to master using bird's wings and flying, so they stick to easier forms to change into. And I imagine squirrels aren't even mad enough to climb up these trees." He prods one of the less sharp-looking thorns and comes away with a cut and bloodied finger.

Grandfather grunts. "And no eldrin would trust a djinn with something so priceless. Eldrin only get the oil from the leaves when a limb has fallen, and they have to get them before the leaves die. Bloodthorn trees are hearty. Their roots entangle with other trees, which keep them all stable. It's incredibly rare to acquire."

Heat from my wound shoots through my body. It surprises me so much I take a step back to keep my balance. I wince as the pain intensifies and turn so no one will witness my expression and be alarmed. My breath is shaky, and I clench my fists to maintain control. The flashes are new, nearly consuming me from the inside out. Terrified is too simple a word to describe the panic that races through my body. It takes me a moment to fight it back.

"My lady, are you okay?" Lucas is instantly at my side.

I raise my hand to stop him. I burned him yesterday when he tried to help me. "I'm fine." Blue flames lick at my skin, running along the surface like fire on kerosene. They're harmless to me. However, I'm afraid of hurting anyone who comes near. Luckily, the flames disappear within moments. My wound is throbbing, becoming cold and numb, which I'm sure is not a good sign.

Grandfather, oblivious to my discomfort, limps around one of the gray-barked trees. "Lucas, you're our only hope. I'll need at least a dozen of the leaves—"

A tall man with wide shoulders steps out from a copse of smaller trees. A rocky ridge runs behind him, leading to dark mountains. He's as tall as us, but brawny with tanned skin. A treller. "What do you trespassers think you're doing in our forest?"

His words have a strange accent, as if he is talking around a mouthful of food. He holds the end of a long saw.

Grandfather stands straighter and eyes the tool. "Last I knew, no one owns Bloodthorn Forest. Not even the eldrin." His smile becomes toothy, showing his not-so-eldrin appearance on purpose. Without his rutch to disguise him, he's taken to scaring anyone who tries to cross our paths.

Startled, the man steps backward, but the saw keeps going, stopping him. He scowls as two others step out of the shrubbery, carrying the rest of the massive saw. They're taller than him and broader chested.

"What have we got here, boys? Intruders?" The third man drops the saw and speaks, his words as thick and rolled as the first man's. He steps in front, pushing the other two aside. A double-sided axe sticks out from behind his left shoulder. His eyes glitter with a hint of defiance and violence. "If you've come to fill the order, you're too late. We've signed a contract with Domicus, and these trees are ours to harvest."

Harvest? He can't mean they're going to cut down these exquisite trees.

Lucas moves in front of me, yet off to the side enough to remain safe from any sudden flare I might experience. Images of an area outside of Anatolia cross my mind. Great swaths of a forest destroyed there, with only the trunks left behind like wooden carcasses across the land.

Though the flames had gone, my veins heat to boiling with the thought of these men destroying this perfect forest. "No one's trespassing. What is it with men in a forest thinking they are kings of the land?" I speak not only to the men, but I mindspeak it to Audhild, who is above us, scouting the area. I reach for the dagger at my hip and the movement triggers a stab of pain to my side. Tears gather in my eyes, but I manage not to let them fall.

"That's because we are, missy. Kings of this forest. And we don't appreciate poachers come to steal our treasures." The second man knocks the other two to the side with his elbows and moves to get in my face. Two broad axes stick out over his shoulders, and he carries a knife sheathed to his thigh.

Audhild's screech gets the treller's attention. A shadow above us circles and she drops out of the air between our group and the lumbermen's. She changes from a marvelous red dragon to a dark-skinned, shriveled woman. She's not as imposing as she had been before my father tried to change her, but she is still fierce. "Is there a problem, youngling?"

Though she's lost some of her regal stature, she is still a head taller than the men. The first one drops the saw handle, his hands shaking. He swipes them down his checkered shirt. His companions shift so they're behind him now. Stupidly undaunted, he frowns at Audhild. "Who're you?"

Audhild grins—a beautiful, terrible sight. "Your worst nightmare." She snaps her elongated, wolfish teeth, and the men jump and turn, leaving their tool without another word. I wonder how they can run with such sharp axes next to their heads. However, if they were up to what I fear they were, I have no remorse for any injuries they sustain.

"Do you think that was necessary?" Grandfather asks. "They're going to report back to Domicus, and we saw how powerful he's become in such a short time. We'll be lucky we don't get stopped anywhere near Anatolia now."

Audhild laughs. "I do hope so. It's been so long since I've had an eldrin for dinner."

Rekspire lands beside her, his black dragon form changing to that of a tall, dark-haired man. "It's not nice to tease the lesser beings, oh, Sovereign." Though teasingly said, he moves so he is between us and Audhild.

She only grins in response, and I wonder at her state of mind since she was hit with my father's Mortuus Irrepo curse. She was temporarily turned into a sluagh, an undead beast, before Rekspire had taken her down. It also hasn't been long since my bracelet released her from his hold, and I still wasn't sure of the lasting effects it has. Though Grandfather showed no signs of ill will, Audhild was much more dangerous if she fell back under my father's influence.

"Shielding your thoughts, youngling?" She spins to face me, her jaw less prominent than when she addressed the men. Her aura, however, darkens.

I narrow my gaze at her. "You taught me yourself how to do so."

"Ah, yes, so I did. However, your thoughts were louder than a hoard walking on dried leaves just moments before."

Lucas steps between us, his chest puffed out much like his magpie form. "Is there a reason you're being so confrontational?"

Audhild hisses and drops her head. "No. I'm afraid I still have a few residuals of the mage's spell that lurk. Though I get surly, I wouldn't act on any of the urges that whisper to me."

I knew the compulsions and experienced the whispers briefly. I understood the way they shifted my thoughts and emotions. Heat flares to life inside me once more, making my wound throb harder. I cringe but am relieved when I remain standing.

I take a moment to gather my thoughts. Audhild's aura clears, heartening me to the truth of her words. "I'm glad to hear you're still under your own control. Let's get on with what we came here for. The sooner we get my wound healed, the better." And maybe then the hot flashes would be gone at last.

I exchange a glance with Lucas as we follow Grandfather into the giant forest. He says nothing, though I detect his concern over our dragon friend's well-being.

"I have never seen trees like these." Rekspire's head swivels from one trunk to another, all of which are covered with thorns. "They are magnificent, but deadly."

"You don't have Bloodthorn trees on Far Starl?" I ask, curious.

"Our trees are not nearly as magnificent and leafy as they are here. Because of the heat, the only trees that survive are succulent ones, which have sharp, needle-like fronds. They can hold water in their leaves, which allows them to survive the arid atmosphere. It's why I was so enthralled with Anavrin when I first arrived. I flew everywhere to see all I could. Far Starl is much different." He glances up. "How many leaves do we need?"

"As many as you can carry. You, too, Lucas." Grandfather speaks over his shoulder. His limp is becoming more pronounced with each day we hike.

I'm not much better with the wound spreading down my right side. My arms itch to join them up in the trees, but since we'd fixed the Zoe Tree's doorway, I'm not strong enough to change. I didn't want to alarm anyone, but the pain and the flashes are getting worse. And they are harder to hide. I pray silently that the cure the Guardian Theocles gave me would do what he said—heal me.

Lucas changes and flies up and out of sight. Rekspire changes as well, and I watch his body circle around until he reaches the area above the thorns. There he lands on a regular tree trunk-sized limb and disappears into the green foliage.

"Youngling, I sense great pain coming from you. And

something more." Concern deepens the creases in Audhild's face.

Grandfather snaps his head in my direction. "Are you all right, Granddaughter?"

Of all the times for Audhild to speak in front of Grandfather instead of mind-sharing. I want to grumble at her, but I sense concern coming from her.

"It's—the pain is getting worse," I admit. I slump down to sit on an old log that's heavily covered with moss, lichen, and half-moon-shaped mushrooms that grow out of the rotting wood. I rub at the bark, which crumbles beneath my fingers.

Audhild turns toward Grandfather. "There's something else. A darkness along the edges of her being." She turns back to me. "Do you feel any different?"

I'm unsure what to make of her change of attitude. The swing from violent and bloodthirsty to caring and concerned is disconcerting. Besides, I have ideas of what it could be, however, I'm not ready to share those ideas yet. "Different, how?"

She gazes at me with her animalistic eyes. It's almost as if she is trying to get inside my mind. I maintain the shield over my thoughts. I don't want her to know my deepest fear. That the curse from my father's talisman is still there, waiting to strike. Though the eel died during our battle, and we thought the Memento Mori curse broken, I fear it isn't completely gone.

I have been careful not to show anyone the damaged area because it has changed from an open red wound to a seeping, death-like black. Each time I experience a heated flash, it grows, spreading down my leg and across my back. Soon it will advance throughout my body.

If this cure doesn't work, I suspect it is only a matter of time before the curse kills me.

2

It's dark by the time we gather all the ingredients for the healing paste. Thankfully, the trellers haven't returned, though I'm sure they're watching us. I have other things, bigger things, to worry about, however.

Grandfather grinds the fire rock, or lava, as Rekspire calls it, with a mortar and pestle. It leaves behind an ashy powder that reminds me of the soot I used to rub into my silver hair to hide it.

Lucas gathers sticks for a fire as I set the last stone in place to seal our campsite from sight. "*Nineno, arodente, ebargofiant.*" The displacement spell snaps into place around a large area, leaving us in a quiet bubble.

"You're getting better each time you work the spells. Stronger." Grandfather's smile is genuine, and I warm at his praise.

"Thank you." I move to sit back on the tree stump at the center of our camp. "What does the fire rock do, exactly?"

"It removes impurities from wounds, draws infections

out." He moves on to the leaves and scrapes them, the oil dripping into the ashy-looking rock powder. A sweet perfume fills the air.

The scent is invigorating and pleasant. "I see what you mean by the perfume of these." I take one of the used leaves and rub it on my skin.

Next in is the blood-red sap he and Lucas gathered from an already scarred tree. I'm excited about trying the mixture. The color reminds me of Audhild's skin when she's in her woman form.

"Now, you'll have to use this before the sap solidifies and becomes impossible to spread." Grandfather stirs it round and round, scrapes his flat metal utensil on the bowl's side, then stirs it again. He dips his finger in and rubs it into his coarse skin. "That should do it."

The sudden realization that I now must undress to use the paste momentarily makes my heart skip a beat. "Where—"

"This way, youngling." Audhild, who had been leaning against a pine tree, takes the mortar and strides off past our protective barrier. She stops to glance back at me. "I won't forget where we are. I found a stream when we were searching for the fire rock. There were no fishkin anywhere in sight. You'll be perfectly safe. Come along."

I'm unsure if I want to be alone with the fire dragon, but I also don't want to be alone on the outside of our site, either. I follow her as quickly as my aching body allows. It's not far, but I'm exhausted by the time we reach the stream. The dark water glitters under a partial moon, which doesn't ease my anxiety.

"Wash in the water first. A clean wound will help the lotion do its job." She must notice my reluctance, for she huffs and turns toward me. "There's no danger here."

"I'm no longer afraid of water, thanks to your swim outfit." I hug my arms to my chest.

"Then what is your reluctance?" Her voice has turned sharp, putting me on edge.

"I'm unused to anyone seeing me—"

Her groan cuts me off. "Modesty. I should've known."

"It's not only that." I stand awkwardly on a rocky beach, unsure how to proceed. After a few moments of deliberation, I realize I can't hide it any longer. I peel off the slick eldrin pants, extra careful around where the skin is open and weeping in the center, which sticks to the cloth. It stings and the cool evening air sends zings of torture throughout the festering wound. I slip out of the shoes and stand, feeling more vulnerable than I have since I'd faced the swamp witch.

I squeal just enough to catch Audhild's attention. Her too-keen eyes gaze at my side even as I limp into the water. "You didn't tell us how bad it is. Do you not trust us after all the time we've been together?"

"It's not about trust. I didn't want to worry anyone." I cup water in my palm and gently wash out the middle, gritting my teeth against the agony. My hands shake, and I bend over and weep. I can't help it. There's no stopping the tears.

Cool hands grip my shoulders. "You should've said something. Rekspire could've tried to fly you here."

I shake my head. "He's not strong enough to bring me this far."

"No, but he could've taken you part of the way, eased your burden by some measure." She makes a deep, throaty clicking sound. "No one expects you to be indestructible. Even dragons have their limits, Tambrynn, as I've proven. Let us help you so you're strong enough to face your father."

Guilt weighs heavily on my chest. "After you suffered my father's curse, I saw how much it affected Grandfather. Rekspire too. And after the battle with the Hulda and then the fight with the eel, I couldn't make Lucas worry more about me than he already does."

"Ah, but you see, we *are* going to worry about you, because we care. How are we to help you when you aren't honest? Have you not heard that a shared burden is lighter than one you keep to yourself, youngling? Come. Sit on this boulder so I can minster to you." Her thin face is grim, though her eyes glow with emotion. Or is it tears? Do dragons cry?

Before I can inquire, heat singes my right side, flying across my body in a heartbeat. I gasp, clench my fists against the sensation, and am relieved when it leaves me. The warmth is gone as fast as it sprung up, leaving me limp.

Audhild helps me out of the cold water and back onto the shore, barefooted, where I stumble over the uneven rocks to sit on a somewhat flat slab of stone near the edge. I tremble from the chill but do not call upon my fire to warm myself lest it lead to another flare.

"I've never seen a fire creature's inner fire act this erratically. At least we are getting it tended to. Now, let me try to sanitize the area with fire." She holds her hand up as I open my mouth to protest. "Just enough to burn off anything that shouldn't be there. Your fire might not be doing what it should at this point."

She summons a ball of orange flames in her hand. She rubs her palms together, dispersing the fire, and then places them on my side.

At first, it burns, but the sensation changes to a manageable sting.

"There. That should do it. Now hold still while I apply the lotion." Instead of using her clawed hands, she produces a flexible wooden spatula wrapped in a thick chunk of moss. She dips it into the dark paste and swipes a generous amount across the edge. "Moss has many useful benefits in healing. Fingernails hold many bacteria and other unseen particles that are unsafe."

"I don't know what bacteria are," I mutter as she makes the first sweep of paste across my skin. Stabs of pain assault my nerves in a rush, and I struggle to stay sitting on the stone.

"Bacteria are what's making this injury infected. I could've treated the wound with something had I known about it," Audhild murmurs as she coats my side well beyond the jagged abscess. She unwraps the moss from the utensil and places it over the lotion, tying it off with thin scraps of white cloth. Around that, she weaves in some leaves, sealing the dressings into place.

"You seem to be quite prepared." I redress, slipping my pants over the bandaged area as painlessly as possible. Luckily, the fabric stretches to fit without restricting me.

"I have not lived hundreds of years to not understand how to tend to injuries." She wraps up the extra leaves into a rolled ball, putting them back in a pocket in her outer jacket. "And I figured you would not want a man touching you in that area. Was I wrong?"

My face heats as I think of Lucas doing what she just did. I cross my arms and glance away from her. "No."

Her chuckle reveals she guessed my thoughts. "I once was a young dragon besmirched with all the hormones and feelings that come with lust and love. Or did you think you are the only one?"

My cheeks flush as I put my slippers back on. "I didn't think any such thing. Grandfather loved Grandmother. I've seen people in love. It's just nothing I've ever experienced before."

Audhild joins me and we make our way back to the

campsite. "So, you are in love with Lucas, not just bonded with him?"

Was I? Wasn't I? "Of course, I love Lucas."

"Tell him, then. After your father killed Halvar, my mate, I had no chance to tell him how I felt. Dragons don't rely on feelings after all. And most mates only join for biological reasons to keep our species alive. But it was more for us. We had a deeper connection. In all the years we were together, I never said I love you." She shrugs her thin shoulders and turns to me. "I will regret that until my death."

We're silent until we reach our camp. Thankfully, Audhild leads the way or I might not have found it in the dark.

"Well?" Grandfather asks. He sits on a log that Lucas dragged past the barrier to sit on. Rekspire sits to his right and Lucas to his left. There's another log on the other side of the fire pit.

"Well, what, old man?" Audhild remains stoic, but I can tell she likes to tease my grandfather. "It will be some time before we see results. It was a curse, after all."

I'm grateful she doesn't tell everyone about how bad my side has become.

Lucas strides over to me. He takes my hand in his and leads me to the empty place and thoughtfully sits on my uninjured side. "We saved you some food." He hands me a plate.

"Thank you." The fire is warm, as is the food which Lucas secured from an old half-djinn lady in a small village we skirted a day and a half ago. We traded some berries and mushrooms for a container of beans and rice with shredded venison and a thick gravy. It is delicious and filling, even though we've been rationing it.

I can't think of anywhere I'd rather be than right here at this moment, despite the pain. I reassure myself it is almost over. The Guardian's cure is in place. I just have to wait for it to heal now. I drink in the contentment of being among those I care the most about.

Suddenly, my necklace heats, warning me of danger.

Howls break the stillness. My father's beasts have found us.

I jerk my head toward the sound. It isn't far. How did we not notice them until now?

Audhild and Grandfather both drop to the ground, thrashing and moaning. Only my father has this kind of effect on them, from the Mortuus Irrepo hex, which turns anyone he uses it on into his undead slave-beast.

Seconds later, the sluaghs arrive, sniffing and circling the trees. Lucas's arm tightens around me.

"Oh, darling daughter of mine." Thoron steps out from behind two large, hulking animals. They're more beastly than any I've witnessed before. Thoron's image wavers beneath a shimmering haze, not unlike an illusion, but it's more material than supernatural. He holds the glowing Eye of Fate, the stolen gauntlet on his hand. "I know you're here, and I know why you're here. I also know your little hidey trick."

The scepter emits a menacing hum. He raises it, and a crackling energy snaps from the stones. "Come out, and I won't hurt anyone else."

"Don't believe him, my lady." Lucas stands stiffly beside me.

"Tambrynn, the stones. Stronger." Grandfather's voice is growly, his body jerking.

I move around the perimeter and, instead of stating the obfuscation spell, I *command* the words. However, I'm unsure if it's working since both Audhild and Grandfather change—their faces contorting and disfiguring. I move faster, yelling the spell. Lucas joins me from the other side while Rekspire watches over Audhild and Grandfather.

I'm exhausted when I rejoin Lucas at my starting point. A loud pop resounds, and we're knocked to the ground.

I land on my right side. A scorching flash engulfs me, as does pain. I shriek as fear blinds me.

I'm burning alive.

The fire I've come to depend upon consumes me with an excruciating wave. In the madness, I sense my father, beckoning the flames on—willing them to devour me whole. A high-pitched note penetrates my ears, and I realize it's my screams.

I can't view Lucas. I can't sense him.

The only thing I feel is torment.

Oh, Kinsman. Please don't let me die this way. I beg it over and over in my mind.

I struggle to breathe. Dots dance in the darkness of my sight. My body moves of its own accord. I have no control over it.

A cool, sweeping breeze washes over me. Gray mist, like a watery shadow, reaches out from the air toward me. *"I am here. Take my hand, Tambrynn."*

The voice is steady. And it's female.

"Mother?"

"I'm going to break his hold on you. Now, Tambrynn. Take my hand."

Closing my eyes, I shut out the furious heat and realize my hand is clutching my necklace, my knuckles white. I take a moment to unfurl my fingers, and then I'm reaching out. Dim voices are like whispers in the wind, some urging me on, others urging the fire to end me.

An aching, frigid hold freezes my hand in place. The searing ice crackles up my arm and across my body. *"Breathe."*

For a moment, I witness a dark-haired woman with tanned skin. Her brown eyes are not my mother's, though they are kind. She is plain, with nothing striking about her to become memorable. Her essence is there and then gone, as is her ghostly presence.

Astralee? Could it be her? No, it wasn't. Her essence isn't the same. This woman's aura is alive in too many ways, where Astralee's was—not.

I gasp. The fire is gone. I'm on my back, dirt and debris covering me as if I have been rolling on the ground. My skin is untouched by the fire, though I'm sure my flesh is no longer there.

Lucas grabs me, and I'm yanked into his embrace. "Tambrynn. Are you all right?" He thrusts me back away, his eyes sweeping me from top to bottom. "You were on fire. How—?"

"Well, youngling, if she had been on fire, throwing yourself at her would not have been the best choice." Audhild pushes him out of the way. "What happened?"

Fear that the inferno will return makes me scoot back away from them. "I don't know. When I fell, I landed on my injured side, and then—" I wave my hand up and down as if to explain the blazing onslaught.

"Yes, but you reached for something, said a word I couldn't understand. Suddenly, the fire disappeared." Her animalistic eyes dilate, and she squints at me. "Something happened. I felt it, but I couldn't see it."

I hesitate. How can I explain? "Someone came to me after I prayed not to die." I swivel to lean more comfortably, away from my throbbing side. "A presence came to me. Told me to fight and to take their hand. So, I did."

"Do you know who it was? Was it Astralee? You said she saved you once." Grandfather joins us. Sweat glistens on his forehead.

I run my fingers through my dirty hair. "No, it wasn't her. I would've known. It was someone else. Someone full of ice."

"I'm glad they saved you." He sits crossed-legged next to my uninjured side. His concern and fear stretch through our bond. "Whoever it was."

I nod. "But, if it's not Astralee, then who could it be? How can anyone else travel through the Betwixt?"

"I've only heard of guardians or strong voyants moving freely in the spirit realm. Voyants can reach out with their visions, but none that I know of have ever had contact with anyone in the visions. They only witness them." Audhild motions for me to come back to the firepit.

Rekspire sits on one log, quietly watching us, an unreadable expression on his face. Anxiety and fear radiate off him.

Lucas is on his feet before I can think to stand.

I take his hand, stand, and drop it. "I don't want to hurt you."

His smile is the same mischievous one I adore. "I would walk through fire to save you, my lady."

"I know. And I would die to save you from it. So, I fear we are at an impasse." I lightly tap his arm with the tips of my fingers. A pang twists inside my chest. I thought after I put the paste on, I'd recover. However, this has been the worst flash so far. How long before I am free from these unwanted flames?

I glance around. "Where'd my father and his pets go?" Instead of viewing a forest through a light haze of the spell, there's only an impenetrable milky wall around the area we'd created for our campsite.

"I'm unsure. After you reset the displacement spell, everything out there disappeared." Grandfather waves his hand toward the border as he sits down next to Rekspire, patting his leg.

Lucas takes a seat on the log opposite the other two, and Audhild sits on the ground. I gently rest next to Lucas. The space between my shoulders pinches, and I stretch to ease the discomfort. "Is that a good thing or a bad thing?"

Grandfather grunts. "I don't know. It's never happened to me before. Not even at my keep. I don't know what power you put in that spell, but it blocked your father and his beasts fully." His stubble bristles as he rubs his hand across his face. "You're becoming more powerful each day."

Lucas rubs my back and then slips over to the ring to build a fire. "It couldn't have happened at a better time. I thought your father was going to come through the barrier."

Fear at what I may have unintentionally created makes my heart race. "Will we be able to take it down and leave?" Another thought hit me. "How will we know Thoron's gone?" I drop my head into my hands. "What have I done?"

"You saved us," Rekspire speaks for the first time. "Your heart is strong. As strong as that of any worthy dragon. You did what any good leader would do if they could, though few of us are as capable as you are becoming. Thank you."

Audhild stares at him for a moment before turning toward me. "Fear not, youngling. Thoron is not a patient man. Even if we must wait, it won't be for long."

We eat the last of the supplies Lucas traded for. Though I try to get comfortable, the discomfort from my injury makes it impossible to relax. Each time I rest in one spot long enough to make it warm, I panic and relocate to a cooler area. So far, I've shifted around six times.

Our campsite isn't big enough to keep moving, so I sit up and lean against one of the oak trees. The bark bites into my back as the ground numbs my bottom. Through it all, my side thrums and aches.

Lucas lays on his stomach on an eldrin-made mat beside Grandfather, who has a separate mat. He sleeps fitfully, flopping around almost as much as I do. It's warm—too warm, Grandfather claimed—to lie inside a tent, so they didn't set it up. Little breeze moves inside our bubble. Will we run out of air?

Audhild lets out a loud sigh and rises from her spot near us. In the blink of an eye, she changes from her dragon form to her womanly one. "Can't sleep either?" she asks as she sits against a tree next to mine.

"Between the pain and fear that I'm going to burn to death by my firebird fire, no." I rub my tired eyes, now gritty from having too little sleep the last few days of travel. "Whatever I did made it impossible to see the moon, so I'm not even sure what time it is."

Despite not being able to view anything, she glances up to where the sky should be. "It's early morning, not quite sunrise yet."

Of course, she would know. "Aren't you tired?" Her eyes are baggy and lined more than normal. Perhaps my moving around had kept her from getting her full rest.

"I am used—" she says and then stops. "When I was

younger, I was used to smaller naps between activities. I will be fine." She twists her head to the side. "I sense a disturbance."

I reach out with whatever senses I have but notice nothing. My necklace is also cool, resting blandly at my throat. "Are you sure?"

Grandfather abruptly wakes. Rekspire snores and jerks, waking up. "Guardians?" he questions groggily.

"We have no guardians here." Grandfather's voice is gruff, his eyes alert.

Rekspire dusts dirt off his clothes. "Well, some kind of magic is happening on the other side of this camp."

"Is there any way to let the shield down, alerting no one to our presence?" Audhild whispers, her eyes closed and head still canted sideways.

Grandfather glances at me. "I don't know. I didn't wield the spell this time."

They all look at me except for Lucas, who remains asleep. I don't wish to wake him. The ache between my shoulder blades twinges. "Do we have to?"

A pulse washes across my senses. My necklace heats for a moment and then cools. I drop my head and twist my fingers through my unkempt hair, snagging them. It's all the answer I need.

Fear reflects in the whites of Grandfather's eyes. "Did you leave any blood behind when you put the antidote on your wound?"

Audhild gasps. "That's how he found us."

Alarm builds in my chest, squeezing my heart. "What do you mean?"

"Tambrynn, do you still have Thoron's gastrolith?" Grandfather scrambles closer to us.

"Lucas—"

Grandfather twists around and shakes Lucas's leg. "My boy, wake up. We have an emergency."

Lucas jumps to his knees. "What? What's going on?"

"The gastrolith." Grandfather stabs his hand out toward him.

Another wave of power ripples across us. The embers in the fire hiss, and sparks dart into the air.

Lucas digs into his pants pocket, handing Grandfather the dragon stone. "Is that Thoron's power?"

"It's the Eye of Fate." Audhild stands and wipes her hands down the hem of her shirt. "Possibly spelled with your blood to direct it into breaking the barrier to get to you."

My heart stutters. "Can he do that?"

Grandfather takes the stone and throws it into the glowing embers at the edge of the pit. "Not if we can stop him." He mutters a few words over the gastrolith. It emits a low whistle in the heat.

"You don't have everything you need to destroy it, old man." Audhild knocks it farther into the fire with her bare hand. "The curse might be gone, but it is still powerful enough to deflect simple spells."

"We're going to have to improvise." Grandfather's voice is rough. Determination shines from the depths of his dark eyes. The stone glows orange. He waits for it to get red hot and then stomps the fire out around it. He kicks it out of the pit. It darkens to black, like a coal.

He and Audhild exchange a look I can't read. He nods, and I'm surprised since I didn't know they could mindspeak to each other.

Grandfather picks the stone up. "Tambrynn, when I tell you to, pull the barrier down. Everyone, get ready. It will take all of us working together to overpower Thoron. And no matter what happens, don't let him capture you."

Fear becomes a hand around my heart, grabbing it and holding on tight. I stand stiffly, ignoring the pang from my still-healing side. My necklace warms as energy snaps around my hands.

"Circle around, younglings. We must have each other's backs." Audhild stands opposite me, facing the other direction.

Lucas changes into a large bird. His claws are long and sharp, and his head comes up to my waist. *"I'd change to a dragon if I could to protect you, my lady. This is the best I can do, at the moment."*

My breath hitches painfully, thinking of him going into danger once again. *"Please be careful."*

"Always."

Rekspire and Audhild change as well, leaving only Grandfather and me in our normal forms. I unclasp the dagger, and Grandfather holds an eldrin curved blade and a walking stick. I close my eyes and pray silently for protection.

Another barrage of energy shakes the ground beneath us. My barrier wavers.

"Now, Tambrynn." Grandfather calls out.

I reach out with my ability and *call.* As with the flood, it takes a moment for it to respond, but then the murky boundary clears, then drops. Noise explodes around us, as do gusts of furious energy that whip leaves and debris into a whirlwind.

The sun is only beginning to rise, and the light is hazy. However, the sight we're met with isn't one I expected. It's much worse.

4

Thoron is not alone. Surrounded and circled by his beasts, their mouths frothing and fur raised, another force stands before him.

The Hulda.

Shadows form a semi-circle around the swamp witch's back. Her bony hands resemble bent sticks on a thin limb. Though I don't witness her power, I sense it when she knocks my father's sluaghs aside as if they are flies to be swatted away.

Thoron screams out, the Eye of Fate raised high and smoking. Dark magic zings from the gems and sails right through the Hulda and her lost spirits.

She cackles in a high-pitched shriek. "No physical weapon can stop me, death mage. You know that."

"We had an agreement, witch. Kill me, and you perish as well." Thoron drops the ineffective scepter and the gauntlet. Crackling red magic bursts from his hands. With a flick, he sends it whining toward his opponent.

It knocks the witch back a step, but she recovers quickly. Her ghostly shadows gather closer, forming an erratic, flickering wall.

"We must get the scepter back before they notice us," Audhild whispers in our minds. Could the Hulda hear her?

I glance over at Grandfather, who stands mere feet from me. As soon as I make a move, they'll notice us. I don't want him harmed. He pays no mind to me, though. He locks his gaze on Thoron.

I reach out my hand and *call* in rapid succession. The Hulda jerks her head in our direction as I send out my demand to the scepter.

"No," she screams at us. She flings her other skeletal hand out, but it's not fast enough to stop the Eye of Fate from reaching me.

The gauntlet settles over my hand a moment before the metal scepter settles in its grip. "Stop," I yell at them.

Thoron waves his arm, slapping my request away. However, he slides back with the force of my demand.

The Hulda shrieks, and her ghostly army dashes toward me. Though unformed, red eyes hover where their eyes should be. Frost accumulates on the ground beneath their shapeless forms, the chill reaching me well before the first one gets close.

I gasp.

"Time to leave," Grandfather shouts. He has grabbed his pack and is stuffing his carved stones inside the outer pocket.

Rekspire and Audhild grab Grandfather's arms, swinging their wings wide to lift him into the air. His bag drops, but Lucas catches it in his large talons as his powerful body lifts into the air.

Pain from my side stabs me when I try to change. Before I can turn to run, I'm bound tight in a grip. I glance sideways at the Hulda where I sense the magical hold comes from. She clenches her hand, and my lungs tighten, choking me.

"We have unfinished business, firebird."

"No! She's mine to destroy." Thoron sends a spell out, lashing the Hulda.

She squeals and drops me.

I swallow air in great heaves.

Thoron flips a ball of black lightning my way. Six of his beasts break from him and dash toward me.

Gasping still, I yell, "Stop." I push as much of my ability into it as I can muster. My necklace is a hot coal at my chest, throbbing to the rapid beat of my heart.

My power clashes with Thoron's spell and the Hulda's magic. A blazing white light bursts from the meeting point. A moment of silence echoes before a mighty explosion rocks the area, assaulting my ears.

I'm airborne, without wings, and the impact of the blast rattles my bones. I'm hot and then cold. My nerves pop in different places across my body. And then, I'm dropping.

Too fast.

I catch sight of the ground coming at me.

I flail and brace myself for the impact.

Instead of the ground, I hit another body. Though softer than land, it isn't without impact. My shoulders jerk with the immediate halt, the motion crushing my chest.

We both tumble to the ground, though I still cannot tell who it is. My arms and legs entangle with theirs, and I struggle to get loose.

"Get up, youngling. We have no time to dawdle." Audhild pushes me off and uses a tree as a brace to rise.

I move to stand, but my right knee spirals with sharp stabs, and I tumble back to the ground. Black haze envelopes us.

Audhild makes a choking sound, and her body spasms. She's changing. Her eyes widen. *"He knows. Do not let him take me, youngling. Your very life is at stake. He'll use the Sovereign power against you. There's no stopping him this time."*

Her fervency alarms me. "What do you mean?"

"Take my essence before he can drain it out of me. It has to be you. You have to take my place." Audhild removes the bracelet I'd placed on her after my father changed her the first time. She slices one palm with a sharp fingernail, clasps her hands together with the bracelet, and breathes fire on them. Light bursts through the spaces between her entwined fingers.

"Go to the lighthouse. You'll find my true heart there." Audhild's words are breathy, her eyes glazed. *"I have loved you like my own child, Halvar's kin.* She holds out her hands, which have changed to beastly claws completely now.

I try to catch her as she falls, lifeless, to the ground. I *call* the scepter, but even with it, I cannot put any pressure on my right leg. All I manage is to catch the bracelet she drops. It's melted together and I clasp it tightly as I crawl closer to her.

Two beasts jump over me and grab Audhild by the arms. She's unmoving, her mouth open and eyes closed.

"Don't." I scream and jerk the scepter from beneath me,

pointing it at them. Light flashes from the gems, but it's weak —like I am.

They break away from a lifeless Audhild, shaking their head at the light. One of them snarls at me, his spit hitting my arm. Tossing the scepter to the ground, I instead summon the faint buzzing in my gut and *push*.

One beast falls sideways, losing its grip on Audhild. The other, however, drags her back around to where I sit, helpless, on the ground.

No hum remains in my gut. Nothing to call upon. I grab the metal handle of the scepter, not wanting the beast to reclaim it. My cheeks are wet as I use the metal pole to get to my feet. No, foot. I can stand on one foot only. The other knee radiates pain, and I cannot put my foot down fully.

The Hulda and Thoron continue to battle each other.

"My lady. We must get away before one of them captures you."

"I can't leave Audhild behind." I limp, screaming with each burning stab, back toward the beasts who drag Audhild to Thoron. Morning light is brightening now, and I can tell how pale she is.

Fear grips me as I realize she isn't moving at all. She couldn't be dead. Dragons are hard to kill.

One beast breaks out from behind a tree, and I swing the scepter, hitting it square in the side of the head. The sluagh squeals before dropping to the ground. Unable to stand without the scepter, I fall against another tree. I push past the unconscious creature. My teeth ache from clenching them against the agony radiating from my injuries. I continue, desperate to get to Audhild.

The Hulda hits Thoron with a shadowy spell. He raises from the ground, digging at his throat and wheezing.

I recall that spell, how it almost tore me in half, but there's no empathy for him. If anything, he deserves it.

Grabbing the necklace in my free hand, I raise the scepter while balancing on one unsteady foot. The Hulda turns toward me just as I'm ready to smack her in the back with my last remaining dregs of power. Though she has no lips, it looks as if she's smiling. I hold back, instead.

"She is mine now. The Sovereign is under my power." Another shadow, this one bigger and lighter than the others, joins the swamp witch. "I will rule over all the kingdoms with —" she shrieks. "Where'd it go? What have you done with it?"

I do not know what she means, so I don't answer. Dawn radiates golden rays. When I glance back at the last shadow—the one with the light—it's gone.

"*Audhild?*" My desperate entreaty comes out in one word. Only silence answers me.

"No. This can't be happening. Not after all my plans." The Hulda is incensed, her skeletal body swinging around as if she's lost something. She stops twisting and pins me with a glowing gaze from beneath her hood. "You!"

Behind her, Grandfather drops from the air on top of Thoron. I glimpse Rekspire's dark tail in the brilliant morning light. Immediately, three beasts are on top of my grandfather, dragging him off Thoron and over to the side. He resists, but his body changes even before Thoron gets up.

"*My lady, watch out.*" Lucas's screeing shout makes me wince. He darts at the witch, who deflects him. He tumbles to the ground and out of sight.

"*Lucas?*" I shift to move toward him, but I'm hit with a spell cast from the Hulda. My protective bubble sizzles and then is gone. All my power is gone. Intense cold envelopes me, numbing me, just like when I'd faced off with the death witch before. I shudder against the memory and the paralyzing chill.

Cackling, the Hulda floats toward me. "You thought you'd steal it, didn't you? You pathetic half-breed. Just because you were infused with dragon DNA before you were born does not allow you to become Sovereign."

I stiffen my back, knowing I have no power to defend myself, wishing I could get beyond the witch to reach Grandfather. There's no humming left in my gut. Even the necklace I wear is dormant, chilled against my skin. "I have no idea what you're talking about."

The sluaghs lift Grandfather, who has fully changed to his beastly form, before their master. Thoron glances sideways at me and grins. He murmurs something, and light from Grandfather leaves him and enters my father. It only takes moments before the light is gone, consumed.

Grandfather is gone. In his place is the thing I've feared since mother died.

A bloodthirsty beast.

"No," I scream, but it's too late. My knees buckle, and I drop to the ground, gritting my teeth. I clutch the scepter as if my life depends on it.

Maybe it does. I'm outnumbered and outmatched. And not only have I lost Audhild, but Grandfather as well. The pain in my right leg is nothing compared to the ache in my heart.

The beast dragging Audhild brings her to Thoron's feet.

"What is this?" he demands, striking it with magic, killing his pet. I sense a spirit depart as its body crumples to the ground. Wind rushes through the massive trees around us and then stills.

Shock makes me speechless. I thought the sluaghs were already dead.

How can this be?

Thoron kicks Audhild's body over. Her bestial face twists upward to the blue sky beyond the lush canopy of bloodthorn leaves. She'd been fiercely beautiful once. She was not any longer. "Save her. I'll feast on her bones later."

"You fool," the Hulda screams.

I'm not sure if she screams it at me or my father. But as the light of dawn quickly brightens, she vanishes along with her shadowy army of lost souls. In their absence, birds start chittering.

With a wide smile, my father turns toward me. "Join me, and I will release your grandfather." He holds out his hand and, like a puppet master, makes one of my grandfather's arms wave at me as if asking me to join them.

I glare hate at him, though something in my mind urges me to consider his request.

"*Don't do it, my lady. Bennett wouldn't want you to. Fight.*" Lucas's words break through the desperate voice's hold on my thoughts. "*Fight on behalf of their memory if not for any other reason.*"

I shake my head. Have I forgotten who I am? I don't make deals with froggen or mergirls. Nor do I negotiate with evil mages. Especially one who would so callously take the lives of those I love. I won't give in to him. Too much is at stake.

"*Lucas, help me change.*" I stare at my leering father, who stands so casually between my mentor and my grandfather. "I will never willingly turn myself over to you."

Thoron chuckles. "We'll see, daughter." He then growls, his face turning red. "Get her." He points and all his beasts, including Grandfather, rush toward me.

Cradling the melted bracelet and scepter to my chest, I lift my free hand.

Lucas swoops down and grips my fingers with his talons. Tingles sweep across my body as our mixed abilities work to change me. But it's not enough.

I squeeze his claw harder as the sluaghs are mere steps away—Grandfather in the lead. His dark eyes show no mercy, no love. He truly is gone.

"I love you, Grandfather," I say as I let him go in my mind.

In a last plea, I shout, "Please, Kinsman." I send all of my energy into my and Lucas's embrace. A flush sings through my body, and then I'm airborne—my wings spread wide.

Rekspire swoops in, landing on Audhild and grabbing her while I've distracted Thoron. His massive wings arc wide, shooting them both into the air.

Thoron throws a dark hex at the black dragon, but Rekspire dodges it at the last moment. And then we're out of range, above the massive forest, heading east.

Lucas screes out his satisfaction as we race off away from my father.

And my grandfather.

My heart is heavy, but I don't look back.

Red skies greet us as we land near Grandfather and Audhild's mountainous keep. We flew a wide arc around any populated area so as not to be seen, and it took most of the day to do so. My whole body aches more than I can express.

My heart is damaged more.

"Are you all right, my lady? All I can feel from you is pain." Lucas rubs my shoulder. Grandfather's pack is on the ground next to me where Lucas landed.

I sit, panting from both exhaustion and agony, the scepter and the mangled bracelet next to me. I manage a nod.

It all looks the same to me in my dazed state. I left it to them to find the correct mountain. However, now that we are here, we must locate the hidden opening.

Rekspire searches the perimeter. "Over here," he calls to us. Audhild's body lies near a rocky outcropping a short distance away.

Lucas helps me stand, places his shoulder beneath mine,

and helps me to walk over to where Rekspire gazes intently at the air. "What do you see, Chosen One?"

"Please ... don't... call me that." A chill has worked its way through my body, and my teeth chatter. My only relief is a numbness that accompanies the cold, which gives me a margin of blessed relief from the pain. I don't focus on how that is probably not a good sign.

"Audhild chose you. The Kinsman chose you. You are the chosen one." He reaches out but grasps nothing. "Can you spot the Wehyah Tree?"

I stand with Lucas's help and gaze around the area. At first, there's nothing. Then I catch a flicker in the corner of my eye. "Over there?" I point, and Lucas assists me closer to the area. Again, I take a couple of moments to search for it, but then I spot the old, gnarled tree wavering like it's there behind a disguise. "Here." Relief is fleeting when an icy shiver rocks me.

Lucas helps me past Grandfather's border, leaning me against the cavern doorway. He then retrieves the pack, the melted bracelet, and the scepter. The gauntlet remains on my hand, though I barely acknowledge it, the pain from my injuries taking up all of my concentration.

Rekspire reverently places Audhild in the area where we'd chained him when he attacked her. "We need to hide her where no one will find her and use her body for dark magic."

Is there such a safe place? If there is, I want to go there myself.

"For now, let's keep her in the cave. Tambrynn, can you help me put up another powerful barrier to keep anything out?" Lucas takes the stones from the pack and joins me at the doorway. "I'll place them if you help me recite the spell."

I try hard to recreate the dense protection I'd accomplished the previous night, my voice clogging as I recite the words. Has it only been a night? Using my sleeve, I swipe away the tears that dampen my face.

Lucas stands still, patiently waiting for me to realize my mind has drifted off into thoughts of the previous eve.

"This is difficult. Take your time. Unless Thoron has the eldrin's Apatestone necklaces, we have time." His eyes are red and his jaw clenched tight. He's suffering just as I am.

I take a deep breath and then recite the spell, "*Nineno, arodente, ebargofiant.*" I demand it and Lucas repeats it with me as we both lay a stone in place. When he reaches the other end of the opening, the spell pops into place, leaving our space dark.

Crackling light from Rekspire's magic helps me to locate the scepter. I tap it twice on the stone floor, and it lights up, a glow bouncing off the speckled rock walls and ceiling. The bracelet I hold tight to my chest.

Lucas heads to where he previously stacked some extra dried limbs, both small and large. "I'll build a fire." Within a few minutes, it's blazing, adding welcomed warmth to the air and allowing us all to move around freely in the now semi-illuminated space.

My eyes droop as exhaustion sets in. At some point, warm hands lift and carry me. I'm too tired to open my eyes to see what's happening, even though anxiety zings through my body, urging it to respond.

There are only darkness and nightmares.

———

The next morning, I awake with a start. My first realization is of water. I thrash, afraid whoever holds me is trying to drown me.

"Wait, stop, my lady. You're not well. Your body is freezing, and I'm only trying to warm you."

Lucas? Pain stabs my joints as the steamy air engulfs me.

"Should I help hold her?" Rekspire's voice comes from behind me. "She is afraid of water, isn't she?"

I stop jerking and the pain lessens. "What? What's happening? Where's the bracelet?"

Lucas sits me up on the edge of the pool. The sky is gray, though there are no clouds. "When we woke this morn, you were shivering in your sleep, and your gauntlet had fallen off. At first, I thought it might be nightmares, but I noticed your lips were blue. We tried to put a blanket on you, but you burned it off. We thought if we put you in the heated springs, it would help to warm you without incinerating anything else."

Anguish and fear radiate off Lucas in waves. Although steam rises from the clear water, the air is cool against my skin, and I quiver. I recall relaxing in the water before. At least until I remember the Mortifer Blade. I reach for the dagger, which is usually at my side, earning me a zing of fresh pain. "My dagger?" I bite the words out.

"It was in the pack." Water ripples as Rekspire walks into the hot depths near us.

"Do you want to try it? See if it warms you up?" Lucas's eyes are bright with eagerness. He's truly worried about me.

"Sure, yes. But, slowly, please." I can't stop the shake in my voice.

He nods and places one arm beneath my legs and the other at my back. "Hold on to me, my lady."

The water is pleasant on my chilled toes as Lucas walks gently into it. He moves until we are against the far side, away from where we'd sat before, and against a shelf that juts out. The water is warm, but its warmth doesn't reach inside of me. There's only a numb coldness.

Lucas places me to sit against the ledge where the water is waist-deep and scoots over to sit next to me. "Is that better?"

I run my hand through the heated liquid. It prickles at my skin like I'd been out too long in the snow. Like frostbite. His face is so earnest. I can't dash his hopes with the truth. "Possibly. Maybe I just need to soak a bit?"

Heat bursts from my injured side and pushes outward until flames lick at my skin, boiling the water around my waist. The fire is there, but I'm empty inside. I jerk away from Lucas, earning me a searing lick of pain.

He jumps away, and I'm glad that he isn't injured.

I dig my fingernails into my palms. "I'm so sorry. There was no time to warn you."

"Here, let me. I promise I'll keep her safe." Rekspire steps up to me with his arms out.

"What are you going to do?" I ask, anxious.

He puts his arms down. "There was this fire dragon on Far Starl who grew ill. His inner temperature became erratic, going from cold to hot without him being able to control it. One of our leaders took him to the pits. That's a place where heated mud is used to draw out infections. They dunked him in it. It cured him."

"So, you want to dunk her in the water?" Disbelief rings in Lucas's voice.

"Only if she's willing. I'll be careful and won't let her drown. Her fire shouldn't injure me." He holds his arms out for me again.

They both stare at me, awaiting my answer. I don't think it will work, but surely it can't hurt at this point. "Fine."

I'm stiff as he picks me up and carries me to the center, where it's deeper. Though I'm willing and have gotten over my aversion to water, I'm unsure and weak.

"Now, I'm going to let go of your legs but not your back."

Carefully, he releases my legs. Panic almost takes over, but I hold it back.

"Okay so far, Chosen One?"

I frown at that, but I don't correct him. Doubtless, getting him to change it is a losing battle. I'm mostly floating. "Yes."

"I'm going to lower you into the water. Close your eyes and hold your breath. It will only be for a few seconds, and then I'll pull you out. Ready?"

I'm not, but I nod anyway. I take a lungful of air and close my eyes. The water is warm as it washes over me fully, my hair floating about my head. Rekspire's hand is firm on my stomach, holding me beneath the surface. True to his word, a few moments later, before I have the urge to fight it, he pulls me out.

"How do you feel, my lady?" Lucas startles me with his closeness. He'd obviously moved when I was under water.

I jerk, splashing water and clutching my chest. Only then do I realize I can move my fingers more than I could before I'd gone under. They're achy but not stiff now. "Better I think."

"Should we carry you, or do you want to try walking back to the edge?" Lucas's arm is around me already, anticipating my answer.

"I'll walk." I take his hand in mine, not wanting to be an invalid, and fearing my erratic fire might accidentally hurt him. My right knee is still sore, but I limp to the shelf where he'd placed me before.

Rekspire settles back in his previous spot. "Let your leg soak for a bit. I recall Bennett saying this water heals."

We sit in silence for several minutes. When I relax enough to want to sit lower in the spring, I note the sky looks hazier than when we first came out. "Is that smoke I smell?"

Lucas darts a glance from me to the sky.

Rekspire frowns. "On Far Starl, it's so dry that a flame could catch an entire forest on fire. Very dangerous."

"Yes, but we've had a lot of rain and the flood lately." Lucas's narrow eyes peer harder at the growing darkness coming from the west. "That's the direction of Anatolia, isn't it?"

Though I am warming up, fear overrules wanting to stay in the water longer. "Maybe we should get back inside the mountain."

"I agree." Lucas sweeps me into his arms and whisks us out of the pool. Water pours off our bodies and my clothes cling to me uncomfortably.

Cool air assails my sensitive body as we rise and dash, making me shiver. The dark sky in the distance chills me more than the air.

Rekspire grabs a stick with a burned end, and Lucas follows him inside the barrier into the mountain opening. We're dripping all over the gritty floor, but I'm relieved to be inside the displacement spell where we're safe.

"You don't think Anatolia is on fire, do you?" I ask when Lucas sets me down. Strangely, my wound is not as painful as it had been last eve, and I'm able to walk back inside to where only embers remain in the firepit.

"It's hard to tell what that was. But I've never seen a fire so big it could destroy a forest." Lucas wrings his shirt bottom out.

Rekspire changes to his dragon form and then changes back. He's thoroughly dry when he's done.

Lucas stares at him for a moment and changes to his magpie form and then back. He's fully dry. He glances at me with a smirk on his handsome face.

I try but still cannot change on my own. "I can't."

"If I remember correctly, there were many clothes items on the backside of the stairway." Rekspire offers.

Only it brings to mind Audhild and Madrigal, my grandmother, whom I don't remember. It's like a dagger to my heart. "Right. I do recall that when I changed into the swimming suit."

"I could help you change if you'd like instead." Lucas holds out a slim hand to me. One side of his smile quirks up higher than the other. His eyes are red-rimmed and thin lines crease his usually smooth skin.

I clasp his hand and squeeze it. "That's okay. I feel better now. You were right, the water helped. I'm sure I'll be able to change again soon. I'll just go see what clothing I can use."

"Maybe you'll find some food while you're looking?" Rekspire remarks as I make my way to the hidden closet full of my grandmother's belongings.

"If you're so hungry, maybe you could go hunt for something and scout the smoke in the air." Lucas's annoyance is obvious.

I turn the corner before I can hear Rekspire answer him. The space is just as we'd left it—cluttered and unruly. I take a dress off the top of the pile and fold it like I'd been trained to do so many years ago. Instead of putting it down, I hug it to my chest, slide to the ground on my left side, and allow myself a moment to cry.

"My lady?"

I'm heartened by Lucas's concern. However, I don't wish him to witness my suffering. *"It's okay. I'm fine. I just need a few moments—"*

"Say no more. Call to me if you need anything."

Visions of Mother fill my mind. Of us picking flowers and roots to make her tinctures. Thoughts of my grandmother whom I never knew. Images of Grandfather's kind but disfigured face, and then of Audhild before and after my father had changed her to one of his beastly sluaghs.

It isn't fair.

None of this is right. Evil should not prevail over what's good and true, noble, and just. I can't reconcile why the Kinsman allows worthy people to suffer or die while the vile, like my father, thrive.

The Kinsman. Am I a fool to think such a being exists?

My mind goes back and forth over all the experiences I've had. Surely Theocles, the Guardian of the doorway to Hevell, would've known had there not been a real Kinsman. Someone had to set the brinicle in place and given him his duty.

What would Grandfather tell me? Or Audhild? Surely, they would've helped me make sense of it all. But they can't. Not anymore. I stifle my sobs into Grandmother's dress.

Time passes, and I'm unsure how long I sit on the cavern floor in mourning. At last, I can cry no more. My body protests enough that I must move. In the meantime, my legs and backside have fallen asleep, so I stretch tentatively. I'm still wet, my drying clothes clinging to me in the damp cavern air, so I strip the outfit off and stare at the leaves wrapping my bandage.

The leaves are no longer green, but an ugly sopping mess from being soaked in the thermal spring's water. I scrape them away and am left with the stained gauze. I remove it to get to the wound inside.

Dark veins run out of the center where the talisman's curse had broken against my flesh. However, the weeping redness has gone, leaving a puckered spot behind. I tentatively touch the area and am reassured when there's substantially less pain than before.

Before Audhild tended to me.

Before my father and the Hulda had shown up.

Before I was powerless to keep her and Grandfather from being ripped from me.

Everything goes back to him.

My father.

He's the center of all the suffering in my life. The blood of those I love the most is on his hands.

Anger replaces anguish. With my side on the mend, I need to figure out how to take my father and the Hulda down. I'm convinced had the swamp witch not shown up, Thoron would've retreated, and Audhild and Grandfather would still be with me.

The haunted look in Lucas's eyes reminds me I'm not the only one affected by their blatant disregard for anyone else but themselves. My gut warms as my determination settles. I will eliminate both of them. Even if I have to die doing so.

———

"My lady, I was worried about you." Lucas's concern wraps around me like a comforting blanket. He sits off to the side of the firepit. Flames blaze from several logs placed in the center, and the crackling and warmth draws me as much as my beloved's beckoning arm.

"Yes, I'm sorry." I sit next to him, unafraid of which side he's on now that I'm healing. "The reality of what happened in the Bloodthorn forest finally hit me." I send him a wane grin as I snuggle under his arm.

I find it strange, however, that my heated flairs have not returned. Perhaps it had all been because of the infection. The salve must be working. It is a minor win, but I will take it.

A thought bouncing around in the back of my mind nags me. What if not having my firebird ability at the ready is due instead to my fire being gone? I couldn't call it while I'd cleaned the disorderly area behind the stairs. I'd left neat stacks of clothes, all of which would fit me if needed, and had organized all the shoes and put them away. The other items I'd sorted and left in tidy piles.

I would never admit that the moments of cleaning and putting an area to rights had been satisfying. Having spent many years as an indentured servant, I could do those tasks in my sleep. After I finished putting everything in order, the small sense of accomplishment grounded me. It gave me the strength I needed to face the others again.

"Where'd Rekspire go?" I soak in the warmth from Lucas's campfire.

Lucas hugs me, then drops his arm to look me over. "He went to check on the smoke and hunt. I never knew how hard it would be to keep a grown dragon fed." He interjects a note of humor in his voice, but I can tell it's for my benefit. Mixed emotions trail through our bond, revealing his feelings are as scattered as mine.

I grab his hand, hold it to my chest, and gaze into his dark eyes. "It's okay to be scared. I'm frightened. I don't know what to do next or how I'm going to overpower my father. Add in the Hulda, and I'm overwhelmed."

He pulls me onto his lap and holds me tight. "I'm supposed to be brave for you, my lady. Your knight in shining armor. I'm terrified I won't be able to keep you safe. When you started turning blue, I just about lost it."

I rest my head on his shoulder. "You brought me back, though."

"Yeah, but only after Rekspire told me about the other dragon. Otherwise, I didn't know how to handle it." His fingers massage the space between my shoulder blades, which are knotted and sore.

I kiss his neck and lean my forehead against him, savoring his reassuring touch. "I don't doubt for a moment you wouldn't have figured out to take me to the pool. Or set me on fire. Something." I try to add a dash of mirth to my voice, hoping to lighten his mood.

"Thank you for having faith in me when I have none in myself." He leans back and gazes deeply into my eyes. "So, your wound, is it healing? You don't seem to be in as much pain. At least, I don't sense much coming from you."

"It's much better." My breath catches, and I swallow. "Audhild explained how I'd let it get infected. I think the salve took care of that. It only slightly aches now."

He rests his forehead on mine. "I'm so glad. I—"

Rekspire rushes into the cavern, disrupting our conversation. "They've destroyed Anatolia. I got us some supplies, though."

He holds out a crate with several items in it.

"They? Who are they?" I dig through the crate and find a bag of flour, sugar, some vegetables, and a couple of wrapped lumps.

He waves his hand. "The eldrin. Your father and his beasts. Possibly all of them combined. It wasn't clear when I was there who was the actual offender, as they were all offending."

"Did you steal those?" Lucas teases him.

Rekspire's chin juts upward. He'd teased Lucas about pilfering food when he had bargained for it before. "It was pure chaos, and there was fire everywhere. I merely saved it from going up in flames." He sets it down. "I have another one outside. I can carry more in dragon form."

He leaves, and Lucas joins me in digging through the wooden crate. When he turns to look at me, he's smiling. "There's enough for several days. And if he has more, we'll be able to survive for a while."

Rekspire drags in a larger crate. This one has several bottles of colored liquid, different vegetables, and more wrapped and bagged items.

"How badly ruined is Anatolia?" I ask as I peruse both boxes, unsure. They might not consider it stealing, but if there were people in need, it should go to them.

"The newer side is still burning. People were running in every direction, which is how I grabbed the crates." He raises his hand at my skeptical look. "The eldrin had taken them from the shop owners. They were also trying to force the tent dwellers to fight the fire while they pillaged the town. No one stayed. They either fled or fought back. I watched the guards kill several of them. I assure you, we are in greater need than they were."

"Guards?" Lucas asks as he unwraps a hunk of meat.

"The uniformed eldrin. I believe one of the tent nomads yelled that title."

"Like the guards of the nomad prison? Were they the ones who stopped us when we traveled with Grandfather?" My heart pinches as soon as I say the words.

"Possibly. Bennett mentioned how strange their presence had been. If that's what they were, one has to wonder what their role was." Lucas takes a bundle of meat over to the firepit and slices it with a knife left beside the stones. "Were they guarding something or stealing unknown persons in the city for their work camps?"

A picture of the crowded metal cages flits through my mind. "I remember Grandfather eluding to the fact you could get lost in Anatolia. If that's true, how many work camps do they have?"

The meat Lucas sliced sizzles on a pan over the fire. I hold back fresh grief thinking of Grandfather's delicious meals. My stomach clenches, and I fear I have no appetite for whatever he is cooking. Guilt creeps in. I should be grateful, having practically starved for years on Tenebris. However, sorrow sits like a large stone in my gut, leaving no room for anything else.

"I saw numerous cages as I flew around Anavrin before I found you. I lost count." Rekspire brings over several fresh vegetables, carrots, onions, potatoes, and a bag of dry beans. He sets a few out and cleans them.

My heart stutters at the thought of so many people being locked up. "How're we supposed to save that many people, handle the Hulda, *and* my father?"

Rekspire rests his animalistic gaze on mine. "I hadn't wanted to bring this up before." He scratches his trim beard. "But there are weapons on Far Starl that might be helpful."

"What kind of weapons?" Lucas halts cooking and stares at Rekspire.

"They're dangerous enough to subdue the mightiest of dragons. They're powerful enough to take on Thoron."

8

Lucas glances at me, his eyebrows raised. "Why did Bennett not mention these weapons, then? Wouldn't he have told us about something so helpful before if we could've used them against Thoron?"

Rekspire sets a carrot down and picks up an onion to slice. "It sounded to me as though he didn't know about them. Or maybe he was intimidated by them and didn't want to mention anything? I don't know."

The dragon-man is acting funny. I contemplate his reasons for a moment before speaking. "You fear them."

His head snaps up. "Wouldn't you be afraid if they steal your will away and leave you nothing more than an obedient animal?" He's visibly shaken, his cheek twitching.

The heat of his response startles me, and I instantly regret my words. "My apologies. I meant no disrespect. I should've stated that differently."

Rekspire heaves out a breath. "I should be the one apologizing. Yes, I'm terrified of them. They treat dragons worse than livestock on Far Starl. I envy the cattle in this kingdom. They're free here." He stops for a moment, his shoulders lifting with a deep breath. He then shrinks back to his humped form. "There are many weapons there. The guardians use shocking sticks, guns, chip implants to monitor you, and electric control collars when you don't comply. The list goes on."

I frown. I don't fully understand any of these weapons or their uses. "What is something we could use against Thoron if we could get it?"

His forehead furrows. "I would think any of them would give us an advantage. Most you use after someone's captured, though, so those would not be as helpful. If we already had him detained, we wouldn't need a weapon against him. The net could be helpful. A stun gun could stop him from afar."

Lucas turns the meat to brown on the other side. It sizzles and pops in the pan, giving off a tantalizing aroma. "What is a stun gun?"

Rekspire hands the chopped vegetables to Lucas to add to the pan. "A device that's loaded with electrical barbs. When fired, the needles dig into your skin, and a strong current stops you, allowing your enemy to descend upon you. They hit me once, on my leg. It was quite painful and left a scar."

"So, it would be like a magical arrow?" I shiver at remembering the arrow that shot me out of the sky. Though it hadn't stopped me from moving, it had allowed the disgusting fat man to get to me before Lucas did.

He stops to think. "Similar, but also different. It is very dangerous." His gaze is low as he shuffles his feet against the gritty ground.

I wonder if there is a story behind the bitterness in his voice. Had another dragon used it on him?

We're silent for a moment, letting his information soak in. The air is heavy with the odor of cooking food. With the opening magically cut off, little air comes through to whip the smoke and scent out. I sniff and rub at my face.

"The obvious question is, how easy is it to gain access to any of those weapons?" Lucas asks in a low voice. He doesn't look up, rather he stares at the food as he keeps it evenly browned.

Rekspire looks up for the first time in several minutes. "There's a stockpile in the graveyard that was my home. I can take you right to them." He uses his sharp fingernails to fish a chunk of meat out of the pan. He devours it in just a couple of bites, unbothered by the heat. "The problem is not in finding them. It's how do we get there when Anavrin's doorway is hidden and its pieces held together with only the displacement stones?"

I almost groan. I'd forgotten about that in all the other excitement. We'd meant to return to the doorway and repair it with spells only Grandfather and Audhild knew. I shove my fingers through my hair, tangling them painfully in several snags. "We're stuck here." Possibly forever.

"We may be, but so is Thoron." Lucas removes the pan and divides the remaining part of the meal equally between us, with a lesser portion for Rekspire. "With Rekspire and Audhild here, away from his magic, he has no access to dragon bones."

"That we know of," I add, uncertain. "Are there other dragon bones here that we don't know about? What was the story you told me about the lighthouse's light being a dragon bone?"

Lucas sets the pan aside and settles down to eat. "Well, most fairy tales we've been told so far have come true. I suppose it's possible, though I'd have thought Audhild would've mentioned it." He digs into his food like a starving man. "I recall setting aside a couple of books that might have some information we could use right now. I'll look for them after we've eaten."

Thinking about the dragon bones makes me think of Audhild. She mentioned the lighthouse and her heart. But what did that mean? "Where did you put Audhild?"

Rekspire's gaze is steady. "I put her in a deeper cave on the other side of the mountain. It's hard to get to, so she should be safe." He pauses and looks away. "It's not as honorable as she deserves, but it's better than being cast away like on Far Starl."

Lucas finishes his portion. "When this is over and done, we will give her a champion's burial in an exalted setting." His voice is so confident I almost believe him. He points to the plate he handed me. "You're still healing and need everything you can eat and some rest when you're done."

I try to give him a believable smile, but fear I fail. "I will." It's a much weaker promise than his for Audhild's remains. I spear a slice of carrot and chew it.

He isn't fooled.

I swallow and send him a more hopeful smile.

"This has been terribly hard on you, my lady, I know. Please try. I couldn't stand it if you got sick again. And don't let him talk you into giving up all your meat."

His concern hits me like a heavy bucket in the chest. It's as if he'd been hiding it and only now opened the doorway to show me his concern. His pain overrules my absent hunger. "I promise."

His smile is genuine. Guilt weighs heavily on my heart. I need to be stronger for him if for no other reason.

Lucas changes to his magpie form, flies up the stairs, and is out of sight within moments.

I slump down on the log and eye the cooling food. It looks good, and I know Lucas was trying to compensate for my grandfather's loss. He'd cared about him and Audhild as well.

"He's right. You need nourishment." Rekspire mumbles around a mouthful of food, giving away that he witnessed us mindspeak. "But if you find you can't eat it, I will not turn it down."

———

I rub the sleep from my eyes, realizing by the silence that I am alone. The fire blazes, so I haven't been by myself that long. A glance around the room reveals the boxes of food along the wall. Grandfather's pack sits among the supplies Rekspire had gathered, but there is no sign of either of the men.

I rise from my prone position and stretch. Still sore, I'm heartened that my body is overall much better than it had been before I'd fallen asleep. My side pricks, though, and I wonder if any of the salve remains in the pack.

My feet crunch against the gritty floor. The air is cooler by the wall where the flame's heat doesn't reach. I caress the rough canvas of Grandfather's bag, wishing he were here to help us. With a shaky breath, I pray for what I know not, then dig into it. Inside, I'm surprised to find more of the shifting stones—some larger and some smaller than the ones Lucas put in place at the cavern entryway.

Deeper in, I pull out more stones, some gems, and my father's talisman—the gastrolith. There's no glow or dark essence to it. I close my eyes to sense what's left of my father's power. However, it emits no magic since the curse is gone, and Grandfather burned it. I rub off some soot and toss it in a pile of other stones where it blends in with the rubble.

I pull out several things, setting aside my dagger and

sheath, the mangled protection bracelet, and Mother's necklace, which I'd given back to Grandfather so my heated flares wouldn't ruin it. Grandfather's netherlight is next, along with a heavy, leather-bound book. I dump the utensils, string, rope, and other essentials out, emptying the bag.

I put Mother's necklace back on. Grandfather always seemed to pull whatever we needed out of the depths of the bag. How could this be everything? Then I recall, we'd left many of the items in the Bloodthorn Forest, such as the tent, the main pan Grandfather used while we were traveling, and the canteens. The ointment is missing also.

There had to be other things I wasn't remembering. "Whatever they were, it doesn't matter," I mutter. "I will never go back to that cursed forest." Sorrow sits heavy on my chest. It was too hard to think about, let alone return to. It was as painful a memory as the small cottage where Mother died, yet I find the forest worse, since there I'd lost two people who I loved.

I gather it all to put back but stop when I get to the leather-bound book. It has a string tied around it to keep it closed. The leather tie is stiff as I untie it, thinking it might be Grandfather's recipes. However, it appears to be a journal.

The spine is the width of my palm, but just. I flip through the worn pages, noticing he's written in it at different times, with faded shades of ink in the first entries.

Keeping the mangled bracelet aside, I stash everything else back inside. I tuck the bracelet into my pants pocket and hug the book to my chest. I try once more to change.

Tingles sweep across my skin in a welcome rush. Giddiness flows right along with them. When I open my eyes, I'm still standing, but I'm not in my girlish form. I'm in my firebird form. I shriek with delight, taking flight instantly.

A wide smile greets me when I land and change back in

front of Lucas. He sits at the table with books in neat piles covering most of the surface. The Sacratus walking stick is aglow and leaned against the end of the table, its light reflecting off the stones in the wall and ceiling.

"Well done, my lady. I take it you had a good rest?" He catches sight of the book I hold. "What is that?"

"I found it in Grandfather's pack. It looks like a journal." I hand it to him.

He opens it and thumbs through the pages, his face set in concentration. "How interesting. I didn't look through the bag. I should've thought to do so."

"It's been a confusing time." I offer. "Have you found anything helpful at all?" I pull out a chair, sit, and glance at the books. The titles contain terms I'm not familiar with. I wish Audhild had had more time to teach me. Though I learned a great deal, there were many things left for me to learn. I grieve not having the precocious dragon here to help me.

He rubs his eyes. "Nothing so far, I'm afraid."

I shift to rub his shoulders. "You're obviously tired. You need rest as much as I do."

"Keep doing that, and I'll fall asleep sitting up." His smile is waning, his shadowed eyes closed. "I'd gotten used to the sleeping mat. Don't know if I can get used to sleeping on the granite of this floor."

I grimace at the wistfulness in his voice. I hadn't realized that was part of what we'd left behind, mainly because I couldn't use anything without burning it to ashes. "Would it be easier to change and sleep as a bird?" Rekspire lets out a loud snorting snore. A glance toward Audhild's stash reveals his sleeping form, his tail curled around to cover his nose. He jerks as if in a dream.

Lucas lets out a breathy laugh at the drake's sudden

interruption. "I suppose that would be best. Do you need anything before I do, my lady?"

"Only for you to get some rest. I'll just find a few books for myself to study while you sleep and try to make myself helpful."

He bends over and gives me a quick kiss on the lips. "You're always helpful."

I stroke his check. In an instant, it goes from skin to feathers. His head bobs back and forth before he darts away to find a spot to settle on. I'm grateful he didn't fight me about resting. However, it's telling how exhausted he is if he changes mid-embrace.

I glance about the tomes Lucas had been studying and tap my fingernails on Grandfather's book. These books are all too advanced for me. Instead, I dig into Grandfather's leather journal.

The beginning is harder to read since it's faded. I get to the middle where there are stories he recounts from fairy tales with notes on the side determining if he believes them to be true. Suddenly, I sense a presence. A look up and around finds no one with me and the men still asleep. Possibly my mind is playing tricks on me. Probably truer is that I am missing Audhild and her careful instruction. That decided, I peruse the next two books.

In the very center is a children's tale with hand-drawn illustrations. A careful note at the top says *Cadence's favorite bedtime story*. I grin at the colorful pictures he'd drawn and then water-painted to go with the narrative. It's all together cheerful and fanciful, and I imagine Mother as a child sitting in rapture as Grandfather read it to her.

The story is about a brother and sister who, after having skipped out on their chores, were picking berries in a meadow all day. As the sun goes down, they realize they must get home before dinnertime. The forest path they need to travel through, however, is now blocked by a large, downed tree, though there'd been no storm. That left them with one way back. Their path leads through a shadowy forest they were warned had monsters hiding in it. At the edge, they find a sad, gnarled tree. Since it's autumn, that tree is the only one that still has leaves and can cover them when rain starts to fall. They huddle together, crying beneath its shelter, and snuggled against the tree's gray bark.

The children cry so hard and for so long, they fall asleep. When they wake, there's a key on the ground by their feet. The brother grabs it as the girl finds the tree has a secret doorway —a safer back way through the forest. They use the key, make it home, and surprise their distraught parents, who are getting a search party ready to hunt for them.

I rub my fingers across the illustration of the tree. Besides being beautiful, it's so lifelike that a familiarity nags at the edges of my mind. Had I seen this tree before? I'd traveled through several forests in the past fortnight. There were the regular trees in the meadows and along the streams. Pine trees lined the mountains in a great swathing canopy. And then there was the Wehyah Tree …

That's it.

The drawing resembles the old gnarled tree at the entrance to the mountain. I grab the glowing metal scepter, the book, and change. The logs in the fireplace are now black with gray ash. I stoke the fire, add some sticks, and a couple of logs for more light. That done, I take the scepter and the book to where the tree stretches across the inner edge of the displacement stones.

I open the book to the spot I had just read and compare the two. Though the sketch is from a different angle, the trees are identical.

What does it mean?

An idea jolts me. I bend to get under the low, sprawling limbs and place my hand on the trunk. "Hello?" I whisper, sure that I'm being absurd.

"Good eve, Chosen One."

9

I jerk my hand away, fall on my backside, and stare at the wizened old tree. I hadn't even believed it to be alive. Surely, I imagined what had just happened. A quick touch of my forehead assures me I'm not feverish or ill.

The scepter at my side radiates and hums, much like a cat's purr. Its metal is warm as if it had sat out in the sun. I glance back at the Wehyah Tree, confused about what is happening.

No wind, nothing moves the tree, yet I discern something within it I haven't noticed before. Slowly, I reach my hand out to touch the bark. Energy snaps my flesh when I brush my fingers against it again. I almost pull back but stop myself.

"Did you speak to me?" I ask tentatively.

"As you spoke to me, yes." The voice is deep, containing a hint of humor.

"Who are you?" I recall the spirit of the Zoe Tree when I had been fighting to restore the flood. Are all of Anavrin's trees sentient?

"I am Nathua." His name sounds like wind as he speaks it. The scepter throbs with the words. *"I am the Guardian of arcane*

knowledge, keeper of unknown paths, and instigator of mysteries." The rugged voice cracks at the end.

I blink, unsure what to think of his titles or why the scepter reacts to this presence. "So, you're a Guardian like Theocles?" I don't mention the Hulda since I believe her to be more evil than good. I hope he is not like her.

"Many are our numbers, yet I am older than he. As old as the mountains, I am. Metal and stone wielder, I began. But Guardian, still I be."

The soundness of his words, though oddly spoken, rings true to my senses. "How did I never sense you here?" I glance around. "How did no one ever see you before?"

"Revealed was I to the Sovereign who is no more. 'Twas she who brought the beastly thief to hide and hole the holy things. I shared with him the secrets of the stones, though I spoke no words lest I reveal his tragic fate."

My heart stutters. "His tragic fate?"

"A sacrifice for thee, no more can I say. Fates be not my forte. But fret not for him, for sealed his reward is decreed."

I have never understood poetry much, with the flowery words and lofty concepts. The only exception was Mother's song about me. Those lyrics, at least, were easier to comprehend. But why is he revealing himself to me?

"You said you're the instigator of mysteries. Why make yourself known to me now?"

The leaves on the tree rustle, and my nerves snap to attention. My instincts will me to pay attention to his next words. *"The time has come for the rise of the Great Sovereign. One who burns away curses and reestablishes unity. Perilous will be your path, you and your Watchmate. Dangerous is your mission. You will only succeed if you wield a dragon's crystal heart."*

I open my mouth to say something, but there are too many questions to know what to ask first.

"Come, follow this, the winding trail. It will lead you to where wisdom flows like water. There you will find healing, instruction, and the answers you seek."

A picture explodes in my mind of a fertile land of flowers, ripe fruits, and rolling hills. I close my eyes to hold the beauty of the image tight, but it dissolves like sugar in hot water and is gone. When I open my eyes, my hand has disappeared up to my wrist inside the tree's trunk. I yank my hand back out, but it is unharmed. Fingers spread wide, I examine them and recall a similar time I'd done the same thing before entering the Zoe Tree.

Can it be?

I carefully reach my hand out again and it disappears into the shadow—a doorway? It's much smaller than the Zoe Tree's door and not lit up from the other side. But it is a doorway all the same.

"Gather what you need for straight is not the path you tread. Do not linger, for danger turns her face toward you and grins."

The presence is gone as if it had never been, but the doorway remains. His last words ring through my mind and a quickening awakens in my gut. I panic, fearing it might be another hot flare and relax when nothing happens. However, the urge to hasten doesn't go away. It sits like an ember radiating in the center of my being.

I reexamine Nathua's words. Most of it was in riddles and as easy to understand as some of Grandfather's tomes. The only thing I fully gather is that we need to travel through the Wehyah Tree to another kingdom, where I'll find what I need to know.

Heartache sticks like too much sawdust in my throat. Grandfather had been the one to guide me so far, and I lost him to my father's spell. Though Nathua wasn't Grandfather, could it be that the Kinsman had sent someone to help us? I am definitely over my head dealing with my father and the Hulda, let alone dealing with Audhild's death and Grandfather's loss.

"Kinsman, thank you for providing when I thought all was lost," I mutter, tears streaking down my face and making my nose run. A strange relief mixes with the sadness which had rested heavily upon my soul, lessening my burden. For the first time in days, I can breathe without tightness.

I gratefully suck in air, expanding my lungs to full capacity. I smile and sag with the small measure of release before moving to rise. Prickling radiates across my healing side and back—not painful or itching, but noticeable. I reach a shaking hand to it and pray it isn't what I think it is. However, Nathua's words about finding healing stick in my mind, along with my intuition about my father's curse.

The eel might be dead because of it, but that didn't mean it left me free from its hold. So, I need all the help I can find to rid myself of it before it spreads too far, and I become a slave to its power. I can't allow that to happen. Too many lives are at stake.

Wiping my tears away, I shut the book and embrace it tightly. I don't wish to wake Lucas yet, so I pack Grandfather's bag with several items we might need. Two canteens sit along the wall, so I fill them with water from Rekspire's stock and glance across the open space and beyond the stairway. I'll need a change of clothes.

I spied a smaller pack there among Grandmother Madrigal's belongings. Possibly it had been hers for her trials. She must've used it for travel since it resembled Grandfather's pack. Whatever its use, it comes in handy now as I pack it lovingly with a few of her items I'll need.

Among Madrigal's possessions is a corded bracelet woven with dozens of different small stones that emit a green aura. A protective charm? I grab it and put it around my wrist. A shock travels through my body and settles against my side and back. The sensation wriggles and burrows until it ceases completely. The pain that has been haunting me for days lessens.

"Thank you, Grandmother." I clasp the bracelet, thankful Audhild had been thoughtful enough to hoard these precious items. The fire dragon had done so many things to help me. I wish I could thank her now. But, as she mentioned about her mate, if you wait too long, you might not get the chance.

Audhild's last words crash into my mind. *"I have loved you like my own child. Halvar's kin."*

But why? I wasn't even part dragon.

The truth hits me hard. Thoron had used Audhild's mate, Halvar, and his magic to turn Grandfather into one of his sluaghs. Mother had been there, pregnant with me. She'd taken some of his curse, which affected me, even with her powerful spells protecting us. But how would I be a firebird unless I have some fire magic?

And it explains so much. Why my star-shaped pupils are so like dragon eyes. The protective magic shield that comes forth when I need it.

Halvar's fire magic had to be why I became a firebird. In Audhild's heart, I *was* her child because of her mate Halvar's signature on me.

Was that the bond between her and Grandfather? My mind spins harder than the brinicle, and I lean against the stone wall to keep from dropping to the ground. "Oh, Audhild. I wish I'd figured this out before you were gone forever." My heart pinches tighter. Audhild's loss becomes even more acute than before.

I'm unsure how long I sit cradling Madrigal's bag, praying my grief out with silent laments to the Kinsman. I swipe away the moisture from my face and neck.

At the firepit, I finish packing Grandfather's bag and place his leather-bound book at the top of Grandmother's pack next to the netherlight. I belt the sheath holding the Mortifer Blade to my side.

Lucas flies out of the stairway opening when I cinch up my pack. I'd been so busy, I hadn't sensed him awake. He lands two steps from me and gives me a quizzical grin. "Good eve, my lady. I sensed deep emotions coming from you when I woke. But it seems you're up to something different than I pictured. Are we going on a journey?"

"Is it eve? I can't tell any longer without light coming from the opening." I stall, trying to gather my thoughts in a cohesive manner. "Did you have a good rest?"

He sits on the log next to me. "I did, thank you. But you didn't answer me." He waves at the packs, now full and with items hanging from the sides. His dark eyes are intent upon my face, which is still hot from crying. "Are we leaving the mountain?"

"Yes, but probably not how you're thinking." His hand is warm in mine as I tell him about the Wehyah Tree, along with the confusing conversation I had with Nathua. I finish by showing him the illustrated tale. "I feel it in my gut. We need to follow his directions, so I packed for us."

"Can I see the tree first?" Concern and confusion leak through our bond. I can tell he wants to believe me, but he also desires caution.

Together, we walk back to the opening and inspect the tree. Lucas touches the bark, and like the Zoe Tree, his hand disappears.

"This is most unusual," he says while scrubbing a hand through his sleek, black hair. Studying him now, I realize it has grown in the past fortnight. Far from taking away from his beauty, it accentuates how handsome he is.

Rekspire's heavy, scrunching footfalls come from behind us. "Has something happened?" he yawns as he asks.

"Tambrynn said a tree Guardian named Nathua spoke to her." Lucas grabs a crooked branch, his eyebrows high, but drops his hand when nothing appears to happen.

Rekspire's face twists as he studies the tree. "I've heard of Father Trees before, but it was always a myth. You never know which dragon tales to believe."

He touches the trunk, but his hand rests on the bark instead of going through.

I reach out, my hand going through when Rekspire's wouldn't. "Why would that happen? Audhild said dragons could get through any doorway without a key." My eyes dart between the two men. "I don't want to go without you."

"Mother trees use keys to gain access. Audhild explained that dragon's hearts are keys." Rekspire steps back, his shoulders slumped. "Father trees are invitation only, if I remember correctly. No one enters without the Tree Guardian's permission."

Lucas places his hand next to mine. It goes through as well. Rekspire's still rests on the other side of the trunk. I'd hoped we could all go through the doorway, though I admit to not considering Rekspire as much as Lucas. "That means you won't be able to go with us."

"Go where?" He lowers his hand.

"I—" I hesitate to recall exactly what Nathua said. "A winding trail. He said it would lead me to wisdom where all my questions would be answered."

Rekspire's face drops. "Did he speak in riddles and vague terms?"

The embarrassment creeping on me eases. "Yes. He mentioned something about being the instigator of mysteries, so I assume that's part of what he does."

"Ah, then the tales are true, after all. He is fabled to give out poetic missions that only make sense after they're accomplished." He holds a hand up when he sees my expression. "Don't worry about me. If the old stories are true, chaos often follows his missives. I'd rather stay behind."

My scalp pricks with foreboding. "Oh. All right."

Rekspire digs around in the boxes of food. "You'll need some supplies if you're going on a journey." He takes a bag and puts some vegetables, a hunk of meat, and a few pieces of fruit inside. "Take these. I'll wait here until you return. Maybe we won't need the weapons from Far Starl after all." Relief reflects in his voice.

Lucas takes the food. The pack now bulges with its contents.

I place a hand on Rekspire's arm. "I'm leaving the Eye of Fate with you in case you need it. Most of the magic it once contained is now gone, but use it as a light or a weapon if you need to. It would be safer if you don't leave the mountain, though. I'm hoping our trip won't take long."

"Where else have I to go?" An unreadable emotion passes over his face.

My heart aches for him. I know what it's like to be left behind or not included.

Lucas rejoins me at the Wehyah Tree and takes my hand. "Here we go again, my lady. Hold tight to me and don't let go." He bends down and steps into the tree's trunk, which stretches to allow him in.

Rekspire waves at me, his expression back to normal. "Good luck, my Sovereign. Until we meet again."

Before I can reply, Lucas tugs me into the Wehyah Tree's dark expanse.

10

I stumble through the Wehyah Tree and into a murky night. No, not night exactly. Unlike the Zoe Tree's passageway, the ambient light isn't bright like the sun. It's more like a bluish-gray moonlight—dim, but clear enough to view the area close around us.

"Watch your step, my lady," Lucas says. Somehow, we'd gotten separated when entering the doorway and he's not next to me. "The landscape here is uneven."

I roll my ankle on a root. I realize the light from the scepter would've been welcome in this space, as would its sturdiness when walking. However, I hadn't counted on needing it and had left it behind.

I narrow my eyes to get a better look, but it doesn't help much. My toe hits a slight incline, and I stumble again. A nearby tree keeps me from falling over completely, the rough bark scratching at my hands and arm.

"It's quite hard to see here, isn't it?" I rub at my scraped skin. The scratch isn't deep, but it still stings. I wish I had something, anything, to help us see.

The netherlight.

I drop the bag, dig the jar out, and shake it. Blessed light glows from the liquid.

Trees rustle and move about, though there's no wind. Small lights wink in the surrounding foliage. At first, I think it's the reflection of light off an animal's eyes, but upon closer inspection, I find it's some sort of insect. "Wha—?" They swarm us, flying in my hair and darting in front of my eyes. One lands on my cheek, so I swing my arms up to cover my head. They scratch at the hand holding the netherlight. High-pitch squeaks drift around and near my ears as they angrily buzz about.

"What are these creatures?" I twist and turn to get away from them, but they're everywhere. When I move the netherlight, they follow it like moths to lantern's flames.

"I don't know," Lucas replies. His anxiety reaches me through our bond. *"They don't seem to care for the glowing jar."*

Heat washes through my veins and spreads outward until I'm flushed and sweating. I clutch my hands tightly to hold back the hot flash. The more the lighted creatures swarm me, the worse my inner flame becomes. "Stop," I yell, willing them to leave me be.

Tiny screeches break out as they drop from the air. My fire tempers and dies off, leaving me chilled. I clutch my hands together, finding them as cold as if I'd been outside in the winter without gloves. Disappointment twists in my gut. I thought the flashes had gone away after the ointment cured my wound.

"Hey! What're yeh doin' with that light? Ye're killin' my pixies." A hearty voice booms over the delicate flutter of remaining winged beings that have backed away from us at last. The man has a thick accent, with rolling *R's* and odd vowel pronunciations. Like a nomad.

Pixies?

Surprised, I glance up at where the voice came from. Had it not been the fact it was a resounding male voice, I would've thought it to be an angrier version of Arrin.

I recall hearing the term 'pixies' before, in the swamp. The nomads there had warned me about them. I fight back indignation. "I'm doing nothing of the sort. We're simply using the light see in this dark passage. And look—they're not dead."

"Weren't none of 'em attacking yeh, yeh nincompoop. Light kills 'em surer'n a heart attack." He grabs for the netherlight, but I'm too fast. I clutch it in my fist and hold it to my chest out of his reach. He scowls, letting me know exactly what Nobbert would look like without his long beard. "How'd the likes of yeh get in here anyways? Especially with that holy relic, which, by'n'the way, is illegal to use here." He's nomad-sized with massive, furry sideburns but no beard to cover his double chin. In his hand is a staff with a forked end, similar to a pitchfork, except it has only two tines.

So, the netherlight was a holy relic? And like with the Zoe Tree, one isn't supposed to use it in the passage? I narrow my eyes at the stubborn little man. Though I sense power coming from his weapon's sharpened metal tips, it's not strong enough to worry about.

"How'd I know why they were attacking? They swarmed over us. Besides, I don't even know what a pixie is." I ignore his last question. If he's anything like Nobbert, and I believe he is, he would twist that around as well.

"That doesn't tell me what ye're doin' here wavin' a powerful object around for no good reason other'n to kill the pixies." He shakes the pitchfork at me. The edges glint in the moonlight like beast's claws. "I'll just take yeh to the intruder's hold, and them seers can fiddle with yeh." He waves his hand by his forehead. "Scour ye're mind and all that business." He flicks the weapon to our right, motioning for us to move that direction. "That a-way."

"We were invited here by Nathua," Lucas speaks up, his anger not present in his calm words.

The man lets out a low chuckle. "Where are yeh headin' then?" A smirk creeps across his lined face like he knows a secret he won't tell us.

I pinch my lips together. I don't want to admit the old Guardian hadn't exactly told me where I was going, just that I needed to go. "None of your business." I move to step around him, but he jabs the weapon close to me. My hands itch to grab it from him, but I'm not sure if it's anything like the shocking weapon Rekspire told us about.

Lucas steps in front of me, outrage coming off him in waves. "I wouldn't do that if I were you."

"Oh, yeah?" A burst of blue lightning flicks between the tines of his pitchfork. "Well, I think I would."

I glance at the paltry show of energy, unimpressed. What is the man's true motivation? If he were so worried about the pixies, he'd not be ignoring them now. However, I have too many questions that need to be answered to be deterred. I step around Lucas to face him. "I tire of this conversation. Do you know who I am?"

"Tainted. Cursed. That's what yeh are. It's clear'n the nose on my face." Spit flies from his lips. The magic from his weapon hums brighter. Possibly, it's stronger than I gave it credit for.

Fury washes over me, but it's not mine. Lucas reaches over and slides the Mortifer Blade out of the sheath at my side. "I don't know who you think you are, but Tambrynn isn't cursed. Say it again, and you'll meet your end."

Lucas's hand is steady, but his body is on full alert. I grab his arm, wanting to calm him down and lower the dagger. It's far too dangerous to use on such an insignificant foe. It isn't the first time I'd been called cursed, after all. And the itching ache along my back confirms the wound from my father's talisman is not gone, even if Grandmother's bracelet helped me. It's still spreading.

Lucas shrugs my hand off and tilts the blade at the man. "He's not correct, my lady. You're *not* cursed."

"But what if I am?" I ask in a low voice, not wanting to voice my fears, but also not desiring to get into a deadly confrontation with this man.

Lucas turns to me, disbelief on his face. "I thought we worked past this reasoning. How could you think—"

"She is, and therefore, she's not welcome here." The man points the forked stick at Lucas.

My blood chills before it reheats. Blue energy snaps around my hands, but it's erratic. With the heat comes a spike of rage, and my eyes grow warm. There's no holding it back, even if I could. "I'm not responsible if you don't drop that weapon. I've killed one worthy enemy with that blade—sliced him clean in half. Do not threaten Lucas again."

"Jarrel, put your Spear of Judgment aside." A woman's voice breaks through the darkness. It comes from behind the man, however, and it's too dark to get a glimpse beyond our sphere of light.

The man's cheeks fill with air. "But—"

"Lower it." The space fills with the woman's voice. She steps out of the shadows, a tall figure wrapped in a full-length, flowing dress. Long hair brushes past her shoulders in dark waves. "Forgive your less than welcoming reception, Tambrynn. Our doorman takes his job a bit too seriously." She turns to Jarrel. "Your job is complete. Thank you for your service."

Though politely spoken, the words hold an edge that gives no doubt as to its dismissal. I'd heard that tone all too often not to catch it.

Jarrel stares at her, but she doesn't back down. He turns and mumbles, "You'll see I'm right when everything's a huffin' and a heavin'." He stomps off, the spear clutched tight in his hand.

The woman waits until he is gone before giving us a wide sweep of her arm. "Come this way, please. The other regents and I have been eagerly awaiting your arrival."

"Your pardon, miss," Lucas says instead of moving. "We were instructed by Nathua to come here, but we don't know where we're going."

Her laugh is light and pleasant. "I apologize. Nathua is a most confounding Guardian, is he not? I am here to guide you to Panacea, the voyant kingdom. I am Verona. Visions have plagued our docent. They foretold your plight and journey here. Our goal is to help mitigate your circumstances to a better end."

I blink at her, not understanding much of what she said. The intensity of her stare is unnerving, despite the hint of a smile upon her smooth face. I sense there's a secret she keeps from us. Could she be an eldrin and a voyant as well? That might explain her strange behavior.

"Nathua said I would find healing, instruction, and the answers I seek."

"Yes, that is correct, though I sense you have figured a few mysteries out." She clasps her hands in front of her in a relaxed, patient stance.

I reach out with my senses and find no ill will or deception coming from her. Guilt nags at me. I haven't confided in Lucas about my link to Audhild and her mate. I glance at Lucas, who has calmed down some. However, there are questions in his eyes about the woman's statement. "Then we have no time to waste. I have much left to understand."

"This way, please. Do follow closely. These paths, unfortunately, have a mind of their own. Oh, and return your blade. Even its magical signature is strong here. Like to like and all of that." She turns and gracefully strides ahead, her skirt billowing. "Many lost creatures from Before roam this passage. They are nocturnal, and, unfortunately, it is fatal for them. Your light draws them to it. If you would, abandon your netherlight for their sake."

I tuck the jar into a side pocket, cover it with the flap, and take the blade from Lucas, replacing it in the sheath. The light is dim once again, and the edges move like shadows as we strive to keep up with Verona. She moves as one used to the landscape, stepping this way and that around objects I don't see. Darkness behind us swallows what light we have to go by. It's disquieting.

The scent of flowers overwhelmed me in the other passageway. Here, there is only a musty, tainted loam mixed with a tang of evergreens. "What is this place?"

"This is the Aversum Way. As light cannot exist without darkness, and day rules the Zoe Passageway, this passage reflects night. It is neither good nor bad, but a darker mirror image of what exists on the other side."

"The other side?" Lucas asks from behind me, having allowed me the lead when we moved between two large trees. There is a rutted path where Verona takes us, though the land is rough, and I must watch where I step so as not to stumble.

"Exactly," she replies without further explanation. "Panacea is a bountiful land, blessed by the Kinsman. A most ideal land, it boasts abundant plant and animal life. We are also a peaceable society, something no other kingdom has."

My side burns, the warmth spreading through my back. The bracelet on my wrist tingles, sending a warmth through me and easing the discomfort some. However, it still prickles. I rub at it, hoping it doesn't mean the flares are returning.

The ground beneath us rumbles, cutting off the woman. She stops and glances around. Though she says nothing, I can tell from her stiff stance that she is concerned.

As am I.

"What was that?" Lucas asks, quicker than I can form the question.

Verona is silent for a few long seconds. "I'm unsure. This passage gets little traffic. Few know of it. Fewer yet gain entry."

Another rolling grumble explodes, jostling us enough that I throw my arms out to keep my balance. Trees rustle and shake.

"Don't worry." She says, her voice wavering. "We've not far to go. Come. Quickly now."

She rushes, and I hasten after her. My blood pumps faster, sensing her sudden urgency.

Lucas is behind me, his hand pushing against my back. "Should we change?"

"Magic is strictly forbidden here, as within the other passage. It brings instability and disintegrates the enchantments that hold it in place."

Again, I'm lost on some of her terms. What I gather is that magic of any kind is detrimental to the passages. My toe snags against something in the undergrowth. I trip as I try to catch where Verona rushes off without us.

"My lady." Lucas catches my arm, keeping me from tumbling to the dark ground.

I twist sideways and squeal when the pain in my hip and back flare.

"Daughter." the call is vague, and I'm left wondering if it

actually happened. However, the pain in my side is grasping, pulling. Like he knows I'm getting too far away from him to reach, and he's trying to yank me back.

Is that possible? Could he know I'm gone from Anavrin? Is the curse from his talisman able to detect where I am? I close my eyes and *push* against the pain, willing it gone. It eases, leaving me breathless.

Lucas helps steady me. I dust my clothes off, more for something to do with my shaking hands than anything else. Telling Lucas is not an option, as I don't wish to alarm him.

"Are you all right, my lady?"

"I'm just shaken. This path isn't what I envisioned at all. Though Nathua didn't give me much to go by." I rub my side. The ghost of pain is no longer pounding. The flicker in my veins, however, has returned. "Stand back. I can't promise I won't turn into flames."

Lucas moves aside, but not far. Lines crease his forehead.

I take a few deep breaths, willing the sensation away. When I look up, Verona is nowhere in sight. Only a few feet before us is clear, and there's no sign of which direction she has gone. There's no telltale rustle of anyone moving. "Did you see where she went?"

Lucas's head snaps up, his silky hair shaking with the movement. "I don't know. I was too worried about you falling. Surely, she wouldn't just leave us here alone in this passage."

Another shudder ripples past us, and, for the first time since we arrived here, the wind picks up and whips through the trees. The shadows remain, though. I call out for Verona.

There's no response.

My throat tightens, remembering when the Zoe Tree's passageway had become chaotic—when Thoron attacked us. It couldn't be him, could it? How would he have found out about this way? Who else could it be? Possibly, it is the lingering dark magic curse I carry. Nothing happened until it flared to life a moment ago.

What I do know, is that we are hopelessly lost.

11

"What do we do now?" I readjust the pack on my back. I'm unused to its weight, which I fear has thrown off my balance and made me clumsier than usual.

"We follow the animal path and see if we can locate Verona." Lucas steps in front of me and leads us. We get no farther than a few strides when the path forks into two different directions.

"Do you think they lead to other kingdom doorways?" I bend over, searching for footprints. If this way was so unused, it should be easy to discern which way Verona went.

However, had there been footprints, they'd been lost when the wind blew through. A light coating of dust and leaves covers the ground. The wind has died down, but it's still tossing the loose undergrowth around like startled critters taking cover.

The ground grumbles again, a new breeze sweeping across the foliage. Goosebumps break out across my arms, and I hold back a shiver as the air around us cools noticeably.

"I don't know how this back way works." Lucas turns in a

circle. Tresses of his dark hair lift, flitting about. His stance is rigid. "It's no use. Unless she comes back for us, we are on our own."

"Let me see if I can sense anything." Closing my eyes, I reach out with my calling ability. Behind my eyelids, streams of light breach the darkness. I open my eyes, and the illumination is gone. "I thought I saw something."

"Keep trying, my lady. Even if it unsettles the passageway, we need to figure out where to go. I don't want to be lost in this darkness forevermore."

Could Jarrel have instigated the turmoil? It isn't his fault he reminds me of Nobbert and his almost better-tempered brother, Debbert. However, I don't trust him or his cranky demeanor. I take in a deep breath and let it out through my lips. I welcome the warmth from Lucas's hand on my shoulder, though his touch is brief.

I reach out once more, my eyes closed. I relax and glance around as if my eyes are open. There, to my right and again to my left, are two different shafts of light. Turning, I find a few more dull glimmers. I raise my hand and call out to the light.

It spreads until it reaches my hand. I open my eyes, but the image is gone. Shutting my eyes one last time reveals the light is still there, a halo around my outstretched hand. "This way." I use the left pathway and tread with more care around the rockier terrain.

We come to another split path. I repeat what I'd done and find the glint once more. A crack in the distance makes me jump.

Lucas is there to steady me. However, my heart races. "You're doing a fine job, my lady. Let's keep going." His smile is tight, but I appreciate his loving support.

"Right." I track the light source again and with a nod, we're heading right. Each time I stop, the light is brighter. I'm sure we're headed in the correct direction. My hair is a tangled mess from the gusts when we make it to a large tree. With my eyes closed, I detect a hint of an outline. I turn to Lucas. "I think this is it."

"Excellent. It might be better for you to open it since you can see it." Uncertainty leaks through our bond. I squeeze his hand, hoping to reassure him.

"Together?" I ask him.

Wind zags past us, making the mottled shadows of leaves above us dance. A warning or a welcome?

"Together, always." He lifts his hand to mine.

We touch the bark of the tree as one. At first, nothing happens. Then a crunch and the tree shakes. Bark breaks apart, swinging open to reveal a doorway. No light pours forth as it had in the other passageway. It's a yawning, blank emptiness that faces us.

It's not wide enough for both of us to get through, so I step in first. I grab Lucas's hand as I enter, afraid to get separated from him. We leave the sound of the rushing wind behind.

Lucas steps beside me. As soon as his feet both touch ground, the tree emits a cracking noise. The void where the doorway was fills in with a rough bark. There's nothing left of the doorway, only a knotty, bent tree.

Though still night, it's not near as dark as the Aversum Way had been. A humid breeze brushes against us, dispelling the chill I'd had. Both of us turn around in a circle. I take in a rocky incline lined with rubble and sticks that surround the tree. The ground here is bare and dry.

Disappointment settles around me as the heat of this kingdom makes my clothing stick to me like thick porridge. Nothing is verdant or even growing—except for the tree. And even it is dead looking, old and gnarled like the Wehyah Tree had been. "This can't be Panacea."

Lucas frowns. "No, you're quite right, my lady. But where are we then?"

———

A stark landscape unfurls as Lucas and I fly in widening circles out from the gnarled tree. The air is thick and foul. Monotonous landscape stretches as far as my bird's eye can see.

We'd changed to get a better view of where we were after morning brought with it a hazy dawn. It must be near noon now, though the unforgiving sunlight gives no sign of time passing. *"I've never seen a place so dried up and barren."*

"They call it a desert, my lady." Lucas swings wide from my left side. *"Though it looks dead, it isn't. I recall Bennett telling me Far Starl is a place of sand and fire."*

I remember Audhild's aversion to the wet swamp. "Fire?"

"Yes. He spoke of volcanoes. They spew melted metal and rock from cracks in the ground. Fire and elemental dragons are well-suited for this type of environment."

A furious blast of wind blows past me, ruffling my feathers. I shiver, but it isn't from chills. *"This place is dreadfully hot, don't you think?"*

"I do, though as a firebird it shouldn't be so abominable to your sensibilities. Are you really that uncomfortable?" He dips as another gust rakes across the area. The thick leaves atop the strange trees rattle instead of rustle.

I open my beak to pant, finding little relief from the action. *"It's suffocating. Even the swamp wasn't this steaming and rotten."*

"It is a curious kingdom. Bennett and I studied some ancient texts he plundered. They outlined that though most kingdoms had their share of dragons after the split, the majority remained on Far

Starl. And though dragons are long-lived creatures, they don't have many hatchlings during their lifetime."

I thought back on what Grandfather and Rekspire had said about the eggs and how the guardians had treated them before they changed. *"I got the impression there were teems of dragons on Far Starl. How can that be if dragons don't have many offspring?"*

"That's the question Bennett never got answered, I'm afraid. Nor did we figure out why dragons disappeared from other kingdoms like Tenebris. They're little more than fables there. They must've left generations ago to have fallen out of knowledge so fully."

Fiery wind buffets us, and I can't imagine who would prefer to live in such an arid place. *"Maybe they didn't stick around Tenebris due to it dampening magic. I can't imagine such a powerful being staying around when their magic and memories deteriorate there."*

"Nor can I."

We swing a broader arc around and find more of the same —sandy hills, rocks, and brushy plants. Light from the sun peeking over the horizon doesn't make the vision below us any better. Everything is different shades of the same hue, a nondescript grayish tan. I miss the green grass already. *"If this is Far Starl, I wonder if we could find where Rekspire lived and get the weapons he spoke about."*

"We'd have to be careful and disguise ourselves. I wouldn't want to get on the wrong side of a dragon—especially the ones he spoke of. Let's rest here." Lucas heads to two trees growing side by side, which have long trunks topped with a mop of reedy leaves. Rings make up the length of the trunk and round fruit hang from the shelter of the foliage. Though not ideal, this tree is better than others which have hairlike needles protruding from the entire surface.

"Maybe Tenebris isn't such a bad kingdom after all." I chuckle to myself.

"The differences between the three kingdoms are astounding. Can you imagine before the split when they were all together? It's unfathomable." Lucas's tail twitches, and he turns in a circle on the treetop.

I, however, am too big to do so without fear of falling. Though I can fly back up, I don't wish to teeter over the edge and end up falling into the thorny desert below.

A dark shadow dots the horizon, possibly a bird. The sky wavers in the heat, making it harder to see. I squint to make it out but cannot tell for sure. *"Do you see that off to your left?"*

Lucas turns his head one way and then the other to get a good look. He ruffles his feathers. *"It's a dragon, my lady. We'll need to disguise ourselves."*

My heart picks up, beating faster. *"As what, though? I can't change to an eldrin up here."*

"I'm unsure, but I do not wish for them to realize who and what you are, my lady. Try a blackbird, or better yet, a vulture. I'm sure every kingdom has scavenger birds."

My brain spins, trying to settle on something that won't be conspicuous.

"My lady." Urgency fills our bond.

I gulp and think of the scavenger birds on Tenebris and settle on a balding, ugly one I'd shooed away from stalking a master's sick cat once. Tingles race across my hide. I stretch my wings for balance when the change is complete. Luckily, I'm now much smaller.

"Did I do it right?" I glance over at Lucas, who has changed to a darker version of what I had in mind.

Relief hits me before Lucas speaks. *"You did a fine job, my lady."*

The shadow moves across the sky seamlessly. This close, I

can make out the shape. It is a dragon with dark blue scales and a yellow belly. Its wingspan is much smaller than Rekspire or Audhild's. The size doesn't hinder its speed, however.

It turns and heads away from us before it gets too close. The tail is also stubbier than any I've seen before.

"That's a relief." Lucas's sigh echoes in my mind. *"Hopefully it didn't notice us. Let's get out of here and find someplace hidden."*

Lucas, still in disguise, leaps into the air. I follow close behind, panting and pumping my wings hard to keep up with his vigorous pace.

It isn't long, however, before the feathers around my neck rise, my chest warming where my necklace is. It has been so long since that happened last, and since the air is burning already, I didn't notice it right away.

A roar from behind us confirms my suspicion.

I send out a shrill shriek. A glance at the creature sends chills down my spine. In between its two eyes glows a magical red one—one of my father's favorite hexes. *"We're being followed. And it's got a third eye."*

12

Flames hit my tail feathers, followed by another mighty roar from the blue dragon. I'm unsure how it came upon us so quickly. Had it hidden? How did we not spot it?

"We need to lose it quick." Lucas squawks at the beast in an earsplitting manner before he spins downward in a dizzying drop.

I follow his lead, though my spins are awkward. I flounder more than I should. My heart thumps hard in my chest. It will be worth the effort if we lose the blue dragon.

It, luckily, cannot make such quick movements and has to swing around before chasing us once more. However, it is fast. And as strong as dragons are, it's troubling to witness the tracking spell on it. If it isn't my father, who would be powerful enough to place it?

Ground comes up fast, and Lucas levels off. My talons graze the sand and rocks, trying to mimic his actions. Farther up, the dragon adjusts his path.

Lucas screeches his dismay. I'm growing tired. Between the

heat and the effort it takes to follow his lead, I'm not sure how far we can get before the dragon catches us.

"I'll find a small space so we can lose it." Lucas lifts, gaining height, then dives once more, this time heading for some cliffs with what appear to be sun-bleached rocky ledges. We fly as fast as we can, but the dragon is not far behind.

Another spout of fire brushes across my back, and the scent of singed feathers hits my nose. *"Hurry, Lucas. It's gaining on us."*

More blistering heat shoots past my talons as I dip and dart to make it harder for the creature to hit me. Pain erupts on my leg from a burn. I squeal in agony. The sound bounces off the hard rock surface of the hills and echoes around us.

We make it to the outcropping of rocks and skim several curved sections of a boulder wall sailing through the center. The space is much too small for a dragon with its wide wingspan to navigate.

A crash behind us lets me know the dragon is following us through the arches. We exit the tunnel and flit across a ... skull.

A dragon's skull? Could this be the graveyard Rekspire spoke of?

The area opens up, and I'm shocked at the view of a valley full of bones. All weather-worn and glaring white beneath this harsh sun.

The roar that comes far too close for comfort makes a lump form in my throat. How do we lose this infernal dragon?

"There must be hundreds of bones." Lucas's strangled words scatter through my thoughts.

"Thousands," I answer him. *"But we need to find shelter or our bones will join them."*

Another gush of fire shoots off to my left.

"Change to a smaller bird. We'll be less of a target and have an easier chance of hiding." Lucas changes as he speaks.

Fear bounces around my gut. Is it possible to change mid-flight? It's never happened to me before. I concentrate but am hit by a streak of heat scorching my other leg. Why isn't my shield working? I set that aside to consider later. My wings pump harder, and I pray silently for a reprieve so I can gather my thoughts enough to change.

"*My lady?*" Lucas's concern does nothing to ease my dismay.

"*Stop.*" I screech at the dragon. It doesn't stop, its red eye unblinking, focused on us. I continue my zig-zagging path away from it.

A rocky ledge is close. I push to get around the corner. I let my disguise go, and I dip like I'd seen Audhild do in the canyons beneath the eldrin's Sanctuary city. Light bursts in the corners of my eyes, but I ignore it.

My heart drops as fast as my descent. I pull up at the last minute, flinging my wings wide to catch the air. The ground is hard when I hit it, my injured legs taking the brunt of the impact. My body rolls, head over tail until I come to a stop. Dirt and sand cloud the air, coating my nose and tongue.

Panicked, I change back to my girl form, concerned only with hiding from this beast. I scramble over the rocky ground, paying no mind to minor cuts from the sharp rocks.

"*Tambrynn? Are you all right?*" Lucas screeches above me. I realize he's trying to catch the attention of the dragon.

The ground beneath me shakes as the dragon hits it, landing just as awkwardly. I find no comfort in that thought, though.

I scramble backward and into the blessed shelter of the cliff I'd flown around. It's jagged and high, the shadow it throws a welcome reprieve from the sun. I spot a crack with a fair-sized cleft and crawl inside. Even though I wouldn't be safe from the dragon's flames, it's deep enough it can't reach me with its claws. Inside it's cool and moist. Water drips from somewhere beyond sight. It's tight, though, and my sheath digs into my side.

Something on the ground crawls around my legs, but I ignore it, focusing instead on getting as far into the awkward space as I can. I wipe away the sand on my palms down my pants. The rock behind my back is damp and I pray it's just water, though this kingdom seems too dry for that to be true.

Dirt billows in the opening before a shadow darkens the uneven hole. Sniffling noises and then a snort sound as the dragon gets a snoutful of gritty dust. I kick the sand with my feet and toss handfuls at it, hoping against hope it will go away. It chokes and smoke joins the cloudy haze. I brace for a stream of fire that doesn't come.

Lucas screeches in the distance. *"Come get me. Leave Tambrynn alone."*

I'm touched by his chivalry and protective instincts, but fear for his well-being makes me tense.

Something else moves against my left side. I curl up in a tight ball, making myself as small as I can get, not wanting to touch it. A strange critter crawls into sight. I've seen nothing like it before. There's a black and red shell on its back, and it crawls out the opening on long, pointy legs.

The dragon snaps it up in its claw, and a crunch follows the sudden disappearance. Horrified, I lean my head back against the rock behind me. My hair becomes wet, and it drips down my neck. I lean forward, but it's too late. It soaks my shirt and hair. There's nothing to be done about it. I'm not about to go out and be eaten by the dragon.

My stomach dips at the thought of the poor creature's fate. If I hadn't crawled into its home, it would still be alive and well. Something else moves, then something else, until the walls around me break into movement. Several more of the black, strange animals swarm the ground and walls near the opening.

I cringe at their tick-tacking sound across the sandy stone ground. Dozens of them in varying sizes creep, often over another one as they pour out of the crevice.

The dragon roars at their presence. Thuds indicate it is moving away from the smaller critters.

My skin crawls and I drop my head to my arms atop my knees. *"Lucas?"*

"Yes, my lady."

"I don't like this kingdom."

"Nor do I. You can come out now. The dragon is being chased by a swarm of crabs."

I wait a moment before I lean forward and inch out on my hands and knees. Though shaded, it's not nearly as cool as the small cavern had been. I stand and stretch, checking my body for burns and cuts. Both of my legs are tender from the dragonfire. Scratches mar my hands, but luckily nothing serious.

Lucas lands in front of me and changes. "That was close. Are you injured?"

"Just a little. Nothing to worry overmuch about." I rub my leg, wishing I had some of the healing ointment we'd made in Bloodthorn Forest. "Where'd the dragon go, and what are crabs?"

Lucas points in the direction we'd come from. "It flew off after it got chased by the crabs. I'm surprised you didn't see any during the flood. They have claws and a protective shell over their body. They normally live in sandy patches on beaches near seas. However, I didn't spot a sea here. They must live within the rock shelves." He fingers my wet hair. "There must be some sort of underground water source they use to survive."

A shiver wracks my body. "It's odd that they scared a dragon away, don't you think? Especially one with a third eye."

Lucas's frowns. "Third eye?" He hesitates before shaking his head. "Perhaps Thoron has been busier than we knew. Anyway, I believe the crabs were poisonous. One of the first rules of nature is if an animal is brightly colored, it's a warning they may be deadly."

I stare at him, my mouth wide open. "Why is every kingdom we go through wrought with dangers?"

His chuckle is low, apologetic. "I didn't realize the dragon was hexed. I hadn't gotten a good look at the crabs until it was too late. Then I worried I'd startle you, and they might attack you instead."

Several creatures side crawl from beneath the outcropping's edge, their feet clicking as they move. They're coming toward us and the cleft.

"Let's get out of here." Lucas holds his arm out for me to go ahead of him and away from the danger. "Stay in the shadows so the dragon doesn't spot us once again. I'm unsure who is controlling the third eye, but one thing I know is it's not anyone we want to deal with. That spell is black magic."

"Shouldn't we head back to the tree? We'd have a better chance in the passage." Though uncertain, I walk away from the crevice.

"Traveling at night might be better. The land between here and there is pretty open. I don't want to attract the attention of any more dragons that have been spelled. Let's find a place to rest and leave when the sun sets. It shouldn't take long to get back to the tree."

I nod, though I want nothing more than to go back to the

mountain keep on Anavrin at this moment. My hair is damp as I wring it out, the heat already drying it. I glance at the bones all around us. How we're supposed to rest is a mystery. "No wonder Rekspire isn't in a hurry to get home."

Lucas sends me a knowing glance as we climb over an area scattered thick with scorched white bones. "I have to wonder how many of these graveyards there are around Far Starl."

"So, you also believe we're in his home kingdom, then?" I ask, fairly certain that's exactly where we are.

"There are twelve kingdoms that we know of. Far Starl is the only true desert kingdom, with Pseminia being the only one close to its habitat with their volcanoes." Lucas helps me over a large boulder. "However, Pseminia also has oceans and islands that are lush, so far as the texts state."

"So, you're saying Far Starl is the only kingdom it could be?" I wipe my brow to keep the sweat from stinging my eyes.

"Most likely, yes. Unless there are kingdoms we don't have documentation for, which is possible. However, Bennett didn't mention a 'back door' passageway like the Wehyah Tree. Nor has anyone I've ever known spoken of it, even in tales."

A shadow passes near us. I duck before I glance up and catch sight of another dragon, this one an emerald green with a tan belly. It's bigger than the blue one with a long, sweeping tail. I don't get a good look at its forehead, but I don't want to chance it.

"This way," Lucas whispers. He takes my hand and leads me over to a gully area resting beneath some bones and large stones. "I wish Rekspire could've come. He would've at least known the area and could've helped us navigate around the worse dangers."

I silently agree. We climb down, rocks and sand falling as we do so. I land first.

A growl greets me, as does the beastly face of a sluagh. Its cheeks, though normally over-large and gaunt looking, are deeply sunken in its face. Because of that, its eyes bulge unnaturally. Teeth bared, it glares at me as saliva drips down its disfigured chin.

13

I grab my dagger, my hands lit with blue energy. Sand coats my head, and with the sweat on my face, it sticks to my skin like a grainy mud. I shake the debris from my face so I can view the beast better, ignoring the grit coating me.

We're in a small area, the width of two large horse stalls and only a few inches above me. There's nowhere to escape unless I can find a way back up. Old bones, rocks, and debris line the ravine.

Wolf-like ears alert, the beast snarls and dives at me.

"Watch out, Lucas." I scream as he knocks me sideways, landing on top of me and against a hard wall of rock and sand. My blade clatters out of my hand and away from me. I swipe sweaty dirt from my eyes. Lucas's weight departs as he changes to his bird form. I try to change, but rocks impede my legs, pinning them. I jerk to free them, worrying about what's going on.

Lucas screeches as the sluagh strikes, catching his tail. Feathers fly as Lucas darts about. He's faster than the creature, staying just out of reach of the being's claws. But this space is too small to get away indefinitely.

I dig the pile of rubble off my legs quickly and roll to my knees. Out of the corner of my eye, I spot a round, glittering object behind where the sluagh had initially been. But I have no time to investigate.

"My lady, you need to escape. I'll hold him off." Lucas makes a sudden move and strikes the beast's eye.

It cries out in pain and cradles the injury with a clawed hand. Its mouth froths and sores are visible across its chest and back. Burns? Beatings? Besides being angry, it doesn't look well even for a sluagh.

The beast stumbles backward, landing on its backside against the wall where it first stood. Another howl of anger and pain burst from its maw. Though there's darkness around the creature, I sense something else. Something less dangerous, like it's only trying to defend itself—not attack us like it seems.

"What are you waiting for, Tambrynn?"

The beast glances up at me with one uncovered eye, shaking its head and moaning. There's something about its aura that seems familiar.

"I think it was as startled at our arrival as we were to see it. I don't think it meant us harm. It was just defending itself." I peer at it, trying to figure out what is drawing me to it.

It snuffs at me, curling its lip in a sneer. One I've suffered before.

"Nyle?" I ask, incredulous that it could be him. I must be mistaken. Hadn't we given him a chance to be free after the flood? Had my father found him since then?

The creature shifts, fear and uneasiness crossing its deformed features. It looks away from me. Pathetic-sounding grunts end in whines as it pants. When it glances back at me, wetness dampens the fur on its leathery cheeks.

"It is you, isn't it? Why? How did Thoron—"

Nyle erupts in growling roars at the mention of my father. He swings his arm around, scratching at the rocks, raining more dust on the ground.

"Don't trust him, my lady." Lucas swoops in, his claws aiming for the other eye.

Nyle yelps and ducks away from the attack, still holding his injured eye.

"Lucas, stop. I want to see something." My movements are slow, nonthreatening. He cowers, his face covered and his tail firmly between his legs. I grasp hold of one of his arms.

At first, Nyle fights me, but he's weak. I grip tight and close my eyes to concentrate. Vivid images of his escape from the bubble beneath the ocean explode in my mind. Resentment for having to rely upon me, someone he doesn't respect, prickles his pride. He leaves us behind to find his way to another kingdom's doorway, one that opens for him without having a key. He doesn't question why. The sluaghs await him there.

My father's pets capture him. They take Nyle to a building on the edge of a walled city, past two dead uniformed men. Nyle is furious at Thoron's demeanor and glassy-eyed disinterest in his pleas. More beatings come. Then a dark hovel of a room where he's locked in and starved. Then, when he's too weak to fight, my father changes him.

Everything from that point is hazy. There's confusion and terror. Some beasts fight each other, fighting over a powerful, shining object. Nyle, true to form, even as a sluagh, takes the object for himself and slips away while the others battle. Nyle's vision changes. It's clearer.

He runs for the Zoe Tree, but this kingdom is full of dragon guards, like the one that tried to burn me. In his changed form, he witnesses the third eyes as well. It terrifies him. The oblong crystalline object he holds hums, allowing him to remain saner, more in control. He would do anything to protect it, and in doing so, protect himself. But, there's no way back through the doorway when it's being watched by a sluagh dragon guard. So, he flees into the bone graveyards.

The dragons are everywhere, including the bone yards. He's attacked and burned by rogue dragons in the first graveyard he finds. His agony and grief pummel my mind in equal measure. He continues, past a few more bone-laden yards until he finds this one. There's shade here and only one or two guards in the sky, unlike the dozen or more over the others.

Days go by, finding nothing to eat or drink. Though his prize has kept him from the haze of my father's spell, he's slowly starving to death. He can't escape, and he knows he has to protect the object or it will be the end of the kingdoms. Without better options, he determines to hide it from any who would use its power. To destroy. To enslave. To fuel dark magic.

"What is the object?" I ask him through my visual trance.

"A true dragon's heart, hidden once on Anavrin's lighthouse." It's Nyle's voice in my mind.

A memory comes back to me of Audhild telling me her true heart was there. Could it be?

"It's rare, coming but once in a dragon's lifetime. Thoron found it after the flood. At first, he thought turning Audhild would be his secret weapon. But no longer. It is now what he will use against you —the same heart he fashioned his darkest curse from to form us, his mindless beasts. If he gets it again, it will be the end of all the kingdoms."

"How can that be?" Why did Audhild not tell me her mate Halvar was a true dragon? Special?

"Your grandfather hid it, using it as the light in the lighthouse to keep it safe. I only know this because Thoron gained his memories when he fully turned."

I cringe at how casually he talks of how my grandfather fell to my father. *"How do you know all of this?"*

"The dragon's heart can reveal truth or perpetuate a grand lie. I know I've done horrible things, acted selfishly most of my life. But because I chose truth, I am now reconciled to my fate. I am a sacrifice for a greater good. My life for the safety of this heart."

I am stunned at his emphatic stance. He is not the same person as before. He has changed in so many ways. *"What makes it a true heart, and why do you have to die for it?"*

In my mind's eye, his image wavers from the beast to a man. He twists his face in a contrite expression. I sense his spirit—a firm truth in his repentant heart. *"A true dragon's heart comes from a chosen vessel, like yourself. Thoron knows I stole it. I'm the only one who's gotten away. I've hidden myself from him since I took it, but I'm growing weary. If he finds me, finds it, he will consume all life, ruining every kingdom. Only death will remain with Thoron as its ultimate ruler—a false god. I cannot let him do that. If I die, he will never find it. I will have redeemed myself in the Kinsman's eyes."*

His image changes back to the beast, and he curls into himself, like a wounded child. But I'd seen him, witnessed the emergence of his soul from the darkness.

My intuition was correct. The beasts are not undead monsters, empty vessels. But can they be saved?

"What if you don't have to die?" My mind whirls at the possibilities. If I could free Nyle, I could free Grandfather, and I could save the kingdoms. I open my eyes. Lucas stands behind me, his hand on my shoulder. His concern rings through our bond. *"Let me try to change you back. Together, we can defeat my father."*

Nyle's gaze never wavers. *"He'll know. He's strong enough to track us, even from different kingdoms. I ask only one thing of you now, Sovereign. Give me the mercy I don't deserve. Kill me. Or I'll forever be a pawn in your father's game."*

I hesitate. My intuition is telling me to save him. *"Let me try to save you. If that doesn't work, I promise to take the heart and protect it. I won't let my father get hold of it."*

He stares at me as if fighting his own inner battle. *"You must promise me if you fail, you will kill me. I cannot be the death mage's puppet any longer."*

My heart is torn. Could I kill Nyle? I'd killed Siltworth without a second thought. However, Nyle is not without merit now. I don't think I could kill him—even for merciful reasons. My grandfather's life and the lives of all the others under my father's spell fall on me saving Nyle. I have to try. *"I promise."*

He nods. His shoulders no longer slump, and his tail is no longer tucked.

Have I just given him false hope? I pray it's not so.

"My lady?" Lucas steps back when I stand and dust myself off.

"It's Nyle." I point to him, hoping Lucas will understand. "He wishes to be released from my father's spell."

"Oh?" Lucas's brow furrows. "Released as in—"

I run my hand through my hair. It's full of dirt and pebbles, so I stop. "He's stolen a dragon's heart and believes he needs to die to protect it." I briefly explain to him what Nyle told me. "But I'm not convinced killing him is the best alternative. Nyle doesn't deserve this fate. No one does. And I sensed he's changed, repented for his misdeeds. I don't want to kill him if I don't have to." Or at all. "If I can bring him back, maybe I can save Grandfather."

"O-kay." Lucas's gaze comes up from glancing at the Mortifer Blade. "A true dragon's heart. Makes perfect sense."

He eyes Nyle and the object he hunches over—the crystal heart which doesn't look like any heart I've witnessed before. "What's your plan?"

"I have an idea. I'm going to try something similar to what I did for the protection bracelets. But I'll need some water and a fire."

I let out a sigh of relief as Lucas scrambles back down into the trench disguised as a rat. Luckily, he'd left as a rat as well, so I'd expected it. What I hadn't expected had been the half-dozen dragon guards who had flown near since he left to gather firewood. Or Nyle's pleas to use the blade to kill him. Between the dragons, Nyle, and the heat, my head is pounding.

"I'm so glad you're back. Any luck finding wood?" I pick him up and scratch him behind the ears. He is cute, as rodents go. His slanted eyes are less beady than a real critter would have. "No trouble with dragons, I hope."

His nose twitches and he waves a pink paw. I place him on the rocky soil and step away. He changes back and drops an armful of dry sticks and dead prickly debris. "I don't think they even saw me. And I found enough to do what we need, I believe." He eyes Nyle before picking the pieces up to make a small fire.

I take a canister of water and wait for him to arrange the kindling, my fingers tapping the container to rid myself of nervous energy. Even though I am sure of Nyle's desire to die for the better good of all, it was unnerving watching him struggle to not give in to my father's curse. He'd rub the crystal heart and become calmer before the pattern started up again. I tried once to take the crystal, but he'd snarled at me, almost raking my arm with his claws. Nyle's sanity was barely holding on.

Lucas raises his eyebrows at me, probably sensing my unease. "All ready, my lady." He digs around in his pack and finds the small pan I'd packed. "We just need fire now."

I take a deep breath, hoping I can do this. I kneel before the tinder, close my eyes, and say a silent prayer to the Kinsman that my fire will come, but not in an uncontrollable blast.

The buzzing starts in my gut, just as it used to do. It's not strong, but it's powerful enough that I should be able to make it work. I hold out my hand and *call* out to my firebird ability. At first, only tingles itch along my palm. I stay calm, waiting for it to come.

After several moments, my hands warm. I work on a flame just like I had with Audhild in the mountain keep. Blue sparks pop around my fingers before flames erupt in a flush across my palm. I press my hand against the wood, and it catches easily.

I give Lucas the canteen and he pours a measure into the pot and sets it on the fire. He sits back away from the heat. I join him. My clothes are damp with sweat and hands clammy from nervousness.

A roar echoes off the stone. Bones rattle. Nyle whimpers.

"What is that?" I ask, sending Lucas a startled look.

He squints at the opening we used. "I think a dragon landed nearby. Maybe they saw me after all. Or they smell the fire." He opens the pockets of his bag and finds the stones. He hands me half. "You take one side and I'll take the other."

I rush to the center of the hole we'd fallen through and place two stones, one at each end. "*Nineno, arodente, ebargofiant.*" Lucas works in the opposite direction, and we make a full circle, reciting Grandfather's displacement spell. When we finish, the air pops around us, sealing us in.

Sudden silence fills my ears.

Nyle, still cowering, glances up at us. His face is unreadable. I settle back against the side, aware of the grit that finds its way under my shirt. It feels like biting ants beneath my clothes. My skin crawls, and I long for a bath, hot or cold. The air is more stifling now that I've secured the spell, and more sweat finds its way down my back.

Lucas nudges me. "The water is almost ready." He sits upright, alert. His dark locks cling to his forehead and neck. Though he'd rested before we entered the Wehyah Tree, lines crease the edges of his eyes. "If you could hurry, my lady, I would appreciate it."

His unspoken 'and get out of here' is clear in his tone.

"Intentions are everything," I murmur as I dig out Audhild's mangled bracelet, cupping it in my hands. I *call* on my fire like I'd done before, uncaring if it grows wilder this time. Flames shoot at my command, melting the metal off the gems. It pools on the sandy ground. When only the jewels remain, I drop them into the simmering water and grab hold of the pot, making the water boil. "*Sanco–sciath–nequitim–maligna–perfecator,*" I repeat seven times.

Smoke from the fire fills the space, so I dump the water over the ashy remains, extinguishing it while siphoning the gems as it pours out.

I turn and face Nyle. "Hold out your hands."

He stares at me for a second before he does as I request. I place the gems in his hands, place mine over them, and re-chant the protections over him. My insides flare to life as my internal flame awakens fully. The itching along my wound grows stronger also, but I ignore it, focusing instead on what I need to do.

My fire builds. It engulfs me and jumps to Nyle's hands as it spreads—growing hotter. I test it, making it flow to different places, to be sure I'm still in control. I am, so I continue.

As the flames flow over him, Nyle jerks back and forth. My fingers dig into his wrists to keep hold of him. "Don't let go," I yell over the sound of my beating heart that's pounding louder than a horse's hooves in my ears. I close my eyes, willing the noise to go away so I can focus on getting rid of my father's curse.

Nyle's panic joins my frantic pulse as I try to lock my mind with his. I try to assure him with visual images that I won't hurt him. He finally gives in, and I'm able to open my mind to his.

Everything becomes blank—a vast empty grayness. And then I glimpse a rope tethered to Nyle's neck. He's inside a cage, shaking the bars and trying to get out. But the cage and the rope are lit up with a dark force that sizzles. It reeks of my father's detestable magic. The essence of death and vileness.

Is this what a bond looks like? I refused to believe Lucas and my bond looks anything like this.

I reach out and touch the rope. Nyle's eyes grow wide and he screams, "NO!"

Pain explodes and something grabs hold of my body. I'm held firmly by an unseen force. I can't move, can't call upon my ability. It's like when I'd faced off with the Hulda. Fear blooms in my gut and works its way up to rest in my throat.

"Who dares to free my beast?" Thoron's angry voice bellows into the cold space of nothingness, save the rope, the cage, and Nyle.

The injury from my father's talisman kindles, spreading painful needles across my back and leg. It warms as if it's swelling, trying to take over my body.

The hold on me tightens, and I whimper. *"Please Kinsman, help me."* I pray silently, fervently.

A howl blasts into my ears. *"Do not utter that name. He's not welcome here. Nor are you."* Boiling anger washes over me. This is nothing like my heat. It sears, burning, scorching every inch of me.

Rot assails my nose and tongue. It finds my ability in the center of my being and pulls. I push back and let out a guttural scream. Thoron's detestable magic burns like acid. It wraps my throat and mouth, trying to stop my cries. I'm choking, gasping for air, but getting none. I understand now why Nyle was so scared.

My vision dims and my heart thuds with the knowledge he could kill me right now, across space, with no remorse. *"Stop."* It's a weak murmur, but Thoron's anger spikes.

Nyle cowers away from both of us. He shakes his head at me. He'd told me not to free him, but I hadn't listened.

I shield my mind. Grandfather's displacement spell calms me, placing invisible stones around myself. I'm almost at the end when the hold lets go.

"Leave." Thoron's demand fills my ears until they ache.

I'm shoved. Hard.

14

My mind stutters, and I'm awake, staring at Nyle. His mouth is open wide, his sharp, yellow teeth bared, and his eyes pinched shut. It doesn't seem as if he breathes and I fear my father is killing him from whatever space he just threw me out of.

I'm heaving, trying to regain oxygen. The flavor of Thoron, the evil that permeates his spirit, is disgusting. I gag.

"Tambrynn? My lady?" Lucas yells at me in a panic. Had he been calling me? His hand on my back is comforting, steady.

"I'm here." I draw in a shaky breath. It ends in a sob. "I couldn't do it. Thoron was there. Somehow." I can't help the panic that surfaces. My eyes sting and my throat aches as if my father had indeed been choking the life out of me.

Lucas squeezes my shoulder. His concern bleeds through our bond.

I clasp his hand, grateful for his presence, and take in Nyle's shaking figure. His eyes move back and forth. I worry about what my father is doing to him. "I don't understand it at all. Nyle and I were talking and then when I tried to grab hold of this ghostly tether—" I run out of breath. My gasp sounds more like a whimper. "Thoron was there. He stopped me from saving Nyle."

"Take a moment. Catch your breath, my lady. We have time." Lucas's voice is gentle, encouraging.

"But, we don't. Thoron has retaken Nyle." I point to him. "He could be killing him as we speak. Grab the heart, Lucas. My father can't find it." I'm still holding Nyle's wrists, the gems in my palm. Shaking him, I pray over the gems, willing them to protect Nyle from my father.

He chokes, drool dripping from his open maw. His eyes have rolled back, and he's seizing.

I don't let go. "I'm here, Nyle. Don't give in to him. Don't let him take you back."

Nyle growls and yelps, thrashing back and forth. I can tell he's fighting it, working against my father's power. Guilt buries itself in my gut. I should've listened to him and done as he asked. It's my fault he's suffering again at my father's hands.

I close my eyes and try to reconnect with him, but I can't. Pain explodes behind my temples like a slap. "It's no use. Thoron won't allow me back in."

Nyle lets out a small yelp. He struggles more, thrashing and snarling, like a cornered animal.

Lucas pulls at my arm, the dragon's heart held to his chest. It is like a crystal, clear and unblemished. "My lady. I don't think it's wise to stay here any longer. If Nyle can't fight off your father, he'll know we're here with the dragon's heart."

I hesitate a second too long.

When Nyle opens his eyes once more, he lets out a long, heavy snarl, his lips quivering over his bared teeth. There's a glint of red just above his bulging eyes. Saliva drips from his curled bottom lip.

"Oh, no." I let his arm go and back up into the other side of the ditch. Embers from the fire radiate a halo of light. It's barely enough to illuminate the space. "He has a third eye. What should we do?"

"This." Lucas shoves the heart at me and jerks the Mortifer Blade from my sheath. Lucas slashes the weapon across Nyle's throat. He drops to the ground, blinking hard as Nyle collapses before us.

"Wha—" I grasp the empty sheath.

A haunted look darkens Lucas's face. "I'm sorry, my lady. I know you wanted to save him. But the dragon's heart—"

Nyle's gasp is more gurgling than breath. His two eyes are closed, the spell for the spying, third eye broken.

I dash to his side. I can't help the anger and remorse buffeting my heart. He looks up at me, the glimmer of life gone to a dull glaze. I grab his hand, place the gems there, and say the protection spell again, praying that it will help.

Nyle's breathing is raspy. Then shallow.

"I'm so sorry, Nyle. I couldn't save you."

His other hand closes around my wrist. *But you did. I can face my Kinsman now.* His voice is in my head. He slowly turns toward Lucas. *Forgive him. He did what you couldn't do. Now, protect that heart.* With a final coughing choke, he stills.

My snagged hair covers my hanging head. I sense Nyle as he's released from his body on the journey to wherever redeemed souls go. My prayer is that it isn't to the Betwixt.

"I had to save the heart, save you, my lady. He asked for it himself." Lucas shakes his head as if trying to convince himself. The tears glistening in his eyes give him away. "He wanted to protect the world from Thoron. It's a mercy given instead of a life taken. He's free from Thoron's control, and we have the dragon's heart."

I know he's right, but it hits me hard. My desire to save him won't let me go—even after Nyle's words. I hang my head, the heart held loosely in my hands. I'm helpless again against my father. Against circumstances I can't control. "Are we just going to leave him here?"

Lucas gathers the displacement stones. "If Thoron had control of him again, he'll know where we are and maybe how to find us. So, unless you can think of a better plan, I believe it's much safer for us to leave him here and get as far away with the heart as we can."

I try to think of a better plan, but my head still hurts, as does the rest of my body. The ache in my heart is almost physical, the sharp edge of grief mixed with guilt at having failed Nyle. I shy away from Lucas when he tries to take the heart.

"My lady." His voice is a plea. "There was no time to ask. He would've attacked you. I had to act fast."

"I know," I whisper. "Thoron was too strong. And you're right. We have to get the heart away from here before my father comes for it." Reason doesn't comfort me.

I close Nyle's beastly eyes. "May you meet the Kinsman this day, and may you find the mercy you seek." A single tear falls down my dirt-crusted face. I don't bother to wipe it away.

Lucas slowly walks around the space, gathering and placing the displacement stones in the pan we'd used. "We need to disguise ourselves to get out of here. There were many dragons when I went searching for wood. Someone or something is monitoring this area closely. Anything out of the ordinary will get their attention. Do you think you can change into a mouse or a lizard, my lady?"

I'm mute for a moment, hating that he can set aside his emotions and carry on as if nothing just happened. My emotions are all over the place and overflowing like a waterfall. I want to break down and cry. I tuck the grief into a ball and swallow a mouthful of spit as if that will make the distaste of this situation go away.

Willing away the guilt and remorse, I clear my clogged throat. "A lizard? What's that?" Dim light and a blustery breeze have returned to the area now that the spell is gone. It is almost a welcome relief. I pull at the damp collar of my shirt. I'm unsure if I'll find anything welcoming or a relief for a while. "And why not a dragon?"

Lucas hands me the cleaned dagger, which I reluctantly take and put back in the sheath. He then takes the heart and gently tucks it inside my pack. "The other dragons would probably know we aren't what we are trying to appear. We cannot give away the precious cargo we carry."

He carefully helps me put the pack on. It's heavy, though my heart is heavier.

Lucas packs the pan and rocks away and puts his bag on. "Lizards are desert animals somewhat similar to snakes, but with legs. The dragons don't seem to bother the sand lizards here at all. They probably won't pay us any attention." He resettles the pack on his back. His sad gaze doesn't settle on me, but on the opening. "Watch me and see if you can do the same."

In the blink of an eye, Lucas changes and drops to the ground. His appearance is similar to snakes with legs. He crawls across the floor and up the stones without difficulty. He is agile in this form. I let out a long breath and close my eyes, focusing on him and how he crawls.

"Ready?"

It takes a moment to pull my abilities together and conform to his image. My body tingles, and I'm changed. I drop with an *oof* to the sandy ground. I'm no longer sweaty and uncomfortable. Everything is brighter, clearer. There are more colors in the rocks than I'd noticed before, and the opening glows with greater intensity—almost radiant.

"Are you seeing this?" I scramble up the wall beside Lucas with ease.

"Yes. I should've used this form before. It would've been much easier for me to get around." He bobs his head. *"Follow me. When we get out of range of the dragons, we can return to our bird forms and fly back to the tree we entered from."*

Along with the ability to climb easily, my new tail helps me balance. I wonder if this is how dragons see. I narrow my eyes when we get to the opening. Outside of it, we have no problems navigating along the shadow of the bones or along the spikier plants. It's almost easier than trying to navigate around them.

A cry overhead alerts us to a dragon's presence.

I freeze, two legs up and two legs down, my tail holding me still. Lucas has stopped beside me as well. From where we are, I can't detect it.

"Let's keep to the shadows until we have no choice." He moves swiftly ahead of me.

I follow closely behind. It's refreshing to navigate so easily over the sand and stones without wilting under the heat as I did in my girl form. The bones aren't a hindrance, either. Being so close to the ground allows for a certain balance I don't have standing on two feet or flying against the wind currents.

Though we move smoothly and quickly, it takes longer to get to the end of the graveyard than I expected. Perched upon a jutting boulder, we survey the outside of the valley of bones and stone. Ahead of us is a wide expanse of sandy ground, brushy weeds, and those same strange trees with long, ringed trunks.

A dragon's roar is answered by another dragon's hiss. I twist my head to look up and spy two different dragons fighting in the sky, their colorful bodies clashing. One has a third eye, and the other doesn't. My heart rate spikes.

"Must be a rogue and a guardian," Lucas says, as if sensing my unspoken question. *"At least it gives us a chance to leave without getting spotted."*

"Should we change then?" I ask, suddenly not wanting to stick around this area any longer. I itch to fly away and leave it all behind.

"Not just yet. Let's get farther from here just to be safe." Lucas darts forward, his tail swinging back and forth as he goes.

Again, I follow him for what seems like hours. The sun is getting low on the horizon now, spilling a brilliant golden hue across the sandy land.

"Make it to that tree, my lady, and then we'll change."

There's only one tree in sight nearby. The sand wavers with heat, but we move quickly, which helps to keep my feet and hands from getting burned. The air is cooling, and despite the warmth, it's curious how the scorching atmosphere doesn't seem to affect me as a lizard.

We make it to the tree and stop in the trunk's shadow. A glance back reveals no other animals or dragons dotting the air.

In a flash, Lucas changes to his magpie form. *"Try something less flashy than your firebird form, my lady. You're too easy to spot in your splendor, even from afar. If we're lucky, the dragons won't have the enhanced vision of the lizards, or they'll catch the glow of the heart you carry. It shouldn't take long to find the tree back to the Aversum Way. Hopefully, we can get back in. I don't relish staying in this kingdom another minute."*

Neither do I. I think of black feathers and change. *"How'd I do?"*

Lucas gives me a sideways glance. *"It's like looking in a mirror, my lady."*

Though the sun is setting and no longer bakes the land with its bright light, it's still hot. And I'm exhausted, both physically and emotionally.

"It has to be close. I remember seeing this tree when we stepped out of the dark passage."

I don't argue with Lucas. He's said it three times already, and so far, we haven't located the gnarled, old tree. *"Maybe if we changed back, we might find the doorway easier?"* I try not to let my dismay show. I don't wish to alarm him.

"It's here. I'm sure of it. My instincts rarely fail me, and I sense something hidden close by."

We'd flown in circles when we'd arrived—small at first and then arcing out in wider swaths to get a better look at the land. I recall seeing the tree we entered from among a few other bramblier-looking ones. From above, it reminded me of the Wehyah Tree on Anavrin—bent and dead-looking.

There's nothing here that resembles that.

But it's getting dark and harder to see.

The stars here aren't nearly as bright as they were on Tenebris. I wish I could ask Grandfather why that is, and then my throat clogs once more at his loss.

I try not to let the raw disappointment of failure dig in, but it pierces me like a sharp dagger to my heart. *What if I can't save Grandfather, either?* The words whisper in my mind—torturing me.

Nathua's words come back to my mind. *"The time has come for the rise of the Great Sovereign. One who burns away curses and reestablishes the true way."*

What did I know about this so-called guardian, anyway? How had I used such poor judgment to leave one kingdom to get to another and then wind up getting so astray? My side itches, the curse tingling like it's spreading. Anger and resentment ignite in my gut, and I clench my fists with the effort to stifle it.

The emotions aren't mine. I know it like I know the callouses on my hand. It's my father trying to influence me through the blasted curse plaguing my body. I need to remove it—remove him. But how? And what will happen if I can't?

Getting nowhere in the sky, we land and change back.

Lucas's hand on my arm stops my mind from whirling in dark circles. "We will find our way, my lady. I promise you."

I nod.

A menacing male voice rings out through the heavy night air. "Whoever you be, announce yourselves, or I'll fill you full of lead and kinstone."

15

I swing around to my right where the voice came from. There's nothing there but brambles, clusters of sharp grasses, and a couple of trees too far in the distance to hide someone we could hear so clearly.

"Don't move, my lady." Lucas changes, dropping to the ground before I can argue. He blends in with the darkening landscape. A flick of his tail in the clusters of grass, and he's gone.

All my instincts tell me to change as well and follow Lucas. However, though I disagree with what happened with Nyle, I've grown to trust Lucas enough to do as he says. I stand, post-still, stretching out with my hearing as well as I can. I clutch the straps of my pack tight.

Dried grass shifts and rattles as if someone is moving swiftly through them.

A screamed oath and a muffled whistle.

Another whistle answers from afar.

Sounds of a scuffle off to my right, where I imagined the speaker to be. Except I spot nothing and no one.

My legs jitter from an urgent desire to know what's happening. My side prickles. Impatience bites at my nerves. What could take him so long?

No, it's only been a few seconds. I clench my jaw tightly to fight the dark impulses bombarding me, trying to stir up anger.

"Nay. Let me go, you dirty grubber. I'll not submit. You can't make me."

It sounds like Lucas has the upper hand. It takes all my control not to go toward the voice. I twist the hem of my shirt to have something to do with my hands.

Two shadowy figures appear out of thin air, the darkness crumbling off them like dust.

Lucas has hold of a man's collar.

Relief sweeps over me.

He leads someone in my direction. "Caught him with my lizard's eyesight. Saw right through his illusion, though I sensed it first." He jerks the man, young by the looks of him, in front of me and lets him go. "It wasn't a strong one. Most djinn are more capable than that."

The man slaps at the wrinkled spot Lucas left on his shirt. His eyes are wide with a fixed gaze. His arms, hands, and neck have crude symbols inked across them. "You two are bonkers. Nuts, really." He brushes his hands down the length of his shirt, or what is a moth-eaten excuse for a shirt.

"Nuts? If that means infirm, then no. But you—why were you sitting in the middle of nowhere hiding behind a weak spell? And who were you trying to signal?" Lucas crosses his arms, his brows furrowed.

I try not to focus on Lucas's annoyance. I'm already on edge.

The guy turns his head away from us. "I don't know what you're talking about."

A small rustle sounds from behind us. My necklace heats and my hands snap with energy. My body is alert to danger. "Stop." I yell.

Sputters and a garbled cry fill the empty air.

Lucas swivels around, trying to locate the new threat.

Now that I know there are illusions, I squint and spy a murky cloudiness in several spots. At least a half-dozen of them. "Reveal yourselves."

The illusions fall like crumbs to reveal six more people. Though they aren't tall, they aren't short like the nomads. They're all young, but haggard-looking. They, too, have amateurish symbols scrawled on their skin. "Are they djinn or half-djinn, then?" I ask Lucas, who has moved next to me so he can face the others.

"I don't know what djinn is." The first one huffs. Once again, he doesn't seem to gaze directly at anyone or anything for long, though he peeks at me and then glances away quickly. When he blinks, I notice more emblems on his eyelids.

"Djinn are shape-changers. I'm part djinn. That's how I changed to a lizard so I could see you better."

They glance at one another, confused.

"Nice cover." It's a woman this time. Though her features are dainty, almost doll-like, antagonism twists her petite features unattractively. Add that to the ink slashed across her skin, and she gives off a menacing aura. "Just let our companion go or reap our wrath." She takes a step toward the first man.

An image of Shellsea flits through my mind. Her aura is a mirror of the mergirl's hunger for vengeance. I hold up my hand. "Halt."

My hold cuts their cries of dismay short. None of them can move. Their eyes dart around, but that's all they can do. I ease my hold so they can breathe. Fear and something else ping my senses.

Realization dawns on me. "You're hiding something. I want to know what."

The woman tries to growl, but it comes out with a squeak. Though I can sympathize, I need to know what they're up to. I grasp her hand.

I'm thrust into her mind but pull back enough so I'm not overcome with her memories. *"Who are you?"* I demand instead.

"Dweller. Livinia," she responds.

"Why are you out here, hidden from view?"

Livinia struggles, but I push harder at my request. *"Protecting the Outerlands from the flyers. Protecting my clan."*

"Flyers, as in dragons or their guardian riders?"

Her mind snarls at me. *"They are not guardians. They're tyrants who use the dragons to do their bidding."*

This matches what Grandfather told me about Far Starl. *"So, this is Far Starl, then? The dragon kingdom?"*

Surprise tingles along our connection. *"What other kingdom would it be?"*

I ignore her question. They obviously didn't know about the other kingdoms. I have other questions more important than trying to get them to believe in the One World being split into multi-kingdoms. *"What were you planning to do to Lucas and me a few moments ago?"*

She fights the question.

"Answer me."

"We were going to kill you and feed you to the Junta and his rogues."

I'm appalled and almost end contact. *"Why would you do such a thing?"*

"We feed them, and they let us live in peace. Mostly."

I have one more question for her. *"What is a dweller?"*

"Mongrels. Outcasts. We either rebelled against the Empyrean guard or were expelled into this vast wasteland by them."

The inequality shouldn't have surprised me. But to be expelled here in this death trap of a desert was worse than cruel. *"How do you survive?"*

"We barely make do. There's little food and less water. Most don't last long." Livinia struggles against my hold. *"We've learned how to survive."*

My hold is weakening. I release her arm. "Return."

They all relax, though all of them are less than happy about my ability to hold them.

"My lady?" Lucas's tone holds many questions.

"These people are fugitives just trying to survive. We are not here to harm you. We are simply searching for something that will take us back to where we come from—a land far away from here."

Lucas's eyebrows raise at that.

I continue. "We wish you no harm. I can offer you something in return for our safe passage." I dig into my bag where I'd stashed several apples. "Food, if you can tell us how to find an old gnarled tree that's close to this area."

All eyes except the first man's, shift to the ripe, red fruit in my hands. His eyes are on my pack. The group is all thin, too thin. Their cheeks sink below the bones, and their torn clothes hang on their bodies. Someone, the tallest male, thrusts out a hand to grab the apples.

I jerk back. "Freeze."

He stiffens and drops to the hard ground.

"I will give them to you *after* you show me the way to the tree. You won't get one if you try to steal them from me." Even though Livinia alluded to the fact they were starving, I can tell they are desperate by how they eyed the fruit. "You help me, I help you."

Livinia scoffs at me. "How can we trust you?"

I knew I had them. They're too hungry. "You can't. Do we have a deal or not?"

"My lady, what if we need that food?" Lucas asks in my mind.

"I get your concern. I'm hungry too. But we're not having any luck on our own. Besides, it's only fair. They're starving." I move to put everything back inside my pack.

Several of the group grunt in disapproval.

"Let Finian stay." Livinia swings an arm toward the first man. "He can't find anything no-how. He's blind."

I stare at her, dumbfounded. "Then why is he out here confronting us like that?"

If possible, her face scrunches more. "He's our first line of defense. He senses things."

"What kinds of things?" I challenge her, nervous at how his gaze rests on my pack—with the heart—and then slips away.

Her cheeks huff out. They almost look normal. "Lots of things. Look, he'll only slow us down. Let him stay here. He's good at hiding."

I wonder at her protectiveness over the man when she would've killed us without a second thought.

"Fine." Lucas breaks in. "But that one stays with him." He points to the one who tried to get the apples.

The would-be thief lets out a strangled noise and stomps off. In moments, he disappears from view.

"How do you do that?" Lucas asks.

No one answers.

"I have half a loaf of bread to go along with the apples." I have a whole loaf, but I don't intend to give them all our food.

"It's a simple deflection spell. Let me have the bread, and

I'll show you." Finial eagerly responds before anyone else can. He oddly wiggles his fingers.

I have yet to discover a *simple* spell, but he has to be just as hungry as the rest. It wouldn't be fair to leave him out. "Only if we can master it before we search for the tree."

Echoes of 'What?' and 'I can't believe this.' break out. None of them are happy about the deal.

My pack moves—as if someone's trying to open it. I jerk around and *push*.

"*Oof.*"

Something thuds on the ground.

"Drop your guise." I reach out and lift him with my ability. He's light. Though I'm sympathetic, he's tried to steal from me twice. "Do it now."

The shadow flakes off, revealing the apple thief.

Lucas moves between us and grabs the man. I let him go. "What do you think you're doing?"

He lets out a pathetic cry. "I'm starving. We're all starving." His shoulders move as he cries. I'm unsure if he's really upset as no tears streak his face. He could be dehydrated. However, I suspect it's a ploy to play on our emotions. I'd seen thieves on Tenebris play the same kinds of game when they got caught.

I can tell the moment Lucas gives in. Possibly he's still emotional about Nyle. "Look, I'm sorry. But you can't go around stealing to get what you need."

"Oh, yeah? That's the only way we get food around here." Livinia elbows her way up to put her arm around the thief's shoulder.

She was apparently the leader of this small group.

I recall the lengths the other indentured servants would go to just to get a few scraps. I also remembered how it was to go without adequate food or clean water. My conscience twinges. "Let's start over—"

"Dragon's coming," Finian yells. His face is upturned toward the sky as if he could see it. "Hide."

Everyone disappears from view, leaving Lucas and me the only people visible in the whole pasture-sized area. And it is too dark to tell where the dragon is coming from.

16

"What do we do now?" I whisper to Lucas.

"Become lizards," he whispers back.

We drop at the same time. I land across Lucas's back.

The sky is lighter using my lizard sight. I catch a glowing spot moving—no, flying—toward us.

"I see it. It's coming from the direction I'm facing." I scramble off of Lucas. *"So, do we run, or do we stay and wait for it to leave?"*

His tail smacks me in the face. *"There's a halo of light this way, my lady. Let's try to escape there and see if it's the tree."*

"You think it's the tree?" I ask, darting after him.

"I think it has great energy, like the dragon heart. It's the only thing out here that shows any intensity." In his haste, his legs kick out sand. I hurry to get beside him instead of behind him. One foot toss of sand in the face is enough for me.

The dragon squeals overhead. Hopefully, out of frustration at not finding us.

Being a lizard doesn't aid in helping me glance skyward without stopping to twist my head.

We dodge plants with spikes, tufts of sharp grass, and

crawl over boulders that stick out of the ground. Soon, we leave the sound of the dragon behind, and probably the outcasts as well. *"I was looking forward to learning how to hide myself like that."*

"Yes, I would've liked to know that trick as well. However, the dragons seem on alert. You don't think your father has ingratiated himself with the guardians, do you? That might account for the third eyes."

I couldn't imagine my father being on anyone's good side. *"No, I don't see him being agreeable with anyone. He's been here for a while. Probably longer than we realize. Maybe he spelled some guardians and got their dragons as a bonus."*

"Sadly, that would make more sense. We're almost there, my lady. Can you feel a trickle of magic?"

I push out with my ability and find it. It's like an invigorating rush that tickles my sleek hide. *"I can."* We top another crest and stop. We'd moved faster than I'd thought and stand before the gleaming tree we were looking for. *"Funny, I don't remember the magic of that passage being this bright. It was like night."*

Lucas bobs his head up and down as he stares at the tree. Had we been in our normal bodies, it would have only been a few strides ahead.

"Magic defies explanation. The doorway seemed smaller before, don't you think?" Lucas asks.

"I can't tell in this form. I'm going to change back." In a blink, I'm back to standing. The tree no longer radiates any form of light. I set aside the disappointment of losing the grand eyesight since I'm certain gaining entry into the door as a crawly creature would be impossible. Had that been true, more animals and critters would have filled both passages. I move toward it.

"Ready, my lady?" Lucas, back in his manly form, says from beside me.

I raise my hand to touch the trunk and stop. I glance at him, but it's hard to make out his features in this darkness. "Are you sure we should abandon the outcasts like this?"

Lucas frowns. "They abandoned us first. Had we not had the ability to change, we would've been dragon bait."

I shift the pack on my back. The dirt and grit that had made its way beneath my clothing grates against my damp skin. Sweat stings along the scratches. I wish I had buttons like Grandfather's pack had to lighten the load now that I have an extra item. "You're right. I just don't feel completely good about it. Any of it."

"Livinia claimed they know how to survive here. Besides, we have bigger problems than Far Starlian outcasts to worry about." His hand is hot on my shoulder.

It takes all my strength not to step away from his touch. Nothing about this kingdom has been good. Instead, I step forward. "Here goes nothing."

The tree creaks, and though I hadn't noticed much noise at all, the area grows silent. An icy shiver ripples across my skin. I'm really going to leave Nyle and those outcasts behind. It's not something that sits well with me.

Lucas's hand squeezes and then is gone. With a deep breath of vile, hot air, I stride into the tree.

But there isn't any ground to land on. The land drops off several feet below.

I fall down, down, before landing hard on my injured right side. Pain shoots up my back and down my leg. I roll, hugging myself and willing the agony away.

"Are you okay?" Lucas is beside me, his hands smoothing away my hair, which sticks to my too-warm face. I flush with heat. "Watch out."

Lucas spins away from me.

I close my eyes and wait for the sensation to leave. Anger and irritation, resentment and hate battle against my self-control. One rises and I push against it. When I think it's gone, a new one flares to life, tugging at me—my mind. And I'm back to battling against the rage again. I place another barrier up in my mind, using the displacement incantation. It takes much too long to set in place, and I'm panting when it's finally done. I'm sweating, gritty, and limp from the strain.

"Tambrynn?" Lucas's voice cracks.

"I'm here."

"I was worried—" He hesitates and blows out a puff of air. His face is only inches from mine. He closes his dark eyes. When he opens them again, the tears are gone. He kisses my forehead. "I'm so sorry for all of it. All—"

"I know." My hand lingers on his cheek. My anger leaves me. "I'll be fine when we get to the voyant kingdom." My voice is more sure than I am.

He sits down beside me, my hand held tight in his, and I notice we're back in the dim passage. However, it's not near as dark as Far Starl had been. I lay on the cool ground, relieved. My laugh is breathy. "Thank the Kinsman. I wasn't sure if we were going to get out of that forsaken kingdom. No wonder nobody ever went there for their eldrin trials."

Lucas stretches on the ground beside me and lets out a low, reluctant chuckle. "I couldn't agree with you more." His stomach gurgles and he laughs harder. "Do you still have those apples, my lady?"

I jerk upright. The heart. I dig into the pack and find it tucked to the side and below several items. "Oh, the heart. It's safe."

Lucas's frown deepens. "We'll have to be more careful. Would you like me to carry it instead?"

"Maybe later if it gets too heavy. I won't forget about it again." I move it to the bottom, hoping it will be safer, and take out the two remaining apples. "Well, I guess they got their snack after all. At least he left us some." I hand Lucas one and crunch into the other. Sweet and tart collide on my tongue. Juice drips down my chin as I chew a large mouthful. I don't bother to wipe it away. I'm already beyond disgusting. "So, what do we do now? Try to find that woman, Verona? Or try to go back to Anavrin?"

I vote for Anavrin, though I don't say so.

"Forward or back, that is the question."

I jolt around. It's Nathua's voice, but I don't spot him amongst the shadows. Lucas twists his head, searching for the voice. I nudge him with my elbow. "You heard that?"

He nods, his body tense.

"It's Nathua," I whisper.

"Meandering was your path. Enlightenment did you find?" The voice seems to come from everywhere at once.

I clench the half-eaten apple in my fingers. A realization hits. "You knew we'd get lost and find Nyle hiding the dragon's heart. Did you know he was going to die?"

"Ah, fates are not mine to share."

Fates my foot. I frown at his elusiveness. "Besides getting the true dragon's heart, I found out I don't want to live on Far Starl."

"Obvious stated."

"We found out that lizards have incredible eyesight. They can find hidden pools of magic." Lucas sits up further, more relaxed. "And that there are ways to hide our presence without the stones and displacement spells. We just didn't learn how to do it."

"Worthy Watcher you are. Knowledge is power. Keep to the narrow path."

Silence.

"Nathua?" I call out.

"I think he's gone. I see why you said he was confusing. He doesn't give you many details, does he?" Lucas finishes his apple and rises. He holds out a hand to me.

"Not so much, no." I take his hand, pick up the pack with my other hand, and stand.

"If only we could use our lizard sight without being lizards."

I narrow my eyes at him. "What if we could?"

"What are you thinking, my lady?" He gives me a crooked grin—the devilish one I adore. It's frustrating and provocative all at once.

"We're able to change to fit whatever circumstances we're in, right?" I'm heartened by his murmur of agreement. "Then why can't we pull from one when we're in another shape?"

"I don't know. I've never tried." Lucas stares off, trying to figure it out. "Is it possible?"

"Why wouldn't it be? We just need to practice it." My grin is genuine this time. I regain hope and embrace it tightly.

"Yes, but we can't use magic here. What we can do is find that narrow path and see where it leads us."

17

I hold Lucas's hand as we navigate the Aversum Way, hoping to find a narrow path. So far, there hasn't been any real path to follow, and we must pick our way through the trees, bushes, and uneven land. Pixies glow and flutter about from afar, not daring to come close, which I'm thankful for. It's hard enough not to trip without having them flitting around my head.

Truly, the only thing I want is to find a pleasant stream to clean up in. However, we've passed no meandering river, or even so much as a puddle. "Besides gaining the heart, what do you think the real lesson was that we were supposed to learn from Far Starl?" That question has circled my mind since Nathua left and hasn't stopped nagging me since.

Lucas holds a low limb back so I can crawl under it. I take his other outstretched hand to balance. "There are many things we can take away from that visit. I wish we'd learned how to make ourselves disappear like the outcasts had. Maybe if we put some stones in our pockets and recite the spell, it would work."

I jerk to a halt, my hand pulling at Lucas's when he doesn't notice I stopped.

"What is it, my lady?"

"The outcasts had symbols on their skin. Do you think they were runes?"

Lucas is quiet as he considers it. "I don't know why I didn't notice it, but I think you're right. I thought they looked familiar, but I've studied so many books lately that their resemblance didn't hit me."

"So, it's possible? Did you read anything about tattoos or using the symbols on a person?" I shift the pack to ease the burden on my shoulders and lower back.

"Holy words hold power, yes." He scratches his chin, which bristles from stubble. "The Clerics on Tenebris, for example, used them to keep the tunnels safe and to show the way to the holy inner chambers. Some of Bennett's special objects have runes etched in them to amplify their power. So, it could be possible."

A figure carrying a stick darts into the shadows at the edge of visibility. He looks familiar. "Was that the guy who tried to stop us when we first got here?"

"*Hmm.* Jarrel? Let's follow him. Maybe he'll lead us to Verona or Panacea." Lucas rushes to follow him.

It doesn't take us long to catch up to him.

Jarrel spins to face us when he hears me step on a stick. He holds his scepter at attention but backs off when he sees us. "Yeh two again? What're yeh doin' wandering 'round this place still? Thought yeh'd be long gone with them voyants by now." His eyes widen. "Ye've got a priceless item on yeh. Where'd yeh get it?"

Using my most calm and polite indentured tone, I answer him without acknowledging we have the crystal heart.

"Verona went too fast, and we got lost. We're trying to find her. Can you help us? Please?"

He laughs. "Yeh got yerselves lost? Now i'n't that just the kind'a trouble troublemakers get into?" The finger he points at me has an arthritic bend. "And yeh expect me to do what? Help yeh? Last time we met, yeh got me in trouble. And I'm not helpin' yeh until I know what it is yeh carry." He points his weapon at me again.

"I have a netherlight in my pack and the Mortifer Blade's at my side." I grab the sheath as if to show him. What I said is true, but not what he was asking about. How is it that the little pest of a man can sense the heart? "Look, we're not trying to get you in trouble. If you remember correctly, you were the one who tried to stop us and got yourself in trouble."

He shakes the scepter, threatening us. "I'd be respectful if'n I were yeh. I'm the keeper of this here Way."

Lucas steps forward. "If you help us, we'll no longer be here to bother you. That's a win for all of us."

I say a silent prayer that he will. Otherwise, we may traipse through this back door passage for a while. "Exactly. Just show us the way or tell us where to go. You don't even have to lead us anywhere."

"I don't have to do anything. Ye're the ones who got lost." His voice changes on the last word, turning it into an insult. "Tried to tell them voyants. They don't listen to nothin' I say. Think they knows everything." He turns to walk away.

"Stop." I use my ability without even thinking. I slap a hand to my mouth. "Oh, sorry."

Jarrel is stiff as a statue facing away from us.

A rumble ripples across the passage.

Lucas and I share a dismayed glance.

"I didn't mean to, honestly." I glance back at Jarrel. "Well, I can't undo it now." I stride around the doorman. "I apologize. Release."

He slumps. "*Humph.* I knew yeh were worse'n problematic. Ye wear that curse like a pair of old, stinkin' socks. Them voyants think they own these forgotten ways and can send any hobbity in here." He stomps around while ranting.

Lucas holds out a placating hand. "Listen, we just need to find the right path. I promise not to bother you again for anything. Please, help us."

"I don't care if'n the Kinsman himself sent yeh here. I'll not help any heathen carrying the death mage's mark and whatever else yeh got stashed in them sacks." He crosses his arms over his chest, the scepter held tight in the crook of his elbow and turns away from us.

I carry Thoron's mark? If he weren't so contrary, I'd ask the man why he thinks so. My head hurts, and I squeeze the spot between my eyebrows to ease the tension. *"What do we do?"*

"If he doesn't help us, we'll just have to keep trying to find that narrow way." Lucas reaches out a hand to me.

Footsteps like horse's hooves thunder. They echo in the darkness so that I can't tell which direction they're coming from.

Jarrel jerks to attention. Forgetting us, he runs off into the shadows.

Lucas tenses. "That can't be a good sign." He slides the pack off his back and takes out a dagger from a side pocket.

I eye his stance, still remembering the last time he held a weapon. I slip mine off as well and take the Mortifer Blade from my side, praying we don't have to use it again.

"Whoa." a woman's voice yells above the clatter of hooves. When they come into sight, it's not horses but two magnificent golden stags. Their racks are wide with many points. Thick, silky fur lines their necks. They're bigger than most horses I've seen and sturdy enough to intimidate any seasoned hunter.

Pixies flit around the animals, their lights blinking bright against the darkness. Somehow, their brilliance makes it harder to view what's behind the noble-looking deer.

The stag on the right bows its head, ignoring the pixies with their high-pitched squeaky voices, and scratches its muzzle on its leg. The other stomps impatiently, twisting its head when one of the flying creatures gets too close to its ear. Tri-colored strands make up a colorful rope that's tied to a gleaming leather collar.

Had I envisioned a team to pull a princess, this would be it. I long to reach out and scratch the creatures' necks.

"Who goes this way?" the woman calls out without getting off her conveyance. Her voice is neutral, neither welcoming nor threatening. She's out of sight behind the team's massive bodies. The flickering pixie lights also leave spots when I blink my eyes. I'm left wondering why they don't like light when they have it themselves.

I reach out to tell if there's any ill intent but find nothing to draw upon. Lucas's arm is around my waist, our bags at our feet. I hold the dagger in my hand, but I don't raise it. Wind picks up, making the stags glance around.

I don't apologize for using my ability to sense the other woman's intentions. "My name is Tambrynn, and this is Lucas, my Watcher." I don't offer any more information. If she is as stubborn as Jarrel, it wouldn't be in my best interest to give out too much information.

"Of which kingdom?"

I'm startled into silence.

"Our home kingdom is Anavrin. We are on a mission, brought here by Nathua." Lucas answers easily, calmly.

A moment of silence. "Ah, I see. And why do you use forbidden magic here?" Her tone changes to a higher pitch.

I dance from one foot to the other, guilt nagging me. "My apologies. We were soliciting Jarrel's help, but he refused. I hadn't meant to push my will upon him, but we're lost and—"

"And it is second nature to you, this calling ability, is it not?" One deer stomps and shakes its head. Its antlers clack against the other deer's massive rack, starting a slight scuttle between the two. "Tut, Durmack. Dunnock, settle down. We'll be on our way shortly."

The ropes move, and a woman stands. I glimpse her dark hair between the points of the second stag's antlers. She looks familiar, yet I can't place where I might have ever seen her before. "Good boy, Dunnock. Don't let your brother lead you astray." She steps out from the passage's shadow.

Lithe, without being slim, her head comes to the tip of the stag's shoulders. She wears a dark cloak over a shirt and pants. Long, curly black hair frames an unremarkable face. She smiles slightly, as if sensing my thoughts. "I'm Areli. I believe you met my apprentice, Verona?"

My shock must've shown on my face since her grin turns into a full-on smile.

"We tried to follow her, but she was so quick." Embarrassment at having gotten lost so easily makes me stammer.

Areli holds up a hand. "No need to explain. You were Verona's first assignment, and I fear she was a little too enthusiastic. She told me she was talking and when she looked back, you were gone. She panicked and returned to Panacea instead of searching for you."

The stag closest to me turns its head toward its mistress and snorts. She answers by scratching its neck, her hand getting lost in the thick fur.

"Anyway, I've diverted Verona to another task." She swings an arm in invitation. "Please, won't you join me? I have some errands to run first along a narrow pass. It's perfectly safe, though. These boys know the path well, and I haven't lost a rider yet."

Lucas and I share a look before turning to follow along the polished wooden conveyance. It's an unusual sleigh, having wheels instead of runners. Like a carriage without the top, it rides smoothly over the uneven ground. Areli sits high on a seat in front of us.

Her destination is near to where she found us. We head straight for the shadow of a tree. A doorway opens wide to allow us entry. Not knowing the doorway could stretch so far, I'm too startled for words.

Light envelopes us as we enter a new kingdom. Green grasses, towering gray hills topped with snow, and a bright sun that doesn't carry the furious heat of Far Starl greets us. We merge onto a stunning cliff.

Several narrow land bridges fan out from the verdant cliff, some going down and some going up. Tall mountains create a majestic backdrop. We bounce in the roomy expanse of the back bench seat that could easily sit four. Our packs slide around at our feet. Luckily, the sleigh has walls, which gives us something to hold and keeps us from sliding off the side of the wheeled sled.

Wispy clouds dot a blue sky. Dew shines like crystals everywhere. The scent of a recent rain is heady to my senses. Tears sting the backs of my eyes. We'd well and truly left Far Starl behind as if that dense, deadly kingdom was simply a dream.

"Are you all right, my lady?" Lucas whispers in my mind.

I rub my gritty eyes, trying to get control of my emotions. *"I just didn't realize how blessed rain and water were until there wasn't any to be had."* The light reveals my grimy clothes. I run a hand through my greasy, tangled hair. Gray dirt lines my broken nails, rivaling my days of cleaning ash from fireplaces and mucking out stalls. I long for a hot bath in the springs beneath Grandfather's mountain.

Homesickness, an emotion I've never suffered before, crashes into me. I'm grateful for Lucas's muscular arm bracing my back, holding me steady against the rumbling ride.

With a flick of her hands on the reins, the stags answer and we're turning wide and racing toward a hilly canyon at the edge of a forested cliff. Though the stags came upon us fast in the passage, I find them exceptionally fleet-footed here. Their antlers bob as they run in unison, their golden fur gleaming in the sunlight.

And then Areli's warning makes sense.

I secure my pack behind my legs into the space beneath the seat. Lucas follows suit. Before I'm comfortable, and with another snap of the reins, the deer team jerks the sleigh, and we're racing at a break-neck speed, headed down, down, down. My heart stumbles as my stomach does a twisty dive. It's reminiscent of the carriage ride on Tenebris's wild jaunt, without the blinding snow. Body tense, I clutch the side of the sleigh tight and brace my feet against the wood beneath Areli's seat.

"Which kingdom is this?" Lucas asks, his voice strained.

"Ah, yes. This is Benario Vale, home of a giant warrior race." She says loud enough to carry over the pounding hoofbeats of the speeding deer. Her dark curls float and flutter with the sleigh's movements. "This sleigh was a gift from them. That's why it's so big."

Giants? I gulp, trying to swallow back terror.

18

Areli turns and laughs. "They're not real giants. They are a brawny lineage of forest-dwelling battle masters who are taller than most people across the divided kingdoms. The closest thing you might recognize to them are the trellers from Anavrin."

I squeeze my lips together.

"Have you heard of them?" she calls back. We hit a rise in the ground, and the sleigh lifts before dropping back down at a jarring speed. The grin on Areli's face is a giveaway she enjoys the ride.

My head snaps, and my insides twist. It would be much smoother to fly. I consider asking her if we can, but I can't speak around the lump of fear in my throat.

"We've met a few trellers, yes," Lucas answers loudly. His knuckles are white from his grip on the side. "They haven't been good encounters."

"Oh? That's too bad. I think you'll like the group we're going to meet. They're considered healers in this kingdom."

We hit another small hill and sail up in the air, landing on one side, tipping me into Lucas.

The second set of wheels set back down, tossing me against my side. My hands are sweaty as I scramble to seize the wooden frame of the sleigh again and steady myself.

Areli whoops in delight.

Nothing seems to hinder the stags or slow them down. The sleigh itself is bigger than any I've ever ridden in. Though the stags are mighty, it's unfathomable how the golden deer can pull everything so easily.

Areli's squeal of laughter is unsettling. "Isn't this the best fun you've ever had?" I'd only known one other so fearless —Audhild.

Tears prick at the reminder of the fire dragon. But before I can get too sentimental, we're arcing in a different direction. The transport's tires swish through tall grasses and bramble, making it hard to hold a conversation. And if there's a path here, it's not visible.

"We're almost at the narrow pass. It's tricky, but the boys are proficient." She yells above the commotion. "Hold on."

There's no time to reply as we clatter onto a stone bridge that blends into the landscape, appearing as if out of nowhere. The land on either side drops off into a dizzying canyon. The rugged strip is one only the most-confident traveler would dare to try.

Obviously, Areli is that confident traveler.

My heart jumps past the lump in my throat, and I have to swallow hard to quell the panic. Though I can change to a bird, and flying no longer makes me nervous, the sight of the deep cavern has my knees quaking.

A view of the marbled white and gray mountains is unimpeded. They rise above a blanket of evergreen forest, forming a silhouette against the brilliant blue sky. Birds fly in large flocks across the great expanse of the ravine. I catch the movements of animals scampering among the trees below. It would be most beguiling were we not rushing into a descent of sure death.

Lucas grabs hold of my waist, his other hand clutched to the side wall of the sleigh. *"Have no fear, my lady. We'll change if we have to."*

But I do fear. I close my eyes, hoping that will help. It doesn't—it's worse. I can't anticipate the thumps and bumps if I can't see. The wind rushes by, lifting my hair into tiny whips that sting my face and neck. It's too close to the feeling of falling off the eldrin's cliff to ease my tension. Bile burns my throat, and I reopen my eyes.

The sleigh jolts at a left turn, which is closely followed by a swift right as the stags navigate the treacherous path. Mountains are a blur as we travel down, down. The stag's fluffy white tails and the bottoms of their hooves are the only thing beyond Areli's dark head I can see.

A dip and then a jerk as the stags work to get us up an incline. Our rumble is no longer smooth and just bumpy—it's jolting, wrenching us back and forth along a rutted, zagging trail.

I can't cover my face since I'm holding on for life. I change my mind about watching where we're going and drop my head. It's all I can do to not scream, though I can't speak at all. *"I think I'm going to be sick."*

Lucas doesn't answer, but dread fills our bond, and I'm assured I'm not the only one doubting our mode of transport. We shift sideways, and I'm thrown into Lucas. His hold becomes tighter. I grapple to maintain my grasp, my arms burning as they're stretched.

A glimpse of the whooshing nothingness that surrounds us doesn't ease my discomfort. I squeeze my eyes shut once more. Dismay quickens my breathing. It makes my throat raw and my head woozy. My panic edges toward hysteria. Even if I tried to change, I'm not sure I could focus at this point.

"Deep. Breaths. My lady." Lucas's words stutter in my mind. His fear wraps around me like a cloak.

"I can't." I'm tense, and the ache in my back returns, flaring to a burning itch. Anger builds inside me, beckoning me to strike out at our gleeful driver or even the stags that lead us. All it would take is one small *push*.

"Stop it," I yell at the thoughts trying to control me. If the deer go over, so do I, and I don't want anyone to fall or suffer. But the voice, the desire continues to grow. I clench my teeth against the coercion. My bag slides, and I grab hold of it. Warmth tingles from where I hold the canvas and spreads through my body. A mental snap, and the mania lets me go, though my mind is now muddled.

Dots build behind the darkness of my closed lids. I open my mouth and pant, hoping that will ease the pressure. In and out, I try to concentrate. After a couple of moments, I slowly regain some of my senses. I tuck the bag back behind my feet.

How long will this torturous ride go on? *"Please,"* I beg the Kinsman in an inadequate, unspoken plea to get off this bridge safely and swiftly.

We're tossed mercilessly once more before the bumping smooths out. We're rolling, rolling, until we slow. And then we stop. The stags blow out great heaving breaths, and a gentle wind whispers around us. Birds sing and call out nearby.

"Here we are. Wasn't that an exhilarating ride?" Areli's voice is full of high-pitched excitement. She's enjoying the entire experience.

I should be grateful we've finally arrived. But annoyance at her delight burns through me. I clench my jaw and fight it back. Only Lucas's gentle hand on my back allows me to tuck the errant emotions away so I can reclaim control enough to open my eyes without fury burning in my gaze. My body thrums as if we're still rumbling along. I shake my hands out, trying to rid myself of the undesirable sensation.

I suck in a gulp of blessed air and let it out slowly before opening my eyes. The stag on the right is nuzzling Areli's hand. A wide grin fills her face, bringing a spark of beauty to her otherwise homely appearance. Too bad she is a madwoman.

A tall woman approaches Areli with a friendly greeting. Her skin is as golden as the stags but with a gleaming mahogany braid, which is pinned around her head in a neat bun. She exudes good humor in the curve of her cheeks, and the tilt of her narrow eyes reminds me of Lucas. She doesn't remind me of the trellers from Anavrin, which is a relief.

We're in a grassy glen, with mountains on three sides and the land bridges on the fourth. Those reach up to the incredible ledge, which is almost as tall as the mountains. Evergreen trees grow intermittently around a village of wooden houses. The bank of a river borders the edge of the town on the right. The scent of the water is strong, and it rushes, splashing beyond some trees. Still in the sleigh, I haven't moved. My stomach tumbles around, not yet caught up with the conveyance having stopped.

These giants must be farmers as goats and sheep fill wooden pens that border the village. The animals graze lazily upon lush grass and flowers. Children's squeals come from somewhere unseen. The vision is idyllic and calming.

"My lady?" I hadn't realized Lucas had disembarked. His outstretched hand shakes as he patiently waits to help me down from the carriage. There are no steps, and he had to help me climb in before.

I take his hand and squeeze it. "I fear my knees are still knocking. If I could have a moment before I disembark, please?"

"Tambrynn, Lucas, I'd like to introduce you to Persimony, Master Healer of the Ravenwarren clan here in Ferndown Valley. Persimony, Tambrynn and Lucas, from Anavrin." Areli curtly bows her head in acknowledgment.

Persimony's wide smile is genial as she bows in return. Her long neck makes the action look elegant. "Pleased to meet you both. Welcome to Ferndown Valley." Her voice is rich, with a refined crispness.

Though it calls back to my time as an indentured servant when I had to curtesy at my employer's orders, I respectfully mimic their nods, as does Lucas.

"I fear I might've frightened my riders a bit." Areli's words are apologetic, though her eyes still shine with pleasure.

"Ah, yes. It can be intimidating if you're not used to it. I have something for nausea if you need it." She bends over to address us, our heads coming up only to her chest. Her green shirt wraps around the back like the aprons I used to wear did. Beneath it, a light, bandage-like cloth wraps her arms in a lighter shade. Tan pants flow down her long legs to stockinged feet and sandals.

Areli wasn't wrong to call them giants. Persimony's shoes are easily twice the size of mine, if not more. Her genial countenance defies the intimidation of her size.

I unlatch and swing the door open, allowing Lucas to help me out of the sleigh now that my nerves have settled enough that I'm confident I won't fall on my face. "Thank you for the offer. I'm feeling better now that we've stopped moving."

"If you will follow me." Persimony turns and heads toward the village.

I grab my pack and tug it on. Persimony's strides are long and quick, so Lucas and I hurry to catch up to her and Areli. They discuss news of people and events, so I disregard their conversation and take in our surroundings.

It's a quaint village with smooth cobblestone roads and polished plank walkways. Everything is neat and well-constructed. Flowers grow in clay pots along the paths and in wooden boxes beneath windows. Smoke drifts lazily from chimneys and birds fly above us, calling out above the lull of water flowing in the stream.

Among the trees growing along the banks are thorny trees which remind me of the massive bloodthorns, though they aren't nearly as large. These, however, have black bark, not the gray of the bloodthorns. Different also are the lovely round, yellow leaves which flutter in the breeze. As we get closer, the thorns come into view. They're in a strange, rounded pattern instead of spikes across the whole trunk. "Are these spiky trees related to the bloodthorns on Anavrin?" I ask, unintentionally interrupting their discussion.

Persimony turns to face me. "I believe they are in the same tree family, yes. Any bloodthorns that grow here would be on the other side of our continent near the ocean. The sap is bright red, if I remember correctly." She smiles when we agree with her. "These are honey robinia trees, grown only in this valley. They are an incredibly versatile tree with many uses."

She swings her arm in an arc to show off the tree. "A decidedly hardwood, its thorns are as strong as nails. The wood's durability is perfect for building with. We also use its honeyed pulp and seedpods in tinctures and teas."

Areli bends behind the tree, picks something up, and produces an orange-red feather. It's long and bright, reflecting the sun with a mirrored iridescence. "So, where is your pet phoenix? I've looked forward to seeing it again."

A loud screech fills the sky. Black birds flying in a *V* pattern scatter and then reform as a ball of light darts past them.

Persimony lifts her arm. "Here she is now."

19

My gut hums as my ability flairs to life, like an old friend that's come back to visit. However, I'm too busy to note that. I'm mesmerized by the sight of an enormous feathered bird. It shines like fire in the sky as it comes straight for Persimony's arm. At the last minute, the bird flings out its wings and lands gently upon the giant woman's wrapped forearm. She laughs while it nudges her with its beak.

Though it is orange and red, and twice the size of them, it reminds me of the peacocks from Tenebris with its colorful and patterned feathers. I'm drawn to it, desiring to reach out and take hold of it. But that's not right, it's not my pet. I slip my arms behind my back and interlace my fingers. "She's beautiful."

"A phoenix? I thought they didn't exist." Lucas's words come out tight. He stands stiffly at my side, his chest puffed out.

I glance at him, unsure what's put him in such an alarmed, alert state. "What's a phoenix?"

The bird squawks, its pink eyes staring unblinkingly at me.

Its head ticks as if it reads my every thought and motive. There's a whisper in my mind, but it's gone before I understand what it is.

"It's a mythical firebird." Lucas's tone is almost accusatory. He runs an unsteady hand through his slick black hair. His dark eyes shine with tears.

"A—" I choke out, startled.

"Firebird. But not mythical." Persimony strokes the bird's long neck. It fluffs its feathers, releasing flecks of embers. They flicker and turn to ash before falling and disappearing. "Unlike firebirds, though, phoenixes can regenerate."

A quake starts in my feet and moves its way up my body until I'm shaking. "What does that mean?"

Areli is the one who answers me. "When their life is over, their flames consume them and they are reborn again."

My heart hammers in my chest, filling my ears with its thrum. "Consume them?" I search for Lucas's face and find it filled with shock and dismay. "As in—"

Persimony tilts her head my way. "As in the flames destroy them, and they start anew as a chick. My great-great-grandfather hatched Emberwing. She has been reborn twice so far."

Reborn? Does that mean it will happen to me? My head spins and I stumble back a step.

"My lady." Lucas is at my elbow, keeping me steady.

"That's why I brought you here." Areli steps toward me. "A vision came to me that you needed to meet Emberwing. My visions aren't always clear, but these were unusual in their intensity. I am confident that your true path intersects here, bringing healing and knowledge you wouldn't otherwise find. I am no keeper of fates, but I believe the Kinsman will bless your journey here and show you the path or paths you need to take."

Visions. Like the one I had in the Bloodthorn Forest? Tears fill my eyes, and I blink hard to clear them. "When did you have the visions?"

"Several days ago. They came upon me in waves." Areli closes her eyes and reaches out a hand as if to touch the visions. She clasps her shirt tightly over her heart with her other hand, as if something grieves her. "Five strands with two destroyed. One was severed completely. Evil and death sparred over your soul. Sacrifices made, revealing more sacrifices to come. Flames upon flames and pain following suffering. Then you disappeared behind a barrier I couldn't follow."

Her eyes snap open and glow with power for a moment before they return to normal. "And I knew I had to find you, so I contacted Nathua to help us." She releases her shirt and smooths it down. "It's not my usual protocol. I'm a voyant, not a warrior. We predict, we don't act. But though Nathua is frustrating, his is the power of the unseen paths and unknowable secrets. Only he could reach you, and thank the Kinsman he did. Otherwise, you wouldn't be here now and we couldn't help you."

I'm speechless.

The phoenix screeches again, breaking the silence. She stares at her caregiver's face as if communicating with her.

Could they mindspeak as well?

Persimony chuckles, a deep throaty laugh. "Yes, indeed. I think she needs to be fed. You're welcome to come along." She twists around, the bird still firm on her arm, heading for the village.

All the houses are much bigger than what I'm used to. The doorways reach well over my head with chest-high handles. We plod along the sturdy wooden walkways and past several houses. Noises of everyday life filter out voices and the clink and clank of people working.

Some giants glance at us as they travel along the cobbled street. Most of them bow their heads in greetings. A few of the sourer folk gaze at me with suspicion. I run my hand across my long hair, realizing it might be because I am quite unruly looking at the moment. Crates of vegetables and wares fill ram-driven vehicles rattling along on wooden wheels. More ornate than a regular coach or carriage, the carved wood gleams. I'm awed by the extraordinary craftsmanship and quality.

Both Lucas and I are silent as we follow Areli and Persimony. We travel past storefronts and side roads to the back of the village, where there is a large barn with towering horses. The goats are the size of a normal horse, and I amuse myself with thoughts about riding one.

And then my mind turns to what Areli said. What truths could I find in this kingdom? If Persimony is a master healer, will she figure out I'm cursed? My eyes travel to the bright phoenix. It twists its head, meeting my gaze. A knowing passes between us. She sees inside me, to my deepest part. My cheeks heat and I drop my gaze.

"Where is everyone?" Lucas asks, breaking me from my contemplations.

We've reached a building with cages built into the sides. There are roofs to stop the sun and rain. Inside the cages are pairs of black birds. Large black birds.

"Many are out doing exercises or checking our borders. We're in a time of so-called peace, but we've had some trouble with the Eaglecaller clan. A few small skirmishes, nothing too alarming." She says this to Areli before turning back to us. "They used to rule Benario Vale until an uprising ended their power. Since then, they've plotted and schemed to return to their thrones. We of the Ravenwarren clan are determined that won't happen." Persimony switches the phoenix over to a wooden stand. She digs in a barrel and tosses a hunk of meat at the bird, who snaps it up hungrily.

I blanch at the sight. Having changed to so many creatures has made me more sensitive to meat sources. I shake the thoughts away, though I can't fully ease the disquiet in my stomach.

"Can I feed your ravens?" Areli sticks her finger in the cage of a single bird. It lets out a quivering cawing sound, which sets the others off with a loud ruckus of caws and calls.

"Of course." She hands Areli a sack, taking a scoopful of grains and berries first to put in a bowl for the phoenix. "It's been too long since your last visit. The group always loves it when you come because you feed them more than I do. Can't let them get too fat or they won't work as hard."

The normalcy of them feeding the birds releases some of my anxiety, and I'm able to relax.

Lucas walks up to one cage and studies the birds inside. One turns its head back and forth while staring at him. The other one in the cage ignores him completely. "Why do you keep so many birds around? What's their use?"

"They were war ravens—at least they were until we won the last battle about fifteen years back. Now they're messengers, and they occasionally impede any intruders." Persimony turns the handle on a metal spout attached to a pipe running out of the ground and fills a bucket with water without having to hand pump it. I watch in fascination. "We don't mistreat them if that's what you're asking. They're well fed, let out to exercise, and safe in our aviary."

Areli pours the final scoopful into the drawer of the last cage. Persimony is behind her with the water and adds it to a different drawer inset with a metal bowl.

She dumps the last of the water on the ground. "Now, let's

go get you cleaned up and fed. Then we can decipher the visions and the prophecy."

I mentally groan at the prophecy part but embrace getting cleaned up. With a glance back at the cages, my heart aches at their confinement, and I follow everyone back toward the village.

————

It's not a pitcher and bowl. Not a hot spring. And it's not even a standing tub. These things I'm used to. What I'm staring at in the "shower" room is something I've never imagined.

The "shower" is encased in glass with a floor drain. I clutch the collar of the fluffy, white robe Persimony gave me, unsure of the bathroom without an actual bath. I'm also surprised the commode is not a wooden chair with a bucket. It's a ceramic bowl with water that rushes like a waterfall, disappears, and refills when I push a lever.

"It's called flushing," Persimony states reassuringly.

The rushing sound reminds me of the sound of the water when I was taken to the froggen castle, and I hold back a shiver at the memory. I would stay well away from it lest I be "flushed" somewhere else.

"This is the shower," she describes how to adjust the handles to get the correct temperature. "I apologize for the height, but I am sure if our children can master it, you can as well."

Only if I had a ladder.

I don't wish to be rude, but my longing to wash away any traces of Far Starl keeps me silent. It's quite unfathomable to need so many instructions just to wash oneself.

"Here is a washcloth and a towel to dry off with. You'll find the soaps on the shelves. Everything else you'll need is here in the basket beside the sink." She hands me a small vial of murky lotion. "This is for any wounds you may have. Use it after you've cleaned up. It contains the honey robinia sap, which eases burns, cuts, bruises, and many kinds of skin ailments. Any questions?"

Although I have too many questions to count, I mutter 'no' as I take the vial. My body is weary and much too ripe, and I don't want to seem overly dense.

Though I admit, I am with this.

Persimony grins. "Wonderful. I'll have someone wash your clothes. They will be ready for you after we dine. In the meantime, I'll set out an outfit for you to use on the bed in your guest room. They're children-sized, so I hope they fit. Let me know if they don't, and I'll find some that will. I want you to be comfortable." She turns and leaves, closing a carved wooden door behind her.

I remove the robe to cover my pack. I tuck it behind the door. Though I couldn't tell on Far Starl, there's a thrum that comes from the dragon's heart. It's powerful. No wonder my father is after it.

The sink has a mirror above it, which exposes how disheveled I truly am. Dirt cakes my face. The area around my eyes and forehead where I sweated is pale compared to the gritty gray of the rest of my skin. My hair is no longer a shiny silver, but a dull, greasy mess.

And oh, the tangles. I may never get through them all. If only I could swim in the sea in the Zoe Tree's Passage. I sigh, hoping I can get through the cleansing process without falling asleep.

I try to recall all of what the giant woman told me about the shower. We had sinks with pumps on Tenebris. The finer estates also had water closets with tubs. However, there was always a water girl who filled the tubs with buckets of hot water. And the servants never got heated water. We used old, chipped pitchers with bowls filled with cold water and a scrap of cloth. If we were lucky, there were streams to sneak off to on a hot summer day.

After a minute of twisting and turning, I finally get the stream of raining water to a comfortable temperature and carefully step in. I fear it will be like working outside in the rain, but because of the gentle warmth of the spray, it is pleasant. I take my time using the labeled crocks of liquid soap to wash with, taking special care of my tangled tresses. They shine in the mirror, reflecting the lights.

When I finish, I'm rejuvenated. It's as if the river of grunge washing down the hole in the floor removed the burdensome weight I've been carrying on my shoulders. As long as I don't bring certain events to mind, I might completely ignore them. At least, for a small amount of time.

I bring the pack out with me. It's damp from my long, hot shower. I sit it down and use the jar of honey robinia lotion Persimony gave me on all my scratches and slather a generous amount on the wound from the talisman's curse.

The clothes on the bed are like Persimony's, with a blue, patterned wraparound top along with a dark gray pair of pants. Tying it in place isn't as bittersweet as I imagined it would be. White, plain underthings with short stockings and a pair of sandals complete my gifted clothes. They fit, and though not as silky as the eldrin clothes, they are fine and well made.

I consider putting on the Mortifer Blade but reject the thought. This is the safest I've been for quite a long time. I don't expect needing a weapon here, though I tuck the bag beneath the bed and out of sight.

A knock sounds on the bedroom door just as I buckle the last sandal. "Tambrynn, it's me." Lucas's voice is quiet.

I stand and smooth away the stray hairs from the damp braid I hastily wove, which swings down my back.

Lucas rests with one shoulder leaning against the doorframe, a beguiling, if lopsided, grin on his handsome face. My chest twinges upon seeing him so at ease. He, too, has cleaned up. His hair is slicked back, with a lock escaping to swoop across his forehead.

Bedecked in a similar outfit to mine except with dark blue and black, the colors compliment his complexion and his hair. My insides flutter, and I realize it has been far too long since I haven't been completely lost to sadness and fear.

"You look most handsome." I cannot hide the smile that stretches across my face. I find I don't want to.

"Not half as beautiful as you, my lady." He takes one hand and kisses it. "I've been told there is a dinner awaiting us." He tucks my hand in the crook of his arm.

My face heats, and my insides warm at his compliment and touch. "I'd almost forgotten what this feels like."

"And what is that?" Lamps that dot the paneled hallway make his dark eyes shimmer. Desire flows off him, enveloping me in a dizzying spin. I embrace it, holding it close like a well-kept secret.

"My attraction to you." I caress his cheek. "Our connection." I take a shaky breath. "I'm sorry I was angry with you about Nyle—"

He leans in and kisses my forehead. "No need to explain. I'm sorry for any action that might have made you angry or sad. You know I always have the best intentions for you and for us." His deep breath tickles the hairs at my temple. "Nothing has been easy since we reunited. When we're not running and hiding, we're having to fight off some rather unpleasant person or creature. And we haven't been alone much. It's no wonder we bump heads once in a while." His arm wraps around me in a tight embrace. "Nothing will break our connection. Ever."

I nestle my head against his neck. A clean scent washes over me, and my pulse races with love and devotion. We hug for several moments before the mouth-watering odors coming from the other part of the house make our stomachs gurgle.

Lucas's chuckle is low. "This can wait, my lady. The need to eat cannot."

20

We travel hand in hand past a spacious kitchen filled with tantalizing scents. Polished wood beams open up into a room filled with conversing people, including Areli, and several children sitting around a long table. A fire blazes in the hearth at the other end of the room. Food lines the table, and each plate is already served.

"Oh, good. Our guests have arrived." Persimony walks by with a tureen of something that wafts delicious scents. Everyone turns and looks our way. "There are two empty seats at the end. Please make yourself at home."

My step falters at the intense attention. I'd almost forgotten how it was when new people viewed my strange appearance. I'm unable to look anyone in the eyes as I find my way to an empty chair. Chunks of seasoned meat, vegetables, mashed potatoes with gravy fill the plates, with two buttered rolls on each. My mouth waters just looking at it all.

"Tambrynn, Lucas, this is my family. My husband, Zenek, and our children, Xamara, Gavenra, Renshaw, and Yesenia."

Persimony waves to each of them. "We gather each night to eat and then discuss the day's events."

She sets the dish on the table and sits beside Zenek, a broad-chested and mighty-looking man. "Now that we have the extra gravy, we can begin." Her voice is full of humor and teasing.

A shy Yesenia taps my shoulder and hands both Lucas and me each a cushion. Her hands are long and gentle, her skin a creamy gold. Pigtails frame a cheerful, round face. She is the image of a younger Persimony. "So you can reach," she mock whispers.

I take the pillow from her, and our gazes meet. Her eyes widen, and her face blushes before she turns to hide her expression. Her sandals slap against the shining floorboards as she rushes back to where the other children sit. She glances back at me once more, before turning her attention to the other children.

Again, I'm reminded of how people used to behave toward me, and it's an unwelcome unease. I'm taken aback by how far I've come that I'd lost that constant alert to other's reactions until this eve. I've either been with people who accepted me for who I am, or I'm in disguise. Unbidden, my old self-doubt wraps around me like a wool blanket—scratchy and uncomfortable, even though it's familiar.

I fight the urge to withdraw and hide.

Lucas grabs my hand and squeezes it. *"I'm sure she meant nothing by it. She seems more intimidated than shocked."*

"Thank you." I squeeze his hand back. As a distraction, I study the still-steaming food on my plate. There's way too much for me to eat, the portions as giant as the people who surround me.

Persimony's voice is indulgent toward the child. "Thank you, Yesenia, for kindly thinking of our guests. Forgive my youngest daughter, Tambrynn, Lucas, and Areli. She's been stuck in a schoolroom all day completing her written questing tests and came home quite rambunctious. Normally she doesn't run in the house."

Yesenia ducks to hide her face. It's the only sign of hearing her mother's rebuke. All the children are engaged in lively banter found only amongst the well-acquainted or siblings.

"We're so honored by your presence. Areli has been filling us in on you both," her husband says around a mouthful of food. With wide shoulders and muscular arms, he makes his chair seem too small. He makes everyone seem small.

"We haven't even uttered the blessing yet, dearest." Persimony sends him a significant look which stops him from taking another bite. A contrite half-grin tugs at his lips.

I sit with my hands in my lap, trying not to seem as awkward as I feel.

He swallows. "I was simply tasting it to be sure it is suitable to be served to our distinguished guests." Several others join his chuckle, giving away his ruse. "Renshaw, it's your turn."

The boy at the end of the table stops mid-sentence and drops his head. "Kinsman, bless this food and our family far and wide. Bring good health and peace to our valley. May we never take for granted all our provisions and gifts. And the rest say—"

"Amen." Everyone echoes the word loudly and raises their heads.

My eyes are wide. Had they just prayed out loud? That's allowed here?

The crowd all dig into the food with gusto—even Areli, who is engaged in a lively discussion with Zenek.

Lucas and I exchange a startled look but follow suit.

"So, Tambrynn, is it? I look forward to getting to know you and your man here." Zenek hesitates, his attention on Lucas.

Lucas puts his fork down and faces him. "I'm Lucas, sir. Tambrynn's Watcher."

"Ah. A Watcher." I'm unsure by the tone of his voice whether that's a statement or a question. Possibly, they don't have Watchers here. Zenek studies Lucas, a fork in one hand and a knife in the other. "Don't mind me, I've been a father to girls for too long. But, please, eat your fill." He waves the hand holding the knife toward us. Persimony has to bat his arm away so he doesn't stab her with the utensil.

The room quiets down to just the clink of silverware on plates. As the group eats, we are no longer the focus of everyone's attention. I'm finally able to relax more. Lucas, I note, has already made a dent in his food. I take a small bite of the roasted meat and find it juicy and seasoned just right. My heart pricks, remembering how delicious Grandfather's food had been. I carefully place the fork back on the table and swallow the meat past the lump of emotion in my throat.

"He and Audhild would want you to eat and be healthy, my lady. As do I." Lucas's voice breaks through my bleak thoughts. *"And after Far Starl, we have much to be grateful for sitting at a table such as this."*

"Of course, you're right. It's been too easy for me to slide into dark thoughts and emotions." I send him a grateful glance and pick the fork back up. The food is delicious. When the meal is finished and after the children are instructed to clean the table, I'm comfortable enough that my smile is genuine.

After the meal, we move into what Persimony calls the family room, a parlor-like space. I settle on a stool next to Lucas by a different fireplace. Clattering and voices come from the kitchen where the children attend to the leftovers and dishes. The fire is warm, and it, along with the amount of food I ate, makes me sleepy.

"This is Ferndown Valley's famous honey-spiced milk. Though I can tell how tired you are. It should help you both to rest fully." Persimony hands us two large mugs, a gentle teasing in her tone.

A glance inside shows a sprinkling of brown powder atop a cloud of white. Its sweet notes dance in my nose and make my mouth water, though I'm already full to bursting from the meal.

"I only filled them halfway," she states, as if in apology.

"It looks wonderful," Lucas says as he holds the heavy crock-like cup with both hands. He takes a sip and groans with pleasure. "Delightful and rich. It's almost as good as a dessert. Thank you."

"My pleasure." Smile lines crease Persimony's eyes. Noise breaks out from the kitchen—children's voices arguing. The lines disappear into a frown. "Excuse me."

When Lucas takes another drink, I cautiously take one myself. Warm, milky smoothness with a burst of earthy spices and a hint of chocolate fills my mouth. It's just sweet enough not to be bland, and thick like a pudding before it's fully set up. "Oh, this is good."

"I'm glad you like it." Zenek carries his mug into the room and sits on a comfortable-looking couch. "It's one of my favorites. I've been looking forward to speaking with you. There are so many things I'm curious about."

Apprehension fills me, and I sit up. "What kinds of things?"

Areli arrives, carrying a glass of water. "Probably the fact that I declared you the newest Sovereign of the split kingdoms, along with your loyal Watcher, of course." She waves her hand dismissively.

I almost drop the mug, the warm contents spilling over the side. "*Um.* What? I mean, Lucas is loyal and my Watcher, yes."

Areli's amiable demeanor drops, and her eyes fixate on the wall beyond me. "When you cried out in prayer during the unquenchable fire, I had a vision of it. Then, during the battle for your soul between the witch and the death mage, I saw you battle them. I watched the strands break, but I couldn't stop it."

Her gaze swings back to me, the blank far-off look gone. "That is why I brought you here to Persimony and her family. I believe the Kinsman has called us to help you find the answers you seek. Information about your lineage that we might help you unravel. Possibly even the mystery of how to end the death mage's reign of terror once and for all."

21

I sit, the heavy mug clutched in my cold hands, stunned into silence. I open my mouth, but nothing comes out. My thoughts scatter like broken glass across a floor.

"How can that be?" Lucas asks, his hand rubbing circles on my back.

"What part?" Areli takes a drink from her glass.

Lucas shakes his head, his hair now dry and swaying with the movement. "Any of it. All of it."

I face Areli, searching her eyes for answers. Realization dawns on me, rushing down my body in tingles. "You were the woman with the ice who came to me when I was lost to the fire? H—how?" Though I'm safe, my body tenses. I replay the dream in vivid detail in my mind, like when I touch someone and relive their memories. Then the rest comes to me. The magic flares. The battle. And finally, my gut clenches at the remembered pain of watching Grandfather and Audhild fall to my father. Air sticks in my lungs.

Areli's brows furrow. "I don't recall any ice, though the entire vision was full of contradictions. There was the bright

"

inferno with you in the middle. There was a darkness that crept at the edges of the flames. It danced as the fire burned brighter." She drops her head and sighs. "You were in agony. So, though it's against protocol, and I've never been able to do it before, I called out for you to keep fighting. I believe now that the death mage and the witch were working together to kill you. I was lucky they didn't sense my presence."

I shake my head to clear the images. "My father was there. His power spurred the flames on. They weren't like my firebird fire. It doesn't hurt me. But those flames? They were excruciating. However, ever since my father's talisman broke while in my pocket, I've been experiencing strange flareups. They take me over—almost overwhelming me. It's all I can do to stop them."

"Then don't." Persimony walks back into the room and sits beside her husband on the couch.

I frown at her calm demeanor, confused.

"What? Why would you say something like that?" Lucas's words are clipped and angry.

Persimony is silent for a long moment before raising a finger. "Just hear me out, okay? The phoenixes, when they're injured or about to die, go up in flames and regenerate. You're a firebird changeling. If this curse from the talisman is afflicting you, maybe you should let your body do what it knows best to do. Let it burn out the evil, so you can start over again —regenerated."

"I—" I'm unable to finish. Again, my thoughts scatter in my mind as I come to terms with something I hadn't expected. I stand up and pace between our stools and the hallway to the kitchen. Twelve paces. Turn. Glance at their expectant faces. Lucas's eyebrows lift in question. In anticipation. "But—"

What was a warm, comfortable atmosphere turns stifling. A tremble starts at my feet and moves its way up my body. I must get out. Get some air. I make for the front door. The children startle as I dash by them, interrupting a water fight between the two who are washing the dishes.

I pay them no mind and head for the door. I reach up and jerk the handle. The door swings easily on well-oiled hinges.

Darkness has fallen, and it's harder to see. Persimony's house is on the edge of the village, facing the forest on the stream's side. In a flash, I'm in my firebird form and take to the sky. If only I had the sight of the lizard.

And then I do. Everything brightens and the shadows clear to reveal the outlines of buildings, trees, and the aviary. The birds inside caw out to me. I sense their longing to be freed from their cages.

I know how that feels.

Above the aviary perches the phoenix, still as a weathervane, its feathers ruffling in the slight breeze. It lets out a squawking roar and joins me in the air.

I know the moment Lucas changes and follows me. His voice calls out my name, but I ignore him. I'm not sure what to say to him, so I push harder, angling toward the trees by the stream flowing beyond the village.

It's not that I want to lose him or fly away from him. I just need a moment to think clearly—*away* from everyone. Find a way to make sense of everything. As much as I love Lucas, some things are too important to rush a decision.

"Friend?"

It isn't Lucas. Even with the land below me alive with nocturnal animals, I know automatically it's the phoenix. Her words crackle with her energy.

"Friend, yes," I answer back.

"Help?"

Irritation mingles with my distress. I want to scream at the bird not to bother me. Doesn't she get that I'm already on edge? My back tingles with a heated flash. Anger and exasperation war for dominance.

A shadow blocks out the light of the moon.

My neck feathers prick and rise at the threat of danger. It's not the phoenix.

My chest heats and energy snaps along the edges of my wings. I've been so distracted I haven't noticed an enormous bird careening for me. *"Watch out."* I yell into the phoenix's mind, hoping it understands my warning. I tuck my wings in, dipping down to get out of the bird's path.

The phoenix lets out a warning scream.

Lucas answers in a panicked scree.

The attacking bird's shrill cry assures me it isn't here to make friends. It wears a crown of feathers upon its brown head which stands up and curves and curls toward the front. White legs with dark speckles cover its lower body.

An eagle? It's bigger than I am and easily double the size of the phoenix.

Though I drop, spinning wildly, I don't move fast enough. It catches hold of me. Luckily, I slip through the creature's pointed talons, thanks to my protective shield. I'm grateful for its return but have no time to consider why it has come back.

I push at the bird, my blue light bursting from me, knocking it back. Its furious scream fills the night air.

I blink. That attack didn't stop it. I just made it madder.

It darts at me again, its wings drawn back, coming at me faster than before. A dark menace pulses off it, warning me of its power.

I try to copy the bird's sleek posture, hoping to give myself more speed. It works, but I'm still tired, making me too slow. It clamps its talons around me, stripping my protective shield away like peeling a potato skin. I skitter off to the side, my wings flailing wildly. Just above the trees, I catch the current, and I'm back to flying again.

Its massive wings keep pushing it toward me. My protective barrier is gone. There's nowhere to hide, but I zig and zag, dodging its more straightforward attack with swift movements. However, stinging pain registers along my back where the talons rake across my feathers.

It barely touched me. How is it possible to be injured so badly with a graze? What kind of magic does this bird have?

I swerve before catching control of my flight. I can't out-fly it. My only hope is to rush down into the trees, where it will be harder for the larger bird to follow. At least, I hope it will be. The problem is that I'm also large enough to have trouble navigating the numerous branches. They are massive, and the trees are close, making it difficult to find a clean spot to enter.

A glance behind causes me to run into a branch with my left shoulder. I spin around and smack my head on the trunk of the tree. Pain explodes, stars dot my sight, and I'm falling. My wing is useless, and I'm a bit befuddled.

Bright red flashes as the phoenix swings by, circling me.

Though I use my right wing to break my fall, I land hard, knocking the air from my lungs. I flip off of my injured wing's side, resting instead on my stinging back. My beak moves as I try to regain the ability to breathe.

"My lady. Tell me where you are." Lucas's yells bombard my mind.

I wince against the added pain. Blackness dances at the edge of my eyes. How badly did I hurt my head?

"Friend. Help." The phoenix's high-pitched voice repeats over and over as it flies in a pattern above me.

I want to tell it to leave, that the brightness of its flame-ridden feathers will alert the other bird to my position. But, unable to breathe, I can do nothing.

Snapping and cracking alarm me, but my sight has grown so dim that I'm unable to tell where it's coming from. The attack bird has not stopped trying to get to me.

More crunching. Though my eyes are wide open, I'm blind. Without oxygen, my body tingles. I can't hold on much longer.

Something slaps me hard on the cheek. The pain comes from far away.

Is this the end?

"Breathe Tambrynn." I'm lifted to sit, but I'm limp, unable to hold my head up.

Another slap hard across my other cheek and my chest squeezes in response.

I gasp, my chest heaving and my face throbbing. The surrounding forest is on fire. I'm on fire. Flames are everywhere. I drop back to the ground, hitting my head. Again.

"Get him. Roll on the ground." More yelling.

Screeching and roaring come from above me.

I maneuver so I'm back on my stomach, wanting to stand. My left arm stabs me with agony when I try to push my body up, so I slump back down. I'm sucking in as much oxygen as I can to make up for not being able to moments before. Dirt and leaves choke me, but I spit them out and keep gasping until I'm no longer dizzy or disoriented.

I rest my right bruised cheek against the cool ground and chance a look up. Ravens and the phoenix battle the larger bird, pushing it away from us. Though the eagle is much bigger, Persimony's bird flock is vigorous in their smaller attacks. The eagle finally relents and flies off.

"Tambrynn? Are you okay?" It's Persimony.

I'm still panting, my throat too raw to speak, so I nod.

"Come. Sit up. It will help you." She puts her arm around my back, wrenching my arm.

I squeal in pain and sink back to the blessedly cool dirt.

"Oh, that doesn't sound good. How badly is she injured?" Areli's voice is near the top of my head.

"I'm not sure. After the eagle got through her defenses and caused her to fall out of the sky, I lost sight of her," Zenek says from somewhere else.

"We'll get the Watcher and tend to his burns if you can carry Tambrynn," Persimony tells him.

Burns?

"Lucas?" I move to get up, grimacing against each injury. I'm on my knees when lightheadedness hits me. I have to stop, or I'll pass out.

"Let me help you." Areli is there beside me. "Which side hurts worse?"

Cringing, I turn my head her way. "My left. And my back. Somehow, that creature scratched me."

"They put poison on their talons." Persimony's voice is angry.

A mournful cry breaks out and something lands by my right side. *"Friend. Help."*

I turn my head to witness the phoenix is still alight with red and gold fire. Some of its feathers are missing and there's a scratch on its face. It had sacrificed its safety to come to my aid. Guilt niggles me at how I'd been so irritated when it spoke to me before. "Yes. Friend, help. Thank you for saving me."

It twitches and lifts its wings, dancing from one foot to the other. Its pink eyes reflect the red and yellow flames as the phoenix watches me with an unflinching regard. With a final roar, it arcs its wings back and up. Then they're moving toward me in a brilliant flash.

Suddenly, I'm on fire.

I'm burning alive.

22

As the fire consumes me, moments of my life that I wish to forget parade before my mind's eye in staggering detail.

Mother's death. The beatings I took at the hands of uncaring employers and the minor acts of retaliation I gleefully committed in return. All the heated disdain and suspicion of my star-shaped pupils and silver-spun hair. Meeting my father and discovering he's not who I wished him to be. The nomad girl—Colly—getting kidnapped, and Arrin's injuries at the hands of the froggen.

But it doesn't end there. I watch Lucas being cursed by my father and then being temporarily lost in his magpie form. The treller whom I had burned and walked away from with no remorse. Shellsea's accusations and my inability to retrieve her crown and the fishkin's treasures. My satisfaction at the murder of Siltworth. And most painful, Grandfather succumbing to my evil father's Mortuus Irrepo hex, making him a full sluagh. Finally, Audhild's sacrifice, which allows me the freedom I don't want without her.

It all sears me with excruciating detail—marking my heart like a red-hot poker. All my failures whisper in my ears. Accusing. They call for my death because I couldn't save them.

I wish it upon myself. My intentions haven't been perfect. Nothing I've done was enough to make up for it. I should die.

At my lowest, I sense him—my father—amid the turmoil whipped up in my soul. Malevolence slithers around me, trying to pin me down with his words of indictment. And I can't fight it off. His amusement grows with my every misstep, fault, or wrong I may have committed.

But who is he, an immoral, evil monster who preys upon anything he comes across to judge me? He who exerts no sympathy but seeks only the indulgence himself. He may be my father, but I refuse to let him overtake me.

I battle him with my mind, raging against the never-ending blazing whips that rip at my body, my very soul.

He laughs at me as if my struggles please him. His mirth expands until it's all I hear.

"No. Stop it." I scream into the nothingness, my eyes clamped shut against the onslaught.

"Tambrynn?"

I don't know the voice.

No, I do.

I open my eyes, expecting Mother.

It's not her. Instead, I find a lovely woman with a crown of colorful feathers atop her head—bright as a sunset. Her pretty face shines with a kindness I can almost touch. However, she has pink, glowing eyes.

"Phoenix?" I ask with disappointment I cannot hide in my tone.

"I'm Emberwing to my friends. We are friends, aren't we?" She turns her head in the curious way that birds do. She has a long neck for a person, which allows her to do so without looking gangly. "I took the only voice I thought would reach you. I'm sorry if it mislead you."

My father's darkness rages but cannot pierce the bubble that surrounds us—a shield she must have brought with her. I reach out to touch it and realize it's the dragon's heart. It reinforces my ability, holding back the flames that no longer barrage me. "What is happening? Why is the true dragon's heart here?"

Emberwing lifts one arm, her fingers long and graceful, resembling feathers, like Lucas's. "Your Watcher grabbed it before he came to search for you. Your body is trying to burn the evil away, but you are fighting it. You cannot regenerate until you allow the fire to release you into something new. Something stronger."

"Stronger? Powerful enough to face my father?"

"I am no fate-keeper. I cannot tell you what you will become. But if you allow the evil in, it will take you over, and the heart your Watcher holds will be lost. He will be lost. Only one can be Sovereign. Do you wish that be your father?" Her eyes snap at me, anger resting behind the glowing pink orbs.

Horror at the thought makes me tense. "No, of course not. But, I—"

"Few can walk through the fire without scars, that is true. The struggle to overcome tests our true selves. If the struggle were easy, anyone could rise to claim the Sovereign title." In a blink, the crystal heart is in her hands. She gives it to me. "Audhild gifted you with the title upon death. Halvar's legacy is more than name. It's his heart that will help guide you. Take their gifts and become the savior the Kinsman created you to be." In a wink, she's gone.

"Don't go." I scream, clutching the crystal heart tightly as the flames once more take control of me. Thoron's darkness seeps back in, circling me. I turn my head from him and reflect on Emberwing's words.

This heart was Halvar's? How? And then I understand. Thoron had used Halvar's heart in his Mortuus Irrepo hex, which turns anyone into his beastly pets. But somehow Grandfather had gotten ahold of it when they battled. It had saved him from being fully turned. That's what the bond was between him and Audhild. Grandfather possessed her mate's heart.

It didn't explain how Nyle had obtained it on Far Starl, a long way from Grandfather's keep, where he must've hidden it.

"Your sacrifices will not be wasted." I hold the heart close. "I will become the Sovereign. I will make you all proud."

With those words, I accept my fate.

I drop my will, which bears up against the inferno and allow the fire to come. I open my mouth and inhale it.

And in the flames, I find peace.

Part Two

I wake up in a strange room, in an actual bed, unsure of how I got there. Sunlight filters in through sheer, patterned curtains on one side of the large, stately room.

A soft, green blanket covers me. There's a plush pillow behind my head. But this can't be right. I hadn't been in a proper bed since Mother died. And what of these fine clothes? They're soft, not woolen. Not something I would have to wear.

Sleep coats my eyes, and I rub it off. Am I dreaming? How can I dream about something I've never experienced?

It takes me a moment to untangle myself from the layers of sheets and blankets so I can sit up. "Where am I?" I ask an empty room.

Across from the bed, a fire pops in a fireplace large enough to cook a side of pork. Yet, though burning, it's clean, not charred or greasy. My fingers pull at my collar, fearing I've fallen asleep somewhere I don't belong and someone will soon be by to discipline me.

Sliding down the side of the bed, I crumple to the wooden

floor with a grunt. Why am I'm as weak as a newborn? Have I been sick? What is going on?

A soft creak of a door opening.

"My lady?" a man's voice calls from the other side of the bed.

Should I hide? I glance at the bed, considering if I could crawl under it. There's a bag there. My belongings? But no. I don't recognize the strange sack. My arms grow weary, and I cannot slip away unseen before two legs appear in front of me.

"Oh, my lady. Are you all right?"

I jump back from his hands, gentle though they are.

"Don't."

"The regeneration probably muddled her mind a bit. Here, let me try." It's a woman's voice. Kind and patient.

"I'm confused." The words come out without my meaning them to. I grimace. This is not like me. I'm always silent. I know my place.

"That's understandable under the circumstances. Please, allow me to help you back to the bed." A hand—a giant hand—reaches for me.

"Stop," I demand and lean away from it, first because no one helps me. Ever. And second, because the hand is so much larger than anything I could expect. I slide myself back along the polished floor but only manage a short distance before I bump into a side table. I hang my head, wishing to disappear into the grains of the wood.

Movements shuffle away from me and then whispering.

Finally, something I'm used to. Had they caught a look at my face? My hair? I run a hand through my hair but am mortified to find it's short. A search with both of my hands confirms it to be true. I let out a sob. "Who cut my hair?"

It had only happened once in my life. When the son of one of my employers took a liking to me. He got handsy, and a rock smacked him square at his temple. I didn't mean to. I was only defending myself. My boss chopped my hair in uneven layers on purpose before hauling me back to the magistrate's office. I cried for hours and was mocked mercilessly for weeks as it grew out.

More furious whispering ensues.

"Look, I'm leaving." My mind draws a blank on where I am again. "If you'll just point me to the kitchens? It won't happen again." I try to stand, but my body does not comply. Tears sting the backs of my eyes. But that won't do. I bite my cheeks to keep them in check. I can't have them witness my distress, my weakness. They'll use it against me.

They always use it against me.

A door opens and shuts. I glance up at the dark man standing beside the doorway, looking decidedly uncomfortable. He shifts from one foot to the other, his gaze never leaving me.

I wish I had a shawl or a hood to cover my head. Growing uneasy about his intense scrutiny, I revisit my plan to slip beneath the bed.

However, the massive woman reopens the door. She carries a large red and orange bird with feathers like a peacock. The man stands with his arms across his chest, watching intently as the woman approaches me. She stops at the end of the bed and lets the bird down on the floor.

It turns its long neck and gives me a one-eyed, pink gaze. I can't look away.

"Friend? Help?"

I laugh to myself. *"I could use a friend, yes. But I don't have any."*

"Many friends." It fluffs its feathers, reaching out wide with its wings. The tips go from one wall to the other. *"No foes."*

I snort and then stop. When had I become infirm in the

head? Animals do not talk to people, even in one's imagination. Instead of the magistrate, I'll go to the workhouses. I school my face so they won't witness my errant thoughts.

An image of the man by the door holding my hand and smiling at me tickles my mind. *"Remember."*

I squint at the bird, suspicious. *'Lucas'*—a whisper in my mind—my voice. I drop my head, frightened. What is happening?

I glance back up at the trio before me. They all emanate expectancy. I nibble at a dry patch on my lip, uncertain what it is they want from me.

"Emberwing?" the woman asks the bird. There's an unspoken question attached to the word.

The bird dances back and forth on its long legs, the talons clicking against the shiny boards. The feathers on the crown of its head rise in a glorious display before it opens its mouth. A loud call breaks out of the bird, filling my ears with its sound.

Before I can brace for it, a flash of fire hits me in the face. I scream and slap at my eyes and my cheeks. It's hot, but it isn't burning me.

But I'm still aflame. I brush at the blue flames that light across my arms and flow down my body to my legs. My slaps sting, so I know I can feel. Why is the fire not burning, then? I whimper and struggle without success to put it out.

I roll into a ball, my knees up to my chin, hands on my head, sure I've become unstable.

The glow grows until everything in view has a blue tint to it. I'm humming. No, my gut is buzzing. I'm vibrating with a strange energy, making me jitter with the power.

Power.

Strength.

Fire.

Fire—*bird.*

The words click into place in my mind, and I remember it all.

All the good. And strange. Along with the bad. Pain lances through my head as the memories settle back into its dark recesses. I'm not on Tenebris. This isn't Anavrin, it's too different. I'm in Benario Vale with Persimony, Emberwing, and Lucas.

And I'm not a weak, slobbering girl. I've been gifted a true dragon's heart. I'm the new Sovereign.

My whimpering stops, and I uncurl myself, stretching my legs and back. Warmth and a familiar purr from the center of my being wash through me—centering me.

I drag my gaze up to Lucas and smile. "Lucas." His smile is the best reward I could ever have. "Thank you, Emberwing." The bird preens before me, her feathers alert and shining. Her tongue clicks, and she cackles.

"So glad to have you back with us." Persimony picks up the phoenix and turns. "I'll let you two catch up."

I wait for the door to shut before I speak. My arms shake, but I ignore them. Urgency tingles through me. "How long have I been out of it, and what do we need to catch up on?"

Lucas comes over and holds out a slim hand to me. I recall the feathers of my beloved magpie in his gallant gesture, and I'm so thankful for him. It takes a bit of effort to climb back up into the bed. When I'm settled, he sits next to me. "It's been a couple of days since you regenerated."

I purse my lips together. "I—regenerated?"

He rubs the back of my hand. "Yes. The war eagle injured you. Your fire became unmanageable again—out of control. Emberwing gave you the dragon's heart and connected with you. I sensed some sort of a bond form between you. But I couldn't reach you. You were lost to me." His dark eyes shine with unshed tears. His laugh is breathy. "I was scared. So scared."

I turn toward him and brush the tears from his cheek. He'd covered the healing mark on his neck with a layer of clear lotion. It's still red and swollen, so I don't touch it. Instead, I drop my hand. "I'm so sorry. I remember bits of it, but not everything."

"This is nothing, my lady. You were burning alive along with the heart. At least, that's what it looked like. Persimony assured me it was going to be all right." He runs a hand through his bangs, which are threatening to curtain his eyes, and I realize how tired he looks. "But it didn't feel all right. What do you remember?"

I take a deep breath and search my memory for the pieces. A shiver racks my body. "My father was there mocking me. Showing me all the ways I've failed. It was horrid. But Emberwing gave me the heart and a convincing talk. So, I stopped fighting the fire, and there was this incredible peace." I put a hand on my chest and then glance down. My necklace is gone.

He reaches into a pocket and holds out a blackened piece of metal—even the gem in the center is but a charred rock. "The fire ruined your mother's necklace. I'm so sorry, my lady. I know it means a great deal to you."

Sadness and loss rock me. Mother, Audhild, and Grandfather. I choke back the grief. "It's expected, I'm sure. There isn't much that can survive a fire that hot." And then another thought comes to mind. "What about the dragon's heart?"

He shakes his head. "When the flames died down, it was gone. There was no sign of it. I had to explain to everyone, of course, how we came upon it and what it was. Areli guessed before I said what it was, voyant and all. And I had to admit that I made a mistake bringing it with me, thinking you were running away." He lets out a huff of air. "We didn't do such a great job of keeping it safe for Nyle, did we?"

I put a hand on my chest. It has a double beat. "But that can't be." I take Lucas's hand and place it above my heart. "What do you feel?"

His eyes widen. "You have a double heartbeat. How can that be?"

"Is it possible that when I regenerated, the dragon's heart became a part of me?" I press my hand harder, feeling the *thump, thump, thump* in swift beats.

"If it did, there's nowhere safer for it to be." Lucas gently runs his hands across my stubble-like hair. "I'm so sorry about this, my lady. There was more of it left, but it was badly singed. Areli trimmed it back so it didn't look like a burned mop before we put you in bed and waited for you to wake up."

My heart skips a beat as I realize it might've changed as well. "Is it still silver?"

He squints at me and turns my head back and forth. "It's more of a silver-white now. Maybe the fire purified it."

"And my eyes?" I dip my head, unsure of what I want the answer to be.

"Are as beautifully starry-eyed as ever, but strangely, they're not gray anymore. They're a beautiful light blue." He squeezes my shoulder. "Your tan from Far Starl is gone, though."

I lift my arm. I'm pale as milk now. My shoulder. It doesn't ache or hurt like it had for so long. I reach around and touch the spot on my side that had been ripped open by my father's curse. "They're gone."

"What's gone?" Concern gives Lucas's voice a growl.

I rustle about touching every place I recall getting injured while fleeing from the war eagle. "All my injuries. The wound from the talisman. And I hit my shoulder on a tree and then hit my head." I rub the spot on my scalp, but there's no pain or tenderness—not even a welt. "When you mentioned regenerating, it didn't occur to me that I didn't hurt. All my wounds are healed."

I reach up to the space between my shoulder and neck, but there's no scar there from the arrow. The skin is smooth as though it never happened. "If it's like starting completely over, how do I still have my memory? Or at least how'd it return? How is that possible?"

Lucas shrugs. "I'm not sure, my lady. I don't know all the details. And really, we don't have much information about it since regenerating only happens to firebirds. Never to a person, not even a djinn. I don't know that it's ever happened before."

"So, what you're saying is that I'm one of a kind?" I tease him and slip my arm around his back.

"You've always been one of a kind, my lady. That hasn't changed."

His lips are tender against mine in a precious kiss. I tuck my head against his shoulder, grateful to be back once more. Living to fight another day. Honoring those who came before me. Ready to take on my father.

24

My stomach grumbles, and I realize I'm starving. "Do you think there's any food around?

A knock on the door stops Lucas from replying. He opens the door to Persimony's daughter Yesenia, who holds a tray of food and drinks.

"Mama said you'd be hungry." She glances shyly up at me, an eager curiosity sparkling in her brown eyes. The tray rattles as she sits it on a table by the window. "I thought so, too, so I gave you my favorite berries from breakfast." She shrugs. "I didn't need them today. Mama said I'm already big and strong like her." She stands beside the table.

Her kindness and sharing takes me aback. Possibly Lucas was correct. The girl was not afraid of me, just simply curious. "Thank you."

"I was glad you didn't fully regenerate like phoenixes do, or you'd have turned into a baby. I don't like babies. They cry all the time, and they can't play with you." She explains about the neighbors who have a baby and how it sometimes wakes her up in the middle of the night. She bounces on her toes, her hands planted firmly on one chair, which is tucked neatly beneath the plain table.

I raise my eyebrows at her, envying her energy, but not knowing how to respond.

"Anyway, Mom said to take your time. You need to regain your strength. Maybe when you do, you can play with us. We have lots of games."

It had been such a long time since I'd played anything. What would giant children play?

Persimony's voice drifts into the room, calling for Yesenia to come help her with something, saving me from having to promise anything.

"I've got to go." Her footsteps slap again as she rushes across the room. She's gone before I can thank her. The door, however, shuts quietly behind her.

I stare at the carved door, at a loss for words.

Lucas chuckles as he helps me out of the bed and across to the wooden chair. "She's become quite fond of you."

"Fond of me? Why?" I sit and take a drink of the milk. It is so delicious I down half the glass before I stop.

"You fought off a war eagle and survived. And then you went up in flames. Nobody except Persimony has witnessed a firebird regenerate before." He sits and removes the lid from his plate. It's heaped with food and still steaming. "And that eagle was from the Eaglecaller clan that's been tormenting Persimony's people. You fought against their biggest eagle and got in a few good blows, too. When the children heard their parents telling others about it, Yesenia became enthralled with you."

I pause with the fork halfway to my mouth. "But I didn't battle the eagle, not really. I was just trying to out-fly it. Then I was injured trying to get away. Emberwing and the ravens chased it off. I didn't do anything glorious."

Lucas stares at me. "I watched you battle it. You knocked it off of you once. As big as it was, that was incredible." He sets his fork down. "Tambrynn, do you realize how big you are in your firebird form? That eagle is a monster. It was fast and powerful, and you fought out of its grasp. Its *magical* grasp. Zenek said that none of their flock that fought this bird survived—not until you came along, anyway. And I have to say, your fiery spinning fall was majestic. Your flames practically sang in this terrible and haunting ballad, filling the air like a tornado." His voice holds a reverence I'm unsure how to take.

Surely, he's only trying to encourage me. "I don't remember any of that, let alone the flames. It certainly wasn't majestic. Clumsy, maybe." I take a bite of the eggs. They're fluffy and delicious with some ham and creamy cheese added in.

His mouth hangs open before he snaps it shut. "You also don't see your own light when you fly or when we were walking in the Aversum Way, either, do you?" A gotcha tone seeps into his voice.

"No. But—"

Lucas holds up a hand. "No buts. You were amazing, even if you were flying away from me." He points his fork at me, reminding me of the dour Jarrel. "Please don't do that again, by the way. I thought you were going to leave me behind. And if you grow stronger from regenerating, full regeneration or not, I can't wait to see what you will do now."

I finish the eggs and move on to the fruit Yesenia brought before I comment again. Lucas's observations of my interaction with the war eagle run through my mind. It all seems too extraordinary to be true. But so were my abilities when I learned about magic. "What is our next step?"

The plate in front of Lucas is empty. He'd eaten faster than

I had. "We'll learn everything we can from Persimony and Areli. They may have some insight into what our next course of action should be." He wipes his mouth with a linen napkin and sets it beside his plate. "We need all the help we can get if we're going to take on Thoron."

"Not to mention the Hulda." All the fuzzy warmth fades as I think of the tasks ahead of me—*us*. I don't relish facing either of them. Especially if I must face them together again, warring against each other or not. I ball a fist against my heart. "Will I be strong enough to take them both on?"

There's a knock on the door before Areli lets herself in. "I wanted to be reassured of your recovery." She strides in, her hands behind her back. "And I apologize, but I heard your last comment. I think I can help you both."

I stare at the fierce set of her chin. "How?"

"We'll train you, both of you, with the ravens and Emberwing."

———

Lucas and I perch in our bird forms on the fence outside of the raven enclosure. Evening whispers to us in the deepening shade of blue creeping across the sunset sky. I slept most of the day and awoke to another incredible meal. Now, well-rested and well-fed, I'm ready to fly with the rest of the Ravenwarren's birds.

"We've grown to expect the attacks to come in twos. First, they scout to find a weakness, and then they hit with more of their war eagles." Persimony instructs as she opens each door of the ravens' cages. The birds flutter out and join us on the fence—but not too close. I sense their hesitation. Can they sense the dragon's heart inside me? "Zenek has taken

Emberwing to the east perimeter. She'll fly back to us once she confirms there's no threat."

What if they attack her? I screech at Persimony, hoping she'll understand. It comes out louder than I normally squawk, startling myself and the birds on the fence. I dance a little, trying to rid myself of the nervous energy coursing through me.

Areli answers. "If they're attacking, she'll let out a war cry with a wave of flames. It's glorious to behold." Her enthusiasm shows no bounds. "We'll see it from here, and the ravens and you two, will fly out in force to help defend the village."

"Is it my imagination or does she sound like she's excited by that idea?" I ask Lucas.

He hops from one foot to another, his wings partially out to balance himself. *"She must be partially djinn. From what I've observed of her so far, she's a definite thrill seeker."*

"Yes, but even you didn't enjoy the ride across the bridge here. If she's djinn, she's full-blooded."

Persimony releases the last raven. There's no room left on the top fence board for it to land, so it arcs around and lands next to Lucas. It is bigger than Lucas by a head, and the only difference in coloring is the small white bib on Lucas's chest.

It flexes its head to gaze above Lucas, scrutinizing me. I don't blame it. We're bigger than they are, or at least I am. My appearance has changed. I glow silver-blue in the dusk, and my feathers are covered in a hard, scale-like coating now. This must be from Halvar's heart, but I'm grateful for it. I'll be harder to injure with the protection covering my sensitive areas.

The bird finally fluffs its feathers and lets out a cry. All the other birds grow restless at its agitation.

Persimony whistles. "Calm, brood." The birds stop shuffling and settle. She nods her head. "Tambrynn and Lucas, follow their lead. And don't forget how big these eagles are. Watch how the ravens make slight attacks before retreating and attacking again. Just because you're bigger doesn't automatically mean you win the battle. To that end, don't take one bird on alone. There's strength in numbers."

Fire shoots into the sapphire sky, followed by a roaring shriek, signaling trouble.

Ravens dance about on the board, awaiting instructions, their beaks in the air.

"Go, my pets. Kinsman be with you." Persimony's whistle signals for them to go.

As one, the ravens alight, shaking the fence.

Lucas and I are not far behind, having waited for them to lead us into battle.

"Lucas, use your lizard sight." I imagine the desert creature in my mind, and my vision becomes clearer, more nuanced.

"That's incredible." His delighted astonishment filters through our bond. *"Why hadn't I thought to do that before?"*

"It was so dark the other eve. I was just wishing I had the ability to see like on Far Starl, and to my surprise, it happened."

The birds split, half heading left, and the other right. Lucas and I agreed to stay together, neither of us wanting to leave the other unattended. We swing right with the second group, following the cries of the phoenix.

I spot six war eagles circling along a fence line with tall spruce trees that appear to be Ferndown Valley's border. Zenek is nowhere in sight, which gives me some relief. Magic or not, the eagles are far too big for one person to take on.

"Friend? Help?"

"Yes, we're here to help. Are you okay?"

Fire erupts once more, and in the dazzling brilliance of the flames, I spy two war eagles attacking Emberwing.

I lift my wings and shove harder. My buzzing ability

bubbles, almost excitedly, flowing through my body like melted metal. I open my mouth and pour out a blaze, blocking the nearest eagle from hitting the phoenix. My fire hits it, and feathers spiral from its long wing.

It screams in protest and turns toward me.

"Watch out, my lady." Lucas feints and drops lower.

"Watching," I reply as I lift, drawing it away from him and the others. It takes my bait and follows me upward.

It's as fast as I remember the last eagle being, but not as big. I twist mid-swing and face it. With a thought, I'm ablaze in blue energy, my shield firmly in place. With a mighty beat of my wings, I unleash blue power on my foe—enough to hinder but not kill it. It catches the bird by surprise, crackling along its immense body, stopping its momentum and making it drop out of flight.

My power dies off, but not before I've flown at a second war eagle. The ravens, seeing the first war eagle's weakness, dart at it, hindering it from following me.

"Wonderful job, my lady."

I screech, relishing the compliment. Satisfied with my first attack, I turn to a second war eagle that's too close to Emberwing's backside. My gut vibrates with untapped energy, and I'm invigorated.

Reaching as far back with my wings as I can, I pull at the heat running through my veins. In the blink of my eye, I'm coated with glowing blue energy. I stretch my wings to swing them and hit the eagle at Emberwing's back.

Wham.

Something hits me, and I'm spiraling through the air.

It's too fast to check where I'm going when I hit another body. A roar bursts forth, and red flames join my crackling blue power. They wash off me like rain on a duck's back —harmless.

However, I've hit Emberwing, and we're tumbling in the air, heads over tails, a swarming sphere of red and blue.

"Friend?" she croons in my head before interlocking my claws in hers.

Like with the visions I've had with Shellsea and Nyle, I connect with Emberwing and view her memories. They're vast, spanning several lifetimes. Unlike the other two, the phoenix has no ill will or selfish motives. There are so many memories. They fly by like a gust of wind, and I catch only the barest hint of what she wants me to see. Treasures in an endless trove of knowledge.

One memory halts—suspended before my mind. It's a man talking with Emberwing. He's not handsome, as common opinion would dictate. There's no smoothness to him. His face is worn but amiable, his hands calloused but tender. Compassion radiates from the conspiratorial bend of his head to the slight smile on his lips. *"I give everyone opportunities throughout their lifetime. Many fail to do what they should. Others give into the darkness around them and never know why they're unsatisfied or keep failing. The ultimate test of one's character is found not in the trying, for many try. It is when an individual embraces the light and rises above their circumstances. When they do what is right, despite personal cost, that they attain a greater calling. That's where destiny is found."*

Lines crinkle from the corners of his eyes, which are neither blue nor brown. *"When we can fearlessly sacrifice ourselves for others, no work of evil can break the impact of such an act."*

Without knowing how or why, I know this man is the Kinsman. Even as that thought comes to mind, his image fades, and I can no longer recall what he looks like. Like ash in the wind, the vision is gone.

Noise bombards my ears, and I'm once more in the Ferndown Valley, my talons interlocked with Emberwing's.

Warmth floods me. Blue, crackling light blasts from the center of my being. It joins with the phoenix's red-hot flames, becoming a beam stronger than Anavrin's lighthouse's radiance.

Our combined light brightens in intensity, so much so that I have to close my eyes. But before we can do anything else, we're hit hard from the side, knocking us apart.

I screech out my dismay and face a larger eagle. It must be the same one from the other night.

Emberwing's piercing call doesn't shake the eagle's glower. It attacks me, but we're too close for it to be immensely impactful. I rake my claws across its belly and am rewarded with its grasping hold of me instead.

We twist circles in the sky. Everything blurs around us.

It snaps its beak at me, and I bite back, our wings stretched and moving to keep us airborne. I *push* with my energy, and it releases me. My protective sphere snaps back into place, and when it comes back to me, I thwart the eagle.

Shrieking, it attacks again, and then again. When it tries a third time, I let it in and grab hold of its talons like Emberwing had with me. With a mighty swing of my wings, we're spinning again. I pull on my fire, and then we're an enormous ball of blue flame and crackling energy.

Its memories play out in my mind. Training. Always fighting. How it was forced to attack sacks filled with stuffing at first. Then small animals. And then people. It knows nothing but what it has been trained to do. It's well fed when it does something right, and then starved when it does something wrong. Now, it won't give up even upon death.

I pull out of the vision, saddened. This creature hasn't lived its own life. It was trained from a hatchling to do its master's bidding, no matter the cost. Like the dragons on Far Starl. Like the indentured servants on Tenebris.

My double heartbeat skips until it's a singular entity. Stronger. More powerful.

We're like a spinning top, going around and around without end. I call on my inner fire to purge the eagle of the warlike behavior, focusing specifically on the violence. I insert my desire for it to be at peace and free instead. My flames build until they're white hot. When I'm sure my work is done, I let the eagle go.

It lets out a small cry before it drops to the ground with a thud. It shakes its head and fluffs its feathers, assuring me it is still alive.

I alone am left hovering above the battlefield.

Emberwing's roaring call breaks the silence of the night. She stands beside two of the other eagles, who lay unmoving on the ground. Close to her is a group of ravens beside another two eagles, and then the other group of ravens with the last eagle sprawled on the ground.

"My lady?" Lucas comes out of the trees, flying straight for me. *"Are you okay?"*

"I'm fine. What happened to the other birds?"

"You don't know?" he says.

"No. The larger eagle caught me and all I remember is spinning."

"You were like a storm, whipping and spinning about. Your power knocked them out of the sky. It was spectacular."

Flames break out below us.

I scree in alarm. All the other ravens jump and scurry away.

Emberwing has caught fire.

Burned feathers and dying embers fill the air. It's thick with smoke and soot. I land beside the singed spot where Emberwing had been standing and change back. In her place is a small red and orange chick. It blinks wide pink eyes up at me as I bend over to pick her up.

She flutters in my grasp, trying to get her balance. *"Friend?"* Her voice is a chitter in my head.

"Yes, the best of friends." Tears trail down my cheeks. I'm not sure why I'm crying, but I can't stop it.

Lucas lands next to me, changing. "Why do you think she regenerated?" He takes the chick, her puffy reddish-orange fluff waving as she moves. He rubs a gentle finger down the back of her head.

"I don't know." The sadness remains as I roll my shoulders. Had she known she was going to regenerate when she gave me her memory vision? One eagle twitches, turning my attention to them. "What happened to them?"

"Blinded by your dazzling light, most likely," Lucas replies.

Emberwing coos to him and rubs her beak on his finger. "I'm not sure if their stupor is permanent or only temporary."

A loud whistle sounds and the ravens, which had been pecking at the grass and wandering around, take flight back toward the village.

Crunching sounds of something moving, or many things moving, break the quiet din. Seven small men crawl through the brambles between the evergreen trees. They mutter to themselves in a language I don't understand.

I have a sense of *déjà vu*. I almost expect Nobbert to amble along with the other nomads ready to shackle me. However, though they look very similar to the grumpy, bearded men, they are not the same ones. They have beards without mustaches, have no hats to cover their bald heads, and wear shoes, something quite different from the Anavrinian nomads.

They stop immediately when they spot us and the eagles. Voices raised, they point to Lucas and me. One of them takes a bow from his back and aims an arrow at us.

"Halt, Eaglecallers." Zenek yells and drops out of a tree on the border, thudding on the ground behind the smallish men. They all jump, startled.

The one with the bow drops his arm and dodges for the cover of the long grasses between the trees.

"Do those little men remind you of anyone?" I ask Lucas.

"Now that you mention it, they do." He gathers Emberwing to him and places a hand in front of the chick protectively.

"Come out and face us." Zenek strides over to one eagle. It snaps its beak at him when he gets close, but it doesn't get up. Zenek swings his hand in front of the eagle's face. It doesn't respond. "What will you do with a group of blind eagles?" A touch of humor laces his words.

I'm horrified at the thought of having blinded them, even if they were attacking the Ravenwarren clan.

One of the small men runs out of cover and over to the giant man. "You'll pay for ruining our kettle." He stands only hip-high on Zenek. His beard is longer than he is, the ends of the white bushy hair grayed from dragging in the dirt. I wonder how he doesn't trip on it.

"You forget you're not in charge anymore, Goddard. And since your birds are on our land, we can take them as part of our warren now. Isn't that the rule your clan agreed upon years ago?" He moves toward the eagle that snapped at him.

"Worthless Ravenwarrens. I don't care 'bout no rules. Don't touch my bird." Goddard yells.

His stubborn fanaticism reminds me so much of my favorite nomad that I'm moved to intervene.

I hold out my hand to stop him, blue lightning sizzling across my skin. It's then that I notice the light that shines from my body, reflecting off the top of his bald head.

Goddard stumbles back, a hand to his chest. "Who—what are you?"

Three other of the Eaglecaller clan join him. None of them look happy.

Zenek nods my way. "This is the new Sovereign, Tambrynn."

A second nomad narrows his eyes at me. "Doesn't look like a sovereign to me. She's not even a dragon. You're trying to fool us." They all break out in loud disagreement.

"I assure you, she has the heart of a dragon." The tilt of Zenek's face is smug.

The man crosses his arms over his chest. "Whelp, I don't believe you. Your clan is nothing but liars."

With a thought, I change to a dragon. I stretch my wings out and roar at them. My disguise is flawless, though it is unfair. I'm not a true dragon. But I am the Sovereign.

They rush into a circle, their arms across each other's

backs, hiding what they're saying. They mutter in that strange language. When they break apart, the bowman has recovered his bow. He aims at me. Before any of us can react, there's a thwapping sound. He releases his arrow, and it comes right for me.

My blue shield flickers into place, but I drop it. The arrow bounces harmlessly against my scaled hide, dropping to the ground. There's not even a scratch on me. I open my mouth and spit blue fire into the sky.

Stunned gasps break out.

Zenek stomps over to me, picks the arrow up, and snaps it in half. "If anyone should pay, it's you for attacking the Kinsman's chosen. You, who held all our clans up to the most holy decrees for centuries, now openly attack the one who is called Sovereign? How the mighty have fallen." He shakes his head, disgust clear on his face.

I change back to my girl form. Lucas comes to stand next to me. "Nice job, my lady," he whispers as he pets Emberwing.

Zenek hands me the two pieces, the arrow looking decidedly tiny in his large hand. "I apologize for their thoughtless attack. Though you could retaliate"—he turns to send a sidelong glance at the men—"I pray you won't use their actions against them." He turns his back on them and winks meaningfully at me.

So, this is his game? Scare them into compliance. Though I don't care for such things, I understand how this could peacefully lead the Ravenwarren clan into a compromise with the Eaglecallers.

I step forward and try my best to glide as I'd seen Audhild do. If I were indeed to be the Sovereign, I needed to learn elegance. I reach Goddard and hold out the broken arrow. I recall the man's words in Emberwing's vision. "What is your goal in attacking the Ravenwarren clan?"

The first man blusters. "They put their noses in our business, warring upon our clan. We only want what we had back."

Zenek stills.

I put a finger up to stop him. "What do you want so badly that you would attack a group of people to get it?"

"It's our kingdom." He bellows, his face turning a deep shade of red.

"You aren't from this kingdom or you'd know." Another of the group spits out. "Who are you to question us, anyway?"

"Do not challenge me." I raise my voice, my eyes heating with anger. The sound of it resonates, and the little men step back from me, fear skittling across their faces. I admit it sounded intimidating like Audhild's voice had. "You who have no fear of my wrath have found it."

They freeze in place, stunned looks on their faces. I walk over and place my hand on the first man's head. I view their history from his early schooling. Nomads set themselves up as the guardians of the holy items when the kingdoms split. They lived in the mountains and mined, growing rich from the minerals, metals, and gems. And then they found the pools of magic—leftovers from before the kingdom split. They used it to lord over the other giant clans, creating armies to guard their wealth instead of guarding the holy items.

Those items they hid as the eldrin did on Anavrin. Then the nomads changed the stories of their history—slanting it to make themselves look grand while disparaging the giants. After years of indoctrination, the nomads got their wish—they became the leaders of the kingdom. Older generations of giants fought back, knowing the lies they spread, but their efforts were fruitless. The nomads batted them down using their vast resources. When the giants finally united, given a single purpose—they overthrew the nomadic rule.

Nomads weren't used to submission, though. They became rabid, like dogs, mad in their quest to recapture their power. They used the magic pools to make their eagles larger and more deadly. Used poison to maim and kill their opponents. Their revenge took on deadly consequences.

Disgusted, I let him go. The glint of his eye reveals he knows what I saw. He's not apologetic, but defiant.

"One clan should not rule over others. It is not the natural way of things. You must rule together, a united leadership. That way, there's harmony and peace. From this point forward, there will be no more fighting. Your clan and all clans in the future will cease creating eagle armies. You will not retaliate for any misdeed you believe they owe you, for you deserve nothing."

They grumble. I stop them with a lifted finger, crackling blue energy zinging across my skin. Fear flickers in each of their faces.

"Your clans will work together to form a panel. You will unify and work together for the good of all the inhabitants of this kingdom, not just one or the other." I glance at Zenek and am relieved that he nods.

The bowman tilts his head at me, highlighting the hair coming out of his ears. His beard twists downward in a frown. "And what if we don't?"

All the injustice I've ever witnessed rises inside of me. I inhale a deep breath and flip open my palm. A harmless, though bright, flame washes across their faces, sealing my words. "If you don't, I will come back and burn your houses, your townships, and your land. I will seize your mines and all your businesses. The pools of magic will dry up. I will leave you with nothing. You will have no resources to bring to the table, and you'll be at the mercy of all the other clans from now until the One World reunites. Have I made myself clear?"

None of them speak. Though there's a heated fury in their eyes, there's also a sweep of surrender that flows from their angry auras.

"Now, who do these birds belong to?" I ask Zenek.

"Our clan can nurse them back to health. Then we will return them to the Eaglecallers. All except for this one." He points to the eagle I'd battled, the biggest one. "This one stays with our warren."

"Is that acceptable to your clan?" I ask the men.

At first, they look like they're going to argue. The first man raises his arms against the others. They mumble in begrudging acquiescence. I wonder how well they will follow my "request."

"Fine. I decree this clan war to be over in finality." I pull out my Mortifer Blade, which I'd placed at my waist before the training exercise. "Let's make this official. Gentlemen, lend me your hands." Though my fire holds much power, I wanted to be sure it would be binding.

I draw blood from Zenek and all the other clansmen. When I slice the last palm, the wind rustles through the trees, power washing over us and setting their oaths in place.

Emberwing chirps happily in Lucas's hands and then tucks her beak beneath a stubby wing.

"Friend. Ally," her chirpy voice squeaks in my mind.

Her contentment filters through a lingering bond between us. For the first time, I have hope that I can defeat my father.

But we must return to Anavrin to do so.

26

I stand in the same area where we disembarked Areli's sleigh days before. The morning is bright, and a gentle rain the eve before has refreshed Benario Vale. The setting is invigorating, and though this kingdom is beautiful, a nagging worry for Rekspire has festered in my gut like a thorn under my skin. We need to get back to Anavrin.

"So, you don't want to ride with me back to the Aversum Way?" Disappointment puckers Areli's face. "I'd hoped to have company for the ride back."

Lucas and I share a brief look. "I think we'd rather spread our wings this time."

I try not to give away the half-truth. We'd rather not go through the harrowing ride again. Ever—even uphill. Flying is preferred. "There is much to get back to," I add, trying my best not to hurt her feelings.

Persimony hands me a cloth with several food items in it. There's a glint of laughter in her dark eyes. "Food for your trip and for when you return home. There are also some herbs and seeds in there and a honey gift for the doorman guard to entice him to show you the way back to your kingdom's doorway without hassle. Areli hinted it was his favorite from our kingdom."

The voyant says nothing as she pets her stags. However, a slight grin forms on her lips at the bribe.

"Wait." Yesenia runs across the grass. A raven precedes her and circles above us, waiting for her to arrive. The girl is huffing when she comes to a stop beside her mother. "I wanted to give this to you before you left, so you don't forget us."

She hands me a cloth-wrapped item. I'm touched by her thoughtfulness. "You didn't have to do that but thank you."

Inside is a corded necklace woven with feathers.

"It's yours and Emberwing's feathers," she states proudly, her smile wide and joyful. "We burned the rest 'cause Areli said hair and feathers can be used against you, and she doesn't trust the Eaglecaller clan. I don't know what that means, but she said I could make this for you so you could wear it. To remember us."

Areli's face gives nothing away, but there's a steely determination in her dark eyes. I bow my head to her.

I hold the necklace to my chest, cherishing it. "Thank you so much. I will treasure it and always remember you."

Yesenia claps her hands and laughs. Voices call to her in the distance—the loudest being her tutor, calling her back to class. There, as well as above us, are ravens flying around, awaiting the children's signals as they learn how to train them. Hopefully, now it wouldn't be for fighting or war with the Eaglecaller clan. She hugs Lucas and me both tightly before skip-running away.

Lucas helps me put the necklace on, though without hair it's much easier to do so. "I'm so sorry I don't have anything to give her in return."

Pride shines on Persimony's golden face. She laughs.

"You've given everyone around here more than enough in tales and stories. I daresay that girl will tell everyone from now until her final breath that she knows the Sovereign Tambrynn, the only person with a dragon's heart. That is worth more than a passing gift. Now, you go. You have tasks to do. Be well, my friends. Know you always have a place to call home here with the Ravenwarren clan."

I pick up the food bundle again. The contents are unknown, but I'm grateful for it and for these people. I tuck the parcel into my pack and shrug it on. There's plenty of room now that the other food and the crystal heart are gone. With my Mortifer Blade in place at my belted waist, Lucas and I wave goodbye. We change and fly over the lush valley, following the land bridges that go up as high as the mountains and to the weathered tree we'd arrived from.

Landing back in the pasture, I change and take a last glance around. The tree Areli used to enter Benario Vale, a frosted spruce, is before us. Blue needles cover its wide limbs. They're tipped in white, where it must get its name. The tree blends in better than any of the other Zoe Trees.

The scent of the evergreens is refreshing. "This kingdom is truly magnificent, isn't it?"

"It is," Lucas says after he changes as well. "Ready, my lady?" He grins, his long, inky hair brushing across his forehead.

I run my hand through it, kiss his cheek, and switch to lizard eyesight. Areli had assured us the night before it wouldn't harm the passage if we donned reptile vision beforehand. "Ready."

We enter a dark passage in chaos.

I stand hand-in-hand with Lucas. "What is going on?" I yell to be heard above the wind. Gusts whip past us, shaking the tree limbs and bowing the grasses low. Sticks fly by us, traveling on the strong current. I hadn't noticed before how much my hair kept me warm and protected my ears until now. My necklace flops around, so I tuck it inside my shirt for safekeeping.

"I don't know, but it can't be anything good," he yells back. Wind flings his hair in different directions. He leans in close to me so he doesn't have to scream. "We either need to wait for Areli to come through the tree or find Jarrel—"

A man with a scepter held high steps out from behind a tree. "Knew yeh'd be along sometime. See what yeh've done bringin' trouble with yeh here to this peaceful place?" He waves the weapon around.

I straighten to face him. His aura is as muddled as before, blending in with the dark space. And though I sense nothing evil coming from him, he always brings a sense of alertness to my nerves that makes me pay attention. So, though I'd promised myself that I would be tolerant of him, my hackles are raised. I fight against them so my abilities don't creep out, knowing he would chastise me for it. "Look—"

Lucas places a hand on my arm. "Tambrynn, why don't you get our gift for him?"

"Right." I slip the pack off and dig inside the wrapped items, taking that moment to resettle my fire, letting it simmer instead of steam. I find the jar, the only one inside, and present it to the nomad guard. "We hoped you might help us back to Anavrin's doorway." At his dark look, I rush on. "This gift is also an apology for any trouble we've caused you." He should notice my father's curse is gone, so there shouldn't be any reason for him to stop us.

He takes a long sniff, though with the wind blowing wildly around us, I'm not sure what he can detect. "Is that Yesenia's honey?" he asks, his voice less hostile.

"It is. We had some on our biscuits this morn." It was

delicious over the warm, fluffy rolls. I'm almost tempted to keep it if he gets hostile again.

He snatches the jar from my hand. "Fine. But that's it. I won't help yeh if'n yeh come back." He tucks the jar inside a wide bib pocket beneath his fat chin. "This way, and don't lose me like yeh did that voyant."

We hustle after him. Luckily, with the improved eyesight, I don't trip over anything. However, we have to lean against the current and dodge some of the flying debris.

We walk for what seems like an age before we come to a wizened tree.

He stops, and I almost run him over. I push the scepter away, not wanting to be impaled by the sharp tines, earning a dark glance from the nomad guard.

"What's the matter?" I ask him loudly.

"The doorway's unlit." He growls out over his shoulder.

"What does that mean?" Lucas steps closer to get a better look.

"Means yeh can't use it." He removes a small cap from the top of his bald head and scratches it. "What in the blazes?" he says it more to himself than to us.

I touch the bark, not sure whether I should believe him. Nothing happens. Fear wraps around my heart in a gripping hold. "So, what do we do, then?"

"Not my problem. I got yeh to Anavrin's doorway. That was our agreement." He stretches the hat back over his head and walks off.

"Wait." I use a trickle of my ability. The Way is already unsettled. A little more wouldn't hurt anything.

He stiffens, stopped in his tracks.

"I don't mean to be ungrateful. But unless you help us find our way, we'll be here with you forevermore. So, not as a favor but as a mutual benefit to us all, I am asking as kindly as I can that you lead us to another doorway. Back to Benario Vale or to Panacea where the voyants live? If you'd be ever so kind." I add in a sweet voice before I release him.

He smooths down his sideburns, fury clear in the set of his bushy eyebrows. When he's finished, he raises the scepter. "I ought to zap yeh and send yeh on yer merry way to the holding pen."

"Ah, but you wouldn't do that would you, Jarrel?" It's Areli. With the noise of the wind, she'd pulled up without me noticing. One of the stags nuzzles Lucas's ear, earning a snort of laughter from him. "It is your duty to help the lost, isn't it?" She dares him with her direct look.

He flings his arms down. "All of yeh are nothin' but trouble. Yeh don't rule this here Way, yeh know."

She steps toward him, her hands clasped in front of her in a deceptive, calm manner. "Ah, but neither do *you*. Our new Sovereign and her Watcher have been invited in by the very Path Master. It is, therefore, your sworn duty to help, not hinder. Unless you'd like to be stationed somewhere less appealing. Such things happen from time to time."

He grumbles under his breath. "Their doorway is dark."

"Then I suggest you bring them to the next available kingdom to look for the Zoe Tree so they can take that passage instead. There is a timely need for their return. If you help them, I'm sure Persimony will find another jar of the honey to send with me the next time I visit." Her eyes glitter with triumph. "Until then, I must return to Panacea. Good day to you all." She swings herself back up into her seat and snaps the reins. The stags snort and take off, clattering away.

"This way." He doesn't look back at us.

No one speaks. It's too windy, and I'm getting weary of fighting the blasts. Soon enough, we're at another doorway.

"Where is this?" Lucas asks.

"The next kingdom over. Good luck to yeh." He hustles away, disappearing into the shadows of the trees once more.

"How does he do that?" I stare after him.

"He has some power here." Lucas grasps my hand, his other holding back his long bangs from beating at his eyes.

For a moment, I'm glad my hair isn't long enough to whip in my face. "I hope it's not that desert kingdom," I say and touch the tree.

A heated sun awaits us as we step into the kingdom. It's stifling hot, almost as bad as climbing into a lit oven. "*Ugh. That oaf brought us back to Far Starl.*"

"It is probably the closest kingdom to Anavrin," Lucas says, frowning. "He might be a curmudgeon, but he does as he's asked when he doesn't have any other choice in the matter."

"Why are nomad men so disagreeable? At least he could've warned us." I adjust the pack against my back, which is already damp from sweat.

"I'm sure he meant to." Lucas squints against the bright sunlight, humor twitching at his shapely mouth. He laughs when he witnesses my sour expression. "At least we know a bit about this kingdom. And from what Rekspire has told us, there's a Zoe Tree outside the walled city. It can't be far from where we met the outcasts."

"Don't forget the spelled dragons." Some of the hope I'd had flees, and I'm left with a sense of dread. "How do we get there without being spotted by them?"

"We blend in." He glances over at me. "Want to change into a dragon again, my lady?"

27

I close my eyes and hold the image of Audhild in my mind's eye. When I open my eyes and glance down, it's not red that greets me, but a silver-white scaled body. I heave out a sigh, which comes out as a frigid puff of smoke. *"I'm never going to get it. And why am I cold, not hot like a firedragon?"*

Lucas, looking remarkably like Rekspire's twin, places a clawed hand on my shoulder. *"Maybe you changed when you regenerated?"*

"Do you have elemental abilities like Rekspire?" I step away and then remember I have a long tail. *"How do dragons use this thing?"*

"They're born with it, my lady, so I'm sure it's much easier for them than for us." Sparks like lightning ignite on his clawed hand. They fizzle and then wink out. *"Hmm. Try holding my hand."*

I do so.

More of the lightning energy sizzles, traveling all across his body. However, it dies out again. *"I don't seem to have enough power myself to fully become Rekspire. But maybe it will intimidate enough to help us if we get spotted. Let's head toward where we were last and search there for the Tree."*

We take to the sky. Instead of the light feeling I have as a bird, flying takes more strength to suspend my larger body, even though my wings are bigger. We don't get far off the ground.

"This is going to take some getting used to." I try to push my wings harder, but they don't respond the same way my firebird forms do.

"It is, indeed." Lucas's voice is breathy. He's wobbling as much as I am. *"Let's change once we get to the edge of the graveyard. We can disguise ourselves easier among the debris there."*

I silently agree, my concentration mainly focused on staying aloft and not looking like I don't know what I'm doing.

We're close enough to the edge of the cliffs when we spot the first dragon circling over the boneyard.

On instinct, I land.

Lucas follows, dropping next to me on the sunbaked ground.

"What do we do?" I ask.

"Too bad we don't know how to hide our presence like those outcasts."

"I have an idea." I patter over to him. *"It hasn't spotted us yet. Let's try to find the outcast group and see if they will teach us how in exchange for some of our food."*

We head in the opposite direction and back around the forest where the old gnarled tree grew. We fly in circles for a short time before I spot a shimmering out of the corner of my eye. *"This way,"* I tell Lucas.

He follows me as I arc around whoever is hiding in the middle of an open area of sand and brushy weeds. I land several feet from the illusion, changing when I touch down. Lucas follows suit, and together we walk toward the person.

"We know you're there. Come out. We have something to offer you in exchange for the ability to hide our appearance." I stop a couple of steps from the wavering area. When nothing happens, I drop my pack and dig out a container of soft goat cheese and a package of crackers.

The wavering image moves toward me, but he doesn't drop his disguise. "Stop. Reveal yourself."

The illusion flickers and flakes to the ground around the blind outcast, Finian. The illusion pops back in place and he takes off running. His whistle is sharp with small bursts. A signal?

Lucas pounces on him, dropping him to the hard ground. "Is everyone in this kingdom as stubborn as you? Tambrynn?"

"Reveal yourself," I demand, my voice snapping with my irritation.

The disguise drops once more.

"I didn't mean to run. It's just a habit," he says while staring directly at me.

"Let him up," I tell Lucas. "But keep hold of him so he doesn't *accidentally* wander off."

Lucas releases him but keeps his arms behind his back in a tight grip.

"I'm going to give you another chance. I am holding food. Cheese and crackers. I'm willing to share with you if you teach us how to hide like you do."

His eyes dart around at that. However, he doesn't give in right away. We wait for a couple of moments before he speaks.

"Why are you glowing like the dragons? I can actually see you."

"We'll tell you if you help us." My shoulders droop. Would

the dragons see my light as well? There may not be a way for me to fully disguise myself now.

"I can't draw the runes or show you how. I'm blind, remember?"

"How do you sense things, then?" Lucas twists the man's arms.

"I—I dunno. I was born this way. Able to see, but not. I know when someone's coming, especially dragons. Now you." He nods at me. "Someone else drew the symbols on me."

"You still have to use the symbols to pull up the disguise." Lucas's frustration leaks through our bond.

I don't blame him. This kingdom puts me on edge too. "Just tell us what you know, and we'll let you have some of the food. We're not bad people. We just need to get back to our—" I almost say kingdom, but remember at the last moment they didn't know about the split kingdoms. "Home."

His shoulders sag. "Fine. The others are coming anyway."

I dip the crackers into the soft cheese and hand him three of them. He barely chews them as he eats. "More?" he asks, his voice and face hopeful.

"Not until your friends arrive and help us."

He licks his fingers, which have no traces of the cheese on them, but he does it twice, anyway.

I hand him one canteen. "Take a couple of drinks, but don't drink it all."

He gulps down several mouthfuls before Lucas jerks the container from him.

"Lucas." I nod toward three oncoming shimmering bodies.

He grabs Finian by the arms and turns him around to face whoever it is.

When they're almost to us, I step forward, my pack at my feet in front of me so no one can try to steal anything again. "Reveal yourselves."

Their guises drop like ashes in the wind. They all scowl at me. Luckily, the girl isn't among the three men.

"Food for information." I will my voice to be calm and even, though I'm still annoyed. First at being in this forsaken kingdom again, and then for having to deal with the impossible outcasts.

They glance at each other, unspeaking. One of them is the thief from the last time.

Finian, however, speaks. "They're not lying. They gave me food and water."

Lucas lets him go and turns his attention to the others.

"Remember the last time—with the apples?" I glare at the thief. "You won't steal from me again. But I will give some food to you if you help us."

His glower is full of calculation, his eyes roaming over us as if contemplating his

next move. "What happened to your hair? And why should we help you?"

The reminder of my nearly bald head puts me on edge. However, I sense another presence and spin around. I catch an arm and brace my mind against any thoughts or memories. "Drop your disguise."

It's the girl, and she wields an axe. Had I not sensed her, she would've smashed it into my head. Ice crackles in my veins as it fills me like my fire had before.

An icy shiver accompanies it, along with an intuitive knowing. I pull at her memories. A childhood spent inside Empyrea, the great walled city of this kingdom. She's the child of a dragon rider and a hatcher—one who cares for dragon's eggs before they're hatched.

Her earliest memories are happy. But they soon take a turn when her mother becomes dissatisfied with her job. Daily she ranted about what she'd been forced to do, and she despised the guardian's treatment of the eggs and hatchlings. As a faithful rider, her father disagreed. They fought and eventually split over her mother's "conspiracy theories" about the government's treatment and use of the dragons.

Her father relinquishes Circe, the girl, to her mother's care after she loses her hatcher job. They're left with only the clothes they wear. Relief is short-lived when they're taken in by some overbearing family, which Circe comes to hate.

The strongest memory is of her mother screaming in a public square at an officer when he mistreats a dragon. They cut her tirade short when they take her into custody after beating her. The most painful part of that memory is having her father there to witness it. He doesn't vouch for her mother as he could've done. The image of his unemotional face when he turns away, treating his wife as if he never knew her, and that he wasn't Circe's father. It destroys her spirit.

Then they're exiled and, for the first time, Circe knows genuine terror. Her mother dies shortly thereafter from the injuries of her beating. Circe is on her own but finds each of her ragamuffin group, pulling them together—helping them all to survive.

But she spends hours staring at the walls of Empyrea, longing to return to a life that isn't so hard. She knows every hole in the wall, all the cracks, but none of them can take her back to the safety she once knew. And she hardens. She and her group are starving but becoming as unyielding as the desert. Her instincts are to attack first and ask questions later.

I understand her disillusionment, her distrust. She was so young when her world turned upside down.

Like mine had.

I pull back from her, letting her memories go.

Startled, she jerks and tries to break my hold. She drops the axe and gets nowhere. I have too good of a grip on her.

Lucas grabs the weapon, anger simmering in the dark depths of his eyes.

"I tire of these games." I hold my dagger loose, but ready. From what I could tell of her life, she will do anything she needs to survive first, no matter what. "We returned to find you for a good faith trade. We aren't stealing from you or trying to harm you, yet you persist in treating us as your enemies." I narrow my eyes at her. Instead of heating like they had before, there's a chill around the edges of my sight.

She hisses at me as shivers wrack her body at my frigid hold.

"We are not your enemy." I jerk her arm closer so I can view the symbols on her skin. Three other of the outcasts each move to stop me, but I hold out the blade. "This is a holy item imbued with the power to do as I bid it."

"It's powerful, dangerous. I see its aura." Finian tells them. His eyes are fixed on the blade in my hand as if he can see it. "I wouldn't do anything stupid." His eyes flick up to my face before setting off into the distance once more.

"Lucas, take Grandfather's notebook and draw these symbols." I kick the pack toward him.

He fishes out the leather journal. "What can I write with?"

I *call* out, hoping one of them will have a writing utensil.

Lucas grabs the two pens out of the air before they reach me.

"Hey, that's mine," the thief growls in anger.

"Stop," I yell at him, halting him from attacking Lucas. The outcast is stronger than he looks, and he tries to thrash around in my hold. "I can squeeze tighter if you like."

He stops moving, but glares hatefully at me.

Finian shuffles his feet. "They're only temporary unless you ink-brand 'em. Or you can burn 'em into your skin, leaving a scar. That works too."

"Shut up," yells one of the other men. "Don't give them all our secrets."

"You idiots." The girl snarls at them. "She's a seer like Finian. She's already read my mind." Circe twists her head toward me. "Let me come with you when you leave. Please." A lone, pathetic tear trickles from one of her eyes. "Please."

"Why would we do that?" I ask her, reaching out to her to sense her actual intentions. All I get is a desperation that wafts off her in waves, slapping against my mind with its intensity.

"Please. This desert is killing me. I won't last another week here." She's sobbing now, but there aren't many tears. I take in her state, the frail bone of her arm in my hand, the sunken cheeks, the dullness of her skin. She's not lying.

I decide to play this out. I'd save them if I could anyway, but they don't know that. "Why would we take anyone who would try to kill us from behind? How could we trust you?"

"We told you before, didn't we? It's what we do. It's not personal. But we can't go on anymore." She shakes her head and sniffles. "Them dragons are all a'roaring since you left us. We can't even sneak around with our concealment. It's like they can see through them now. They never did that before you two came here."

And then she's quaking with soundless cries.

Lucas finishes drawing the symbols on blank sheets of the journal.

"Well, if you take her, take us," the last man speaks up. His voice is raspy. He's as gaunt as the rest of them. I don't recall seeing him the first time we encountered them.

"Where are the others in your group?" I ask, not wanting to revisit her memories.

Circe's crying fit is over, her arm held out straight in my grip, her fingers white from frost. "The dragons got them two days ago. Ambushed us."

Though I shouldn't be, I'm shocked. "What do the dragons do with them?"

She shudders. "They're walking dead men now."

My heart stutters. *Sluaghs?* How did Thoron return *after* we closed up the doorway on Anavrin?

Lucas winces at her words, no doubt sharing my same thoughts. His hands shake as he replaces the notebook in my pack and seals it.

Circe glances up at me. "We'll do anything you say, won't we boys? Just don't leave us here."

They reluctantly nod, not liking her plan. Finian shows no emotion as he stares unseeing into the distance.

She droops further, and I have difficulty keeping her up.

I tug her to standing. "What about Finian? You would've left him out of the food last time."

She shakes her head, some dark strands of hair flittering with the motion. Hair loss, I knew from experience, was a symptom of starvation.

Lucas hands me the pack, a question in his eyes. He tucks the axe in his belt by his side.

I let the girl slide to sit on the ground. It isn't a ruse. She is close to death.

"You help me get to the Zoe Tree with no one hurting either Lucas or me, and we'll help you however we can."

I don't promise, however, to take them with me to Anavrin.

28

Lucas scouts an area of trees near to where we encountered the outcasts. They can't handle walking far, and since their ink marks no longer hide them from the dragons, we need cover in case the dragons do a sweep of the bare, sandy area.

"Now, take it slow. If you eat or drink too much, you'll make yourself sick. Your stomach can't handle a lot of either until it gets used to eating and drinking again." I take two tin cups Lucas retrieved from what I'd packed in his bag. "Sip and nibble."

"What do you know about it anyways?" the thief retorts. He dragged his feet in coming. I almost left him behind.

"More than you might realize." Lucas digs into my pack to get out the food. "Our supplies won't last long." We mind spoke and agreed not to use the stones and displacement spell until we can trust the group a bit more. If we must, we'll sleep as birds in a tree.

I stare at the thief, wondering what to tell him. The Far Starlian kingdom doesn't seem to have any form of indentureship. I doubt they'd take the news of other kingdoms well. "I've had experience with starvation."

He scoffs, not believing me. I hand him the cup that holds a small amount of water. "You can believe what you will. However, I'll not have you waste precious resources by gulping everything down and then throwing it all up later."

"Go on, Neldrick. If you don't want to be here, leave." Finian kicks at the dirt, making it cloud. "None of us has to be here. Most of you wouldn't have given me a chance if you didn't need me. I've heard you talk. I'm blind, not deaf." He laughs, but it's bitter. "These people will give us some of what they have in exchange for information. But none of you are the sharing kind, are you?" He holds out his tin cup. "You're nothing but a pack of vipers waiting for your next strike."

My heart twinges at his lot in life. His bitterness is paltry compared to the heartache he's suffered. And I knew a little something about resentment and how hard it was to overcome.

Neldrick, the thief, doesn't say anything else. He finishes the water and shoves the cup at me. I take it more graciously than I feel. Then I help Lucas pass out the crackers and cheese with a slim slice of apple on top. Only a couple per person, and the food is gone.

The sun sets, the bright sky darkening.

"Dragon coming at us," Finian says, his face slanted toward where we'd been before.

"Run," another one screams as he stands and rushes away from the group.

"Don't," I start, but it's too late. He's gone. I could try to stop him, but a screaming roar from the dragon breaks the stillness. It spots the runner.

The others are twitchy, possibly wondering if they should take their chances and run in a different direction.

"Don't leave the shelter of the trees. It's safer here." My hands are shaky as well, but I control my voice enough to keep it steady.

"There's no place safe from them." Circe lifts her head and stares out at the darkening landscape around us. Her stare is dull, accepting she may not survive this encounter.

A shadow from the dragon flying above us stops any more discussion. It roars, and the man screams.

"We have to help him," I say to Lucas.

"In what form?" He glances up at me.

"Ravens." I am changed immediately to a war bird upon the thought, hoping not to give away who and what we are. I shift my sight to that of the lizard's and spot the man running from the dragon. In his haste, he stumbles.

I'm on the dragon before it reaches the outcast. To distract it, I peck at its face. However, I falter when the glowing red eye comes into view.

It opens its mouth and a ball of fire shoots at my face. It hits my protective shield, sizzling against the icy barrier.

My heart sinks. If anyone is watching from the spelled dragon, my protective barrier just showed I'm magical.

Lucas drops from above and gets a scrape across the dragon's hide. It does no harm, though, just like he hadn't injured Rekspire all that while ago. Ravens against war eagles are one thing. Dragons are another.

"This isn't working." I change mid-flight to my firebird form. A blue glow surrounds me.

The dragon swings its head away from my light, growling out a roar of agitation. When it swings back toward me, the man has already risen and shuffled to the next group of trees.

The dragon, not red nor black, but some shade in between, turns back to me, its wings keeping it aloft. I envy its ability to hold its massive body up. It doesn't stop me from pulling on the hum in my gut to blast it with a sphere of pure ice.

Its piercing cry echoes across the space, and I worry it will alert more dragons to our position. If only I could use the Mortifer Blade like I do the lizard sight. As that thought settles over me, my wings stiffen—in answer to my wish. The final dregs of light glint off my sharp wing tips.

"My lady?" Lucas must sense the change within me. He circles, but far enough away to not gain the beast's attention.

The dragon comes at me, and I have no time to react. Its body rears back, and the beast bares sharp talons. I push up just in time to miss getting hit. My body rolls, and I strike the back of the dragon.

It roars and flails.

"The Mortifer Blade," I tell him, hoping he'll understand. I'm elated that it's working. Keeping the animal in my sight, I spot blood dripping off the dragon's back.

"My lady, your wings. Are you bleeding?" The strength of Lucas's concern hits me.

"No. It's the dragon's blood."

The dragon turns and faces me again. A shudder rocks its hide and then it's attacking again. The red eye glows brighter than before, which is disconcerting. We'll be tracked if I don't stop it. But how?

This time, when it gets close enough, I drop and swivel, catching its underside with my feathers. Their razor-sharp edges catch the beast's body.

I sense my father when I touch it this time. The death and destruction sit on my tongue like a flavor. I gag, unable to spit it out.

The dragon's roar is deep and guttural. It flounders, its wings trying to keep it in the air. But the dragon's flight now resembles Lucas and my awkward flying dragon attempts. It drops to the ground like a sack of potatoes, crashing when it collides with the hard land. Dust and sand cloud the surrounding air.

The outcast who had run breaks out of the tree cover. "Cut its head off. There's a spell that can reanimate it if you don't." He runs past the dragon and back to his group.

I land, changing as I do so. The Mortifer Blade is in my right hand. I don't question, just as I don't question what I know I need to do. I raise the dagger and instead of beheading the animal, I dig at the third eye, cutting an *X* through it.

The moment the spell breaks, I'm knocked backward. I land several feet back. My chest heaves, and sand coats my lips. I spit it out and wipe my sleeve across my lips.

"My lady." Lucas is beside me, helping me stand. "What did you do?"

I look up at him in elation. "I broke my father's spell."

29

"Y ou what?" His mouth hangs open.

I try not to take offense to Lucas's surprise. I'm just as astonished. So far, nothing I'd done had come close to accomplishing this. I'd only hoped to blind or cripple it. "I broke the spell of the third eye on the dragon."

The beast is heaving, dirt blustering when it exhales against the gritty land. Several cuts trickle blood from its back, forehead, and belly.

Lucas and I go over to the animal. It doesn't move when we draw closer.

"It's still alive, my lady. Please be careful," he tells me as though he knows what I'm about to do.

"I will." I place my hand on its leg. Pain greets me first. Then some mottled memories. It doesn't represent the clarity Rekspire had. It's been controlled its entire life. I sense something holding it back, a muffle over its mind. "It's not a rogue. I can't tell how my father got his hex on it."

"What do we do with it?" Lucas kneels next to me.

"Now that the spell is gone, I'm going to see if I can break

221

the guardian's hold on it." I reach out with my mind. The creature stirs beneath my hand. I settle the barrier around my thoughts to conceal my presence.

Like auras, I can make out the strings that bind the dragon. It's like a spider's web, all sticky strings wrapped around it, holding it hostage and imbuing someone else's will upon it. And then I realize the "conspiracy theories" Circe's mother believed are true. It matches what Rekspire told me when I'd broken through to him after he'd attacked Audhild.

The guardians and dragon riders bind the dragons when they're first born to keep them obedient. I raise my hand and call upon the frost. It crackles along the strings, hardening them, making them brittle. I'm heartened that, unlike my father, there's no actual presence or mind behind the binding to stop me.

But I need my fire. I rest in the hum of my ability and allow the thumping of my heart to strengthen the buzzing in my gut. My mind turns to Emberwing's warmth, of the glowing coals in the fires Lucas builds, the blaze flowing along my veins. I am fire. I look up and open my mouth to a gush of flames. The sparkling web melts as my flames burn it—leaving the dragon's mind freed and unharmed.

Lucas catches me as I'm tossed backward, away from the dragon and out of its mind.

A ripple travels across the dragon's scaled hide. It jerks its head up, trying to rise. It makes a couple of attempts before it gains control of its body and wings and can get up on its feet. The coloring of the dragon keeps his injuries from sight. With a mighty roar, it bows its head before me, its wings and tail held high. Smoke curls out of its nostrils as it blinks at me.

"Are you okay?" I mindspeak to it.

It rises and gazes down at me. *"Yes. Sovereign."* It garbles the reply, but it's mind is clear enough that I understand the meaning. Thankfulness rushes at me like a gust of wind.

I smile, for the first time welcoming the title. *"You're welcome."*

The runner jerks my arm. "What're you doing? Don't let it live. It'll kill us all."

Lucas is there in an instant, knocking the man aside. He falls to the ground, and the others rush over to stand behind him. There's suspicion in their gazes.

Except for Finian. "That's incredible," he grins at the dragon. "There's no more darkness to its aura." He crooks his head. "You freed the dragon. How did you do that?"

"What? What did she do?" Circe's glance swings from the blind man to the dragon, and then to me.

"I destroyed the hex and then the spells the guardians put on the dragon." I reach up and stroke the solid scales of the dragon's neck. "But it's still hurt. Lucas, did Persimony give us any of that healing ointment?"

He digs in his pack and produces a small jar of the honey robinia cream and hands it to me.

I hold it out for the dragon to sniff. "It will help your wounds."

When it doesn't protest, I put some on the scratches on its belly. And then I change to a bird and land on its back, where I change again and cover the cuts on its back. "There. Now, I need to put some on your forehead."

It arcs its long neck and blinks at me. I take a generous amount to cover the wound. It huffs out a growl but doesn't protest. "Do you have a name?"

"They aren't given names," Circe says, a frown on her face. "They give dragons numbers. And eventually, they'll notice this one is missing and come search for it."

"Then we need to find a place to hide." Lucas puts the jar back in his pack as I wash my hands off with a trickle of water.

"Rekspire's boneyard," I tell him.

———

It takes most of the night to find the area the outcasts describe as the only place they knew where rogues lived—or hoarded, as they call it. Lucas and I changed to dragons and carried two of the outcasts, while the freed dragon carried the other three. Luckily, they weighed less than a child in their condition. However, with the way my scales shone like a beacon, brighter than the moonlight, it was a tense trek.

We only had to hide once when Finian foresaw another dragon on our horizon. I'd changed to a lizard while the others sheltered behind shrubby bushes. It worked since the dragon didn't come close to us.

"How do the rogues stay hidden so close to Empyrea?" I ask Circe when we get to a clearing inside the graveyard's border.

"The rogues don't bother the guardians, so they don't bother the rogues. Mother thought the leaders somehow put the Junta in place. I agree after seeing how the rogues live— somehow getting food when there is no way they could. It makes sense if it's true because the guardians love control over everything else."

"So, the guardians aren't ignorant of their presence?" Lucas stretches his shoulders and back. It isn't easy carrying someone on your back, even if you are as big as a dragon.

She makes a *pshaw* noise. "The rogues escape them as younglings, sometimes by accident. On purpose, if they're thought to be defective. We were always taught dragons were simply animals to train and use as we wished. Mother discovered that wasn't true. Instead of immunizations, the shots the dragons receive bind the dragons so they can't shift into their other forms. She called it unethical. They exiled us as liars or for trying to induce riots." Her voice takes on a hard edge.

I don't blame her.

The freed dragon sniffs the air and lets out a rumble resembling a cat's purr. I pat its side. "I don't like it much, either."

The dragon bone graveyard is more of a hole in the ground where it seems the guardians dump the dead dragons—without burials or honor. I stand in front of a larger bone, the hazy moonlight showing the splintered remains of a wing joint.

Yet in the distance, I spy smaller bones and skulls. There are no other crystal hearts set among these dried-up masses that look like old logs rather than bones. I wipe my hand across one, and it crumbles, leaving a white dust residue on my skin.

Were these the ones my father feasted upon?

I shake my head. It's all too horrible. The unfairness and maliciousness in all the kingdoms. I can't imagine why the Kinsman would split the One World apart, even if the first people had rebelled. But as I travel to each kingdom and witness the destructiveness of one race over another, it is making a sad sort of sense.

"We'll make it right, my lady." Lucas's gentle words bolster me. "Somehow."

Circe faces the great wall, her eyes stuck on the sight. "We'll need to make camp before the sun comes up. Or at least find safe places for everyone to hide. They'll be sending the morning scouts out when the sun rises." She glances at me. "You might need to find a covering for your head. It's sunburning."

I ignore her words. The heat was unmistakable, and I knew

my scalp was burning. I'd come up with something tomorrow. *"Should we use the displacement stones?"* I mindspeak to Lucas.

He takes a deep breath, his shoulders moving up and down. *"It is safer. I just don't completely trust them yet."*

"What if we wait for them to fall asleep and then use them? They won't even know, and we can rest easier as long as we find somewhere shaded."

Circe turns to glance at us, her eyebrows up and questioning.

"Let's find a nice, shaded spot and settle in." I motion to the dragon. "C'mon, we're not leaving you behind."

It takes several minutes before we find a spot big enough for all of us, including the freed dragon. It circles uneasily before finding a spot to lie down. It tucks its tail around its nose like I'd seen Rekspire do. The outcasts set a schedule for a watch, though they're all exhausted. But with them watching Lucas and my every move, we choose not to change. Instead, we sit among the others, my mind on the food reserves we have left. It's not enough to last past another meal, especially given the dragon could out-eat us all. Eventually, even the outcast watcher nods off.

I take the stones Lucas hands me. We tiptoe a perimeter around the dozing group, placing the stones, and quietly muttering the displacement spell. It snaps in place when we put the last stone behind the dragon. It lifts its head, curving its neck to gaze at me. With a blink, it lies back down and goes to sleep.

We settle in next to the dragon's body, against the debris-filled backdrop. With the curse healed, the flares should be gone, making it safer to sleep next to the dragon. However, I leave some space between us just in case. Lucas kisses my hand, and before I know it, I'm asleep.

The next thing I know, I'm awakened by men in blue

uniforms. They carry sticks with metal ends. They hum with some sort of power, and I recall Rekspire's details of the weaponry they have.

Before I can think to change, they've grabbed Lucas. He yells as one man puts a knife to his throat. I take in our surroundings. Someone moved the stones, and the displacement spell was gone, allowing the—guardians—to find us. But how?

There are half a dozen of the uniformed men. The rest of them grab hold of the other sleepy outcasts—all but Circe, who isn't here.

I inwardly groan, mentally berating my judgment. Her motives had been present in her memories. I just hadn't seen it. It's clear why she turned on us. She longs to be back inside the walls, the only place she'd ever known comfort.

However, the betrayal burns.

30

"Stop." I scream, my heart beating out of my chest. If they hurt one hair on Lucas's head, I will burn their kingdom to the ground without regret.

The men freeze in place, but the dragons they rode on behind them shudder as my order washes across their scales. All of them are different shades, ranging from ice blue to a deep burgundy red. Each of them swivels to focus on me, their dark gazes piercing. Each has a glowing eye.

My hands shake as my mind whirls. Panic hinders my thoughts. And though the sun is barely peeking over the horizon, it's already sweltering.

I place my hand on the freed dragon. *"Help me?"* I beg.

His hide wavers as he changes into a man.

The Empyreans gasp.

Their dragons become restless, their focus now on the freed dragon. Their third eyes glow brighter. I pray there's no way my father made his way off Anavrin. However, even if that's the case, he's infected these dragons with his magic, which has put us in greater danger.

"My fellows," the dragon-man starts, his voice rough. He coughs. "Please, no harm." He waves his arm at me. "The Sovereign. Freedom now."

Lucas changes while the guard still cannot move. He lands next to me and changes back. "What are we going to do with them? How long can you hold them?"

A man appears from behind the dragons. He holds Circe's arm and guides her over to where the other Empyreans stand, unmoving. She doesn't look hurt, though her eyes flick to me and away.

Good. Let her feel guilty. I should never have trusted her—helped her. Did she even understand the cost of her actions? The Mortifer Blade slides easily from the sheath, its handle now almost a part of my hand.

He jerks Circe forward, some sort of metal weapon held to her side. "Are these the ones you reported who attacked our dragon, broke its bindings, and attempted to steal it—all capital offenses?"

I remember that term from her memories. It's what they charged her mother with, two capital offenses of inciting a riot and willful lying. They had downgraded the sentence from death to banishment. As if there was any difference between the two.

At first, she doesn't respond. The object in the man's hand emits energy, like my crackling ability, and she stiffens, jerking in place. It stops, and she reluctantly nods her head once, never looking at us. "Yes."

He squints and then points at my weapon. "And somehow, she's stolen a precious artifact from our archives. Another capital offense." Giddiness makes his voice rise. He's enjoying this torture. However, he doesn't seem to understand his fellow guards are under my control.

I could tell him—stop him. But I want to know where he's

going first. Find out how far Circe's double-crossing leads. I will, however, answer his charge. "This is my blade, and it's not from your kingdom."

He sneers. "Fool. It disappeared several years ago and has been missing ever since. And because you are in possession of it, we will sentence you for theft of the highest order. Guards, seize her."

The other men's eyes flick at each other.

I hold back my grin. He still doesn't realize they are under my control. A thought comes to mind. "Sleep," I order them.

They collapse.

Circe's captor's surprise turns to fury. He jerks her closer. "Dragons, attack."

Lucas grabs one weapon, a stick with a metal-pronged end. As the dragons move to do as ordered, he changes to a bird.

I follow him, attacking the first of the six hexed dragons. It's a deep blue one having smaller scales than most. I use my razor-like wings as I had before with the freed dragon.

Lucas is dodging a green and black one. His wings snap as he hits it, possibly from using the stick he'd grabbed. It howls, and the wind picks up around us.

The blue dragon's tail whips around, but I push up with my wings, evading it. It turns in a serpentine fashion, reminding me of Audhild's flight pattern. Thoughts of her bring a renewed desire to save it. I fly by it, my feathers grazing its forehead and across the flashing eye. It's squeal echoes around the boneyard, making some bones tip and fall over.

But the injured dragon isn't done. I dip and hit like the ravens had in their attacks on the war eagles. Finally, I break through the hex. The power splinters, knocking me tail over beak in the air.

I collide with an ash-colored dragon, the smallest one. I

wonder if it's a youngling. It glows red around its scale's edges, and fire rushes over my protective shield.

"My lady?" Lucas screes in the distance.

"I'm fine. Keep fighting." I roll when I hit the ground and kick off with my legs back into the air.

A glance alerts me that two of the outcasts are running for cover, and Circe is nowhere to be seen. The freed dragon has changed back and is battling with a slim, horned red dragon with small wings. It's an even battle between the two. They spit and hiss, sending sparks and bolts of lightning at each other.

Elemental dragons, like Rekspire.

Energy zaps Lucas's dragon, and it finally falls.

That leaves four others.

Two team up to attack Lucas—a sandy one that blends into the surrounding desert, and a darker brown one.

I screech in protest, but the remaining two come for me. One hits my shield with a powerful explosion as the other's tail whips, making it through my protection, and hitting me square in the stomach.

Pain explodes, and I tumble to the ground. I roll beneath a dragon's skull to get away from its talons. A loud thump alerts me to its position. The skull moves aside, and then I'm on the run.

I scan the sky above to catch sight of Lucas. He isn't faring much better. One dragon hits him from behind with its horned, spiky head. Lucas's cry as he is flung away from the beast ignites a fire inside me.

And then I glimpse a dark dragon flying against the sun.

I blink away the brightness. A hand on my arm has me spinning around, blue energy flying from my fingertips.

It's the guardian who held Circe. He stiffens as my energy crackles over his body. Seizures overtake him until they dissipate. He collapses to the ground with an *oof* but doesn't get back up.

One dragon sends a ball of fire at me. With a thought, I call upon my ice. I become ice. When the heat hits me, it's absorbed by my crystalline body. I shiver, and it dissipates, leaving me unharmed.

A shadow circles above us. A familiar roar resounds, and I snap my head up. Rekspire is in combat with Lucas's attackers.

"Lucas?" My heart thuds painfully.

"Here, my lady. I'm okay."

Relief is short-lived as my dragon sends another wave of smoke and flames my way. I kick up and am only grazed by the heat as I take flight.

"I tire of this battle." My shrieking call pierces the air.

The fire dragon is on my tail. I tuck my wings, spinning wildly until I hit its body in a whipping frenzy of flames and ice. I grab hold of its tail and swing it around as I push with all my strength toward the ones fighting Rekspire. *"Grab hold,"* I tell my storm. I will it to suck them into my tempest. It works. The other dragon is powerless against my onslaught. We continue to spin.

Soon I'm whirling so fast I'm unaware of what I'm doing. I sense when the last dragon has succumbed to my storm. With a last yank, I pull back the whorl I've formed.

It's silent for a moment before a resounding *boom* explodes in a brilliant icy blue light. I close my eyes against the radiance, unsure if I'm still flying or falling.

And then I collide with something, stopping me immediately. My *oof* is accompanied by another one, and we're both tumbling into the bones below, bruising me. I change back to a girl's body to make myself smaller so I hit fewer objects.

Sand and dirt cloud around me when I come to a stop at

the bottom. I choke on the fine particles of bone dust and spit it out of my mouth. Whatever, whoever I hit is above me, the bones creaking with their weight.

"Rekspire?" I call out, hopeful. My body throbs and everything aches.

The weight shifts as the dragon above me changes.

It's not Rekspire. It's the freed dragon.

"Help?" He holds out a hand to me. I take it, grateful for the help as my feet sink into the whitish-gray powder. He pulls me out with ease.

When we emerge, we both have scratches and red marks that will soon bruise. "Thank you," I tell him.

He bows to me. "My Sovereign."

Rekspire lands on a solid square of land next to us. "She doesn't like it when you call her that." He stops and assesses the new dragon. "I don't know you. Who are you?"

The freed dragon-man turns his head as if not understanding the question.

"I freed him. He's one of the Empyrean's dragons." I smile at them, proud of my accomplishment.

Shock spreads across Rekspire's face. "You—freed him? From the Relligo spell the guardians use?"

"And the hex my father had placed on him, a third eye spell, that allows him to see and control the person from afar." My body tingles, starting at my chest and spreading out in warning. My gut hums to life like angry, buzzing bees. "Where's Lucas?"

The three of us look around. All the dragons and the guardians are prone on the ground, none of them moving. There's nothing in the sky indicating Lucas is flying around, scouting, or doing anything else. None of the outcasts remain, all have disappeared.

"*Lucas?*"

No response. I step forward, almost tripping over a jagged piece of bone. Rekspire grasps my hand, helping me past the obstruction. *"Lucas?"* I scream at his mind, hoping the intensity will catch his attention if something distracted him.

Rekspire winces. "He was just here, battling the dragons. Where could he have gone?"

Fear ties my insides into knots. "How did you get here? You shouldn't have been able to come back. What's happening on Anavrin?"

His face twists. "That's why I came here. Thoron's taken over the kingdom. He left few unchanged. I escaped because I slipped past our barrier hiding the Zoe Tree. But the death mage knows it's there since he's used it several times before. He's sent a dozen sluaghs to the island to search for it. It won't be long, and he'll have access to the Zoe Tree's passage. And then possibly here to refuel."

31

At the moment, I couldn't care less about what was happening with Thoron—the situation feels as though it's more than a kingdom away from me. My only concern is for my beloved Watcher.

"We have to find Lucas." I can't help the high squeak in my voice. I'm immediately in the air. They follow me, and we separate and scan the area.

I call out to him over and over, but there's no response. I search for any hint of his presence or emotions, but my seeking comes back empty. My body is crackling with energy.

"Sovereign, I don't mean to stop the search for your beloved. But I need to remind you, if Thoron makes it here, he will grow stronger. We need to stop him before he arrives." Rekspire's hesitant logic angers me.

"I can't think about that now. Not until I find Lucas." I snarl with my reply. I can't help it. My panic has turned to fear, which is quickly growing to terror. *"Let's go back to the graveyard. Retrace our steps."*

He doesn't argue with me. The other dragon is silent, which in my agitated state irritates me as well.

We land next to the group of bodies we'd left behind and change. I count the dragons. There are only five of them. There are seven of the guardians, six asleep and snoring, and the last one not awake but twitching as if he were.

"A dragon is missing." I count them—noting the one missing is the slim-horned one the freed dragon fought. I turn to him. "Do you recall what happened to the dragon you were fighting?"

He glances around, confusion puckering his features. "No. Gone?" He darts about, searching the area.

Rekspire touches my arm, and I fight the urge to jerk away. "What did it look like?"

"It was red and black, kind of slim. Smaller wings. Not like any dragon I know. More like a snake with horns." I dash to the pile of weapons and kick them, needing a way of expending the energy that's building in my bones. The items go tumbling aside, but my outburst is not as satisfying as I'd hoped.

Rekspire jerks his head my way, his golden eyes glowing. "Did you say it was like a snake with horns?"

I fling out my arms in frustration. "Yes. Red and black with smallish wings."

"The Junta," he says through clenched teeth. "Was he hexed?"

"Yes."

Circe appears out of nowhere, standing several feet away from us on the other side of the pit we'd slept in.

My anger deepens. I step toward her, but Rekspire places a hand on my arm. "What are you doing here?"

"I'm sorry. He made me do it. It was all a ruse." She hangs her head, her dull hair hiding her face.

"Who made you do what?" Rekspire answers her in a clipped tone.

"Junta." She scrapes a hand across her nose. "He saved us the other day during the raid. I owed him. He told me to give away our position, or he'd come back and kill me outright." She lifts her head to meet my heated gaze. "I had no other choice."

"But he's a rogue dragon. How was he here with the guardians?"

I'm grateful Rekspire is taking the lead. All I want to do is strangle her until she tells me where Lucas is.

She bites her lip. "He's not. He's a spy sent by the guardians to help keep the rogues in check."

Rekspire takes a step back. "I can't believe—" He bends over and clutches the hem of his shirt to his thighs. "That explains so much. How they always knew when we were attempting to infiltrate the squads. How our current Junta found food and water. It's how he won over our last leader. He cheated."

Her glance at me is apologetic. "He said he was going to grab you and take you to his master on some other kingdom. I didn't believe him. There aren't other kingdoms, and he seemed crazed. That's why I asked you to take us. I wanted to get away from him. From this." She waves at the boneyard. "But we ran out of time. I'm so sorry."

Though her motives weren't what I thought they were, I couldn't comprehend how she kept that from me. "How did you hide it from me when I read your mind?"

"You learn to hide a lot of things when your mother is a fanatic and then you're an outcast. I hide some things I've done from myself, so I don't have to dwell on what I've had to do to survive." Genuine tears glitter in her eyes. "I'll do anything. Let me help, please."

Three of the other outcasts drop their disguises.

"Us too." Finian breaks in. "And by the by, we didn't know what Circe was up to with the Junta."

The others glare at her and agree with the blind outcast.

I lift my head skyward, feeling the time tick by, knowing the danger Lucas is in. "Fine, but we must figure out where he took Lucas." I turn in a half circle, thinking. We'd need a faster mode of travel if we were going to hunt down the Junta.

"The dragons," I murmur to myself.

"Sovereign?" Rekspire steps in front of me. "I sense something different about you. A power draws me to you. You're usually aglow, but this is something more. What's happened?"

Tears prick in my eyes, remembering Nyle and the crystal heart. I mindspeak to him, telling him what happened.

He drops to his knees. "So, you're a true Sovereign, then. You should be able to call upon the other dragons to assist you. Maybe even remove their spells without having to touch them."

The other dragon follows Rekspire's example and now both bow before me. "Stop doing that. I'm just Tambrynn, dragon's heart or not." My eyes close as I will my inner mind to search the other dragons' thoughts.

There are the bindings, the glowing web of spells and hexes they each have. I sense more in the distance and allow my focus to expand. I raise my hand as I bring forth my ice and then my fire. As one, they break the dragons free from the guardian's spell. I stagger back when the last bind snaps. I glance in the distance. Had I pulled from one that was nearby?

There's no time to think about it, though, as I move onto my father's hex. It takes longer to grab hold of the malevolent magic. It fights back, but I dig my feet into the sand and peel the repulsive threads away. They're tough with strands like a strong rope, yet they turn to smoke when they're broken. I'm exhausted when I release the last one. Sweat soaks my clothes and my hair clings to me. I collapse to the ground, panting and wiping away the moisture from my eyes.

Circe meekly hands me one of my canteens and a slice of bread with the meat Persimony had packed for us. She doesn't look at me. Guilt and regret permeate her aura like a rain cloud.

"You need to keep your strength up," she whispers.

I take it all from her without a word.

Rekspire takes the canteen from me after I'm done and gulps down a long drink. "If we're to use the dragons, we need to wake them up." He caps it and hands it back to Circe. "I believe you know how to call things?" He winks at me, but there's a seriousness behind his humor.

"Objects, yes." I roll my shoulders, trying to release some of the tension, and stand again. I'd rather be out trying to find Lucas, but we need all the help we can get. "Stand back. I don't know for sure what I'm doing."

I close my eyes and raise my arms. "Awaken, dragon hoard. I beseech you to come and help me." I send a wave of cold energy out, visualizing it to be an icy splash that awakens them all.

The green and black one shakes its head as it rises. The dragon-man changes to his beast form. He and the other dragons stare at each other, clicks and noises coming from their throats.

"He is explaining what's happened to them in dragon speak. Telling them to trust you and take you where you need to go, that they owe you their allegiance because you freed them and are their Sovereign." Rekspire adds some clicking noises to the fray, the other dragons' heads swinging to include him. More of it continues as I grow edgy, wanting to get moving.

In the distance, the sky darkens. It's not a cloud, it doesn't move like one. "What is that?" I ask, afraid of what the answer might be.

Rekspire glances up and smiles. "That, Sovereign, is your hoard."

32

I'm stupefied. There must be hundreds of dragons headed toward us—different colors, shapes, and sizes. They fill the sky with shrieks and calls, lightning and fire. A streak of ice and a whirl of dust accompanies many of the powerful dragons.

"What am I going to do with these dragons?" I turn toward Rekspire, who stands mesmerized by the sight.

"You are their Sovereign. You will lead them." He steps away and greets the first, who lands close to the edge of the boneyard. They communicate with dragonspeak, the clicks and noises making no sense to me.

"But I don't know how to lead dragons," I say, seemingly to the wind.

"Your pardon." It's Circe. She stands straighter, a ghost of a smile on her lips. "They've been trained to listen and do what they're told. All you have to do is figure out what you need them to do."

The freed dragon comes to stand by me. "Sovereign. Help?"

"Yes. I need help. How do I manage all of them?"

He bows his head and changes back to his dragon form. He lifts into the air and roars. *"Hoard. Bow to the Sovereign."*

I wince at his words, spoken forcefully in my mind.

I'm not the only one. The others cringe and cover their ears as well.

With a rumble, all the dragons bend low, starting at the front and moving through the throng of bodies to the last ones that flew over the great wall.

I'm dumbstruck at the display. Rekspire returns and places a hand on my shoulder but faces the crowd. "This is your new Sovereign, who freed you from the bonds that held you captive, unable to change, a slave to the guardians. This is a fulfillment of the prophecy given years before her arrival. See her hair? It's like the light of the moon—she's moon-born. See her eyes? They're the mark of the Kinsman's chosen one—a firebird. Inside her beats the heart of a true dragon, Halvar the Honorable. Audhild the Great passed her the Sovereign's title before her untimely demise at the hands of the death mage. He's the son of a dragon racer and grandson of a guardian."

Grumbles break out at the mention of my father.

"How do you know so much about Astralee?" I whisper to him.

"I ran into the Hulda on my way to the doorway. She was very chatty and not very pleasant," he mutters.

I stare at him, wondering how badly that went.

Rekspire holds a hand up, stopping the mumbling. "Tambrynn's fate is to save us all and restore balance to the kingdoms. But she cannot do it alone. It is our duty, now that she has freed us, to help her fulfill her destiny. Are you brave enough to answer her call?"

Dragon roars and shrieks fill the air. Heat shimmers off the surrounding ground, but it doesn't seem to bother them. The sheer number of dragons is intimidating. Which is probably why the Far Starlians thought they needed to control the creatures. But it's a cruel practice that I am glad is over.

My heart races, thumping twice as hard as normal. I rest a hand on my chest over Halvar's heart.

If only Lucas were here to share this with me.

Rekspire pats my shoulder. "You have their attention and undivided devotion now. Gather a force you can take to find Lucas, as many as you think you can handle. Then let the others sort this kingdom out. The guardians cannot control them now that the bonds are broken."

I turn toward the freed dragon, who stands close to us. Now that it's light, it's apparent that he's not black and red, but a dark green and red. And in the sunlight, his eyes shine like the stones in Mother's protection bracelet. An idea comes to me. "You are free to choose, but I need help to defeat my father, for I cannot do it alone. If you are amenable to joining us, I rename you Tourmaline, and you will become my shield."

He nods his acceptance.

I glance at the others and call out to the brown one. "Will you join me?"

"I will." His voice is weak, but the gleam in his golden eyes is not.

"Then your name is Quartz," I tell him and turn to two others, both female—a purple dragon and a tan-colored one—an amethyst and pearl. They nod in acknowledgment. "You two will be my guard. Accompany me, please, to Anavrin as we search for Lucas and to locate my father."

I step back toward Rekspire. "You are my second in command, for I trust you as no other besides Lucas. Whatever you say will also be my word."

He snaps his head down and back up in a rare show of honor. "I am forever in your service."

My cheeks heat. "You are a free dragon. I am not your master, but your friend."

"As you say." There's humor in his eyes, but he holds himself stiff like a servant would. I'll have to work on that.

"All other dragons," I yell out, hoping my voice carries. "Take these guardians back to the walled city. Destroy the machines and the potions for the binding spells and then burn anything that documents the ways of slavery. Leave no trace behind. Let the guardians know their rule over you is over, but do not punish them. Give them the city, for it is only a small part of this kingdom. Take the rest as yours and may you be a blessing to this ravaged land."

I dig out the seeds Persimony gave me from my pack. "Plant these in a fertile place and bring life back to the desert. There are fruit trees and plants that will feed you, enrich the soil, and give you shade."

"Well done, Tambrynn," Rekspire whispers to me in passing. He leads some dragons who have changed to people over to the guardians who still sleep.

Word spreads as dragons "talk" to each other, their clicks and noises becoming a drone as they separate into groups and make plans to do as I've asked.

Circe stands back from me, by Finian. "Will you still take us with you?"

"Do you want to go or do you want to stay and be an influence here?" I ask them.

She shifts her feet in the dirt. "If the guardians won't be in charge anymore, I'd like to stay and find my family." She motions to the blind outcast. "Help him find his family."

"Then I welcome you to remain." I don't tell her I'm relieved. Going to Anavrin would be too dangerous for them in their current state. "May the Kinsman bless you on your journey."

Rekspire returns to my side. "Ready to continue the search?"

"More than ready."

We travel east, away from the bone graveyard, the view of the walled city becoming smaller as we fly. I use my lizard sight, hoping to spot the Junta or Lucas somewhere along the way. Though I call out to him, there is no response. My fear becomes a shard stuck in my heart.

The dragons ride behind me toward the Zoe Tree. In the distance, a green area comes into view. It's out of place among the barren expanse. *"How is this growing here?"* I ask Rekspire.

"The doorway tree feeds from the stream in the passage, I believe. At least that's what I've come to understand since the flood. When you left, I studied some and found the kingdoms still share the same stream that flowed through the One World, which keeps the doorways valid. Should a tree die, the access to the passage would be gone."

A flicker of fear races through me. Could this door also be unusable like the one in the Aversum Way? On one hand, it would seal my father in Anavrin. On the other hand, there were many innocent people like Arrin and all the nomads who would suffer. I couldn't allow myself to think too long about it.

As we draw closer, the scent of water and plant life replaces the dusty air. Rekspire leads us above a lake in a sunken space. Water, such a rare commodity here, sparkles like a precious stone. Groupings of the strange, ringed trees and brushy grasses cover the banks.

Crabs scramble as we drop to land, scuttling into holes and beneath rocks. In front of us is a Far Starlian large ringed tree. I land beside it on the ground and change. It's sandy, but there's sharp-bladed grass growing in tufts everywhere. I've seen this grass in the Passageway. "What kind of tree is this?"

The others land near me, their gazes traveling around the area.

Rekspire is the last to change. "Frond trees. They used to grow fruit, but there haven't been any for many moons. This is where the Junta kept his nest. It's probably how the death mage happened upon him and then hexed him. He will have taken Lucas back here to get to Anavrin and his master."

"Sovereign?" Pearl, the tan dragon, digs something out of the tall weeds at the base of the Zoe Tree. She holds up an inky black feather.

Though I know the Junta must have Lucas, the bottom falls out of my stomach, and I almost drop to my knees. I brace myself against the tree, but my inner heat rises, making me dizzy.

"Lucas." I breathe out and grab the feather from her. It's soft against my cheek. My fingers are clumsy as I dig the necklace Yesenia gave me from beneath my shirt. It's worse for wear, having survived my sweaty travel. I twist the new feather into the woven strings at the center, between mine and Emberwing's feathers. A spark of heat and the string melts to the quill, securing it.

Once the shock has worn off, anger sets in. My eyes heat, and energy washes over me, covering me in a sheen of blue from head to toe. The dragons all step away from me. "My father won't take him from me. I will burn him and spread his ashes over the swamp for the Hulda to feast on if I don't destroy her first."

33

We enter the passage with no problems, though a stiff wind blows through it, shaking the leaves on trees. The grasses and plants, however, are all grayed and dead. Dried muck, mud, and debris left from the flood, lines the tree trunks and accumulates in low areas.

Though the brinicle had removed much of the dead fish, the odor remains. It's worse than the scent on the island where Anavrin's Zoe Tree was located. It's strong and burns my nose and makes me gag. "Let's get out of here. Do you remember which way to go?" I glance around, confused. It all looks the same now that the flowers and grasses are dead.

"This way." Rekspire takes the lead.

The stench makes the walk seem longer, the glowering light hurting my eyes. With nothing to absorb the brightness, it is glaring.

"What happened here?" Tourmaline asks, his nose scrunched.

"A great flood caused by a bad guy." I fill them in on a few of the details about the froggen and how they tried to take over Anavrin. I can tell by the skeptical looks they send me they don't completely believe what I tell them. "Just be aware. There are different races on Anavrin. Some may seem peculiar."

We arrive at the broken doorway. The pieces are there where I'd put them, except for one corner where Rekspire must've entered to get to Far Starl.

"Hoard, this is the doorway to the kingdom of Anavrin. It differs from Far Starl. Be on alert." I turn to Rekspire. "So, do I just bust it apart, or—"

"Do you have any of Bennett's displacement stones?" he asks.

"They were in Lucas's pack." I swing mine around to check anyway and find the leather journal. I caress the soft cover and open it to find the drawings Lucas made from the symbols on Circe's arm. "However, I can try these. The outcasts use these to disappear. It may seal it up without the stones. If I use them on this side of the entryway, maybe no one on Anavrin will destroy them. I just need something to draw with."

We search the area but come up with nothing but mud. I dismiss the idea because it will dry and flake off. "It's pointless. There's nothing we can use, and I don't want to start a fire here with all the dead plants. It would probably set the whole passage on fire and possibly kill the trees with it."

I swing my arms down in frustration and rub my wrist against the sheath. "That's it." I take the Mortifer Blade out and start at the bottom of the door's frame, carving the symbols as they are on the page and adding some detail from memory. The edge cuts through the hardened wood easily, sizzling as it does so, leaving behind a dark image burned into the grain.

Like the displacement stones, I add the symbols at equal spaces around the frame, even cutting into the ground at the base of the door to make sure it can't be accessed. When I finish, I cut my palm and place it in the center, where the doors join.

I speak from my heart, hoping my ability will be enough to fix the doorway. "Seal this door against any unwelcome hand. Set it apart so it is its own entity, guarding over both Anavrin and the passageway in equal measure. Take the broken and make it whole, as it was in the beginning."

The ground shakes, and the wind dies down. Light shines from the cracks in the door. It grows and glows until I shade my eyes from the glare.

Pop.

Thud.

I glance up, and the double doors are whole. The wood is smooth beneath my hand as I rub it to be sure of what I'm seeing. It's not just an illusion. "How can this be? I simply wanted to keep the doorway protected."

"As Bennett always said, intentions are everything and words hold power." Rekspire joins me in inspecting the doors. They gleam as if polished, not splintered from the weight of the flood. Even the black handles gleam in the radiant light.

Delight at having repaired the door is short-lived. "Let's go get Lucas."

The doors open silently to a destroyed island. Though the flood damaged the grass, and lines on the trees where water rested against the trunks show, someone dug holes everywhere. No doubt it was my father's pets. The sun is high, signaling midday, and I soak in the rays that don't scorch or bake me alive.

We quickly exit the passage. I shut the doors, pressing my still-bleeding palm to the renewed structure. With a large crack, the tree disappears from sight. And from my senses.

Three sluaghs are on us immediately, their maws bared,

and their fur bristling. Two more struggle to climb out of a hole they've been digging with their claws.

All of us change, they to their dragon forms, and me to my firebird one, before they can touch us. There's no need to disguise ourselves since we are looking for my father. With a glance back at the hill, and using my lizard sight, I view the glowing tree. However, the sluaghs stumble around the area as if the tree isn't there. They simply walk through it.

I blink. It is like the Betwixt now—there, but also not there at the same time. Assured of its safety, though not completely settled on what it might mean in the long term, I turn my beak toward the mainland. *"Do you know where Thoron is? Where can we find Lucas?"*

"The last I saw of him, he had entered the swamp to confront the witch about something. Because he distracted her, I got free." Rekspire takes the lead. *"This way is the quickest I've found."*

I admire his flight, recalling how difficult it had been for Lucas and me when we tried to change to dragons. The three other dragons follow behind us, their gazes taking in all the water and the trees, despite the carnage the flood caused. *"You never told me why you left the safety of the keep? What were you doing in the swamp?"*

I sense rather than hear his sigh. *"It is a long story. Let me attempt to make it short. The nomads showed up on the mountain, seeking refuge from the death mage. They were overtaken by your father's beasts, and I had no choice but to leave the mountain to save them. I knew you would want me to."*

He's correct. *"I would, yes. But how did they know where you were?"*

"They never said how."

The industriousness of the nomads never fails to surprise me. *"What happened then?"*

"I headed to the swamp to save the stranded in the treehouses. When we got there, Thoron was attempting to tear down the trees and burn them. That's when I met the Hulda."

"I'm sure that was a pleasant visit." I shiver, recalling my experience with the swamp witch.

"It was not. However, when she realized what the death mage was up to, she stopped torturing me to go save her swamp. I got the nomads to safety and went back to Far Starl to gather some weapons to help me fight off the beasts."

A warmth of pride fills me that he chose this path instead of staying in the keep as I'd requested. *"Did you bring any of the weapons? I didn't see you grab any?"*

"I brought you and your hoard. That's all the weapons we'll need."

We're flying above the Sunkin Forest, where Lucas and I paddled to the mainland. The water churns with fishkin. A sea of heads bobs in the dark water. Boats bearing sluaghs have them barricaded in the shallows along the hilly dropoff. It's too steep for them to climb up, with far too many limbs sticking out of the water. I grimace, recalling what might be among the debris here.

"Chosen one. Save us." The voice is Shellsea, though I cannot make out which one is her. There are too many of them with green, seaweed hair. Murmurs start when the others spot us, their voices becoming a frenzied riot. They must've been captives for a while. Bodies float on the edges of the throng, whether dead or just exhausted, is unclear.

The bank behind her is a sludgy mess, the top layer dried and peeling like old paint. Trees dangle along the eroded edge over the water, but they don't look steady. Most were ready to fall in if any creature were to climb on them. However, there's one I should be able to land on safely.

I screech and circle them. The sluaghs hiss at me. But they are captives as well, since none of them have oars, and they gathered together numerous boats like a crookedly sewn seam.

She bobs in the water, her hand raised to wave at me. I land on the most stable-looking tree. Her greenish skin is pale, and she sneers at me. "Why did you desert us?"

I change back and crouch on the limb. Her question rubs against the last patience I have. I owe her no explanation. "What is happening here?"

She hisses. "The swamp witch tricked us. She is aligned with the death mage to turn us into his beasts."

I shake my head. "That can't be right. They were fighting each other the last we knew."

Rekspire lands on a tree with exposed roots. It tips and falls with a splash along the edge of the sea. It capsizes three of the small fishing boats holding six sluaghs. The beasts go under, but only four make it back up out of the stream in a mad dash to keep afloat. However, their sloshing attempts at swimming do little to keep them from drowning.

In the mayhem, several of the fishkin use their adept swimming to push past the flailing sluaghs to get to the tree. There's not enough room for them all, and it becomes a fevered brawl. Rekspire flies back further on ground, where my hoard has settled to watch the chaos.

Only two of the overturned sluaghs remain clinging to the bottom of the overturned boat. In the turmoil, I've lost sight of Shellsea. I change and fly an arc back over the group and find her treading water farther back, away from the frantic mass.

With a thought, I'm a dragon again, and I reach down and catch the mergirl with my talons, dragging her out of the water while the others focus on swimming to shore. I let her down beside the other dragons and change back. By now a few of the waterkin have made it onto the bank.

I turn to Shellsea. "How did the Hulda trick you all?" I rub my twitchy hands on my pants, wanting to get back to my search for Lucas.

"She claimed to have our crowns." Shellsea wrings out her long, green hair. The scales along her neck reflect in the sunlight.

"Our trident too. She showed us the trident," someone yells from the gathering group near the soft edge of the bank where several climb out of the water. They trampled several as stronger merpeople climb over others to get out. All of them seem to be exhausted, however, and I wonder how long they've been held captive.

Shellsea sighs. "The trident, too, yes. Her affiliation with the death mage and a few of the lost souls made her privy to where Siltworth had hidden our treasures. She told us she was storing them in the swamp, and her ghosts guarded them for safekeeping. We had no choice but to agree to her terms. The death mage has turned several of our kind. Without our crowns, we are vulnerable."

I turn to Rekspire, who changed back into a man. "Do you think the Hulda was telling the truth? Would she have their treasures?"

"There's only one way to find out." He frowns. "Go back to the swamp."

"But we need to find Lucas." I want to stomp my foot. The Hulda needs to be dealt with, but *after* I retrieve my beloved. My nails bite into my palms. "Where'd you see Thoron last?"

A few voices answer different things.

Shellsea stands taller, a twinkle in her eyes. "Help us find our treasures. In return, we will help you with your Watcher."

I study her. She stands far enough away that I can't reach out and touch her without her moving away. We both know I can compel her to stop, but I won't. I had planned on finding their items, but too many things kept getting in the way. So, it's not exactly a bargain I'm making as much as a concession that gains me what I need. "Do you know where the death mage is?"

34

Like the passageway, the flood has changed many things. The Hevell River is muddier and wider than before. The grasses and flowers I adored are now gone, the land mired with silt and whatever else the deluge washed up. Animals are nowhere to be seen, and neither are their owners. Did they move to higher ground? Or did my father get hold of them?

That is too bleak a thought to ponder.

The farther we go north, though, the less the dead fish stench permeates everything. Some hills here are undamaged, though the farther we get from where the flood touched, the greener it gets.

This is where the land of the sluaghs begins. Groups of them roam the empty villages, forests, and meadows. When I think I spot a small animal, it is a nomad who has been turned. My heart plunges at my father's destruction.

I fly with Rekspire and the hoard, who carries Shellsea and two of the strongest of her kin, on the guardian's special-made saddles. Since the swamp is the last place anyone witnessed Thoron, we head there. The closer we get, the more I want to reject the plan. If I'm truly honest, fighting the Hulda scares me more than fighting my father, which terrifies me. She has no qualms about killing me. My father needed me to bolster his magic. He wouldn't kill me—at least not at first. That alone gives me an opportunity to defeat him.

We're on the edge of the Shadowlands near the swamp. A muted sunset glitters on the snowy tips of the lower Meridian Peaks.

Rekspire dragonspeaks to the others and guides us to a field outside a grove of large trees, where he lands and changes. Fire has touched these trees. They're charred, but the ground is wet, keeping the damage contained. My hoard lands, lets their passengers off, and then changes. I land last, exhausted from calling out to Lucas since we took flight.

There'd been no response, though a moment or two along the way I sensed something. Maddeningly brief, it could have been my imagination. A faint wisp of smoke from the fire remains in the heady air.

"We're entering the swamp witch's territory. Be on the alert. Don't follow any of the lights. And stay away from the water. There are monsters in the depths." Rekspire's lip twitches, and he glances at me.

"We'll fly in. Stay together, and if you're attacked, try to stay near our group. We're stronger together." I repeat Persimony's words, which she'd spoken to me, confident in their truth. "Shellsea, do you have any kin who can tell us about Thoron?"

She shakes her head, her seaweed hair rustling with the movement. "The Hulda expelled them after the flood and sealed her borders."

"Then we go in blind." I think of Finnian. My senses reach out, brushing past the death that permeates the soul of the swamp. Beyond that, anger and reckoning greet me in a wave of dark emotions.

A scream breaks into my mind. The Hulda is aware of us. "Saddle up. The witch is on her warpath."

I snatch the Mortifer Blade from my side and change to a firebird. Inside the cover of the trees, it's dark.

And silent.

Not a good sign. *"Lucas?"* I cry out in desperation.

Anger, pain, and fear hit me. He's injured. Afraid for me. Angry at his captor.

"He's here. Lucas is here." I try to locate where the emotion is coming from, but I don't get any kind of direction. He's close, but that's all I can tell.

My wings push me upward to get beyond the witch's reach. Moss-covered vines hang from the limbs, brushing over my feathers like a caress. And the tree houses come into view. They're hanging like flies in a spider web—vines and limbs keeping them from falling to the brackish water below.

What could have torn them from the trees? They were solid before. My mind switches to the nomads fleeing for their lives. This must be where my father and the Hulda fought.

A rip and a whoosh, and I'm in the Betwixt. Shadowy mist surrounds me.

I'm standing in my girl form on the wooden bridge alone, facing an angry Hulda. She stands atop the skulls as before in the water, not close enough to reach, but too close for comfort.

My body hums, alert to the danger. I clutch the dagger in my hand tighter.

My light reflects off her. Circles, where her eyes should be, are aglow with dark holes in the center through the hood she wears covering her skeletal head. Several spirits gather behind her on both sides.

"You insipid, stupid girl. I'll teach you for returning to the swamp. Stay out of my domain." A ball of the Hulda's shadowy magic spins toward me.

My chest throbs, the dragon's heartbeat, and her power hits my blue shield, a pressure not a pain, and flows away like water off a rock.

"What have you done?" she shrieks, her eyes flashing white. "You can't have it."

I stifle the disbelief and elation her ineffectual attack has on me. Has the dragon's heart been the thing she's been searching for the whole time? Why she was fighting Thoron in the Bloodthorn Forest and then again here, if not?

"I have the one true dragon's heart. I am the next Sovereign," I tell her, my voice raised and echoing in the spiritual realm. "Where is my Lucas?"

Her hood creases where a mouth should be, curling up in a wicked smile.

Though I don't have a necklace that heats a warning for danger, my skin prickles to alert me.

"Bring my newest soul." Her voice is a coo to her lost ones.

Four of the spirits drag a light with them to the witch. It pulses, a throbbing beat between them.

I glance back at the Hulda. She waves a bony arm over them. "I have your beloved. He's not dead yet, but he will be soon."

I prod the presence with my mind but get nothing from it.

She laughs, a menacing sound bordering on hysteria. Her shadow bobs above the skulls. "That won't work. I said he is not dead. Yet."

Realization dawns on me, and fire starts at my head and cascades down my body in a mad rush, taking my stomach with it. She wants to bargain for Lucas's life. I peer around the shadows, searching for Astralee, desperate for her help. Any help.

"Your grandmother is tied up at the moment. There is no one who will come to your aid." Her bony fingers point toward a spot on a tree. There, a light is pinned to the trunk. It juts back and forth, trying to get free, but whatever is holding it won't let go.

"Don't listen to her. Do nothing she asks, Tambrynn," Astralee calls out.

The Hulda whips her hand out, and the light held to the tree disappears. My grandmother was already dead, but could the swamp witch do something worse to her?

Anger boils over inside of me like a rage ready to kill. I hold up the Mortifer Blade. "I promise you that if you have harmed Lucas or my grandmother, I will send you from the Betwixt to meet your Kinsman for your final judgment."

Her shadow is silent and glowering. "Kill me, and you will never find him. I promise you that. All I desire is the heart that beats in your chest. It won't hurt at all. You'll still be alive. And you'll still be able to battle the death mage."

I'm aware of what she doesn't say—that I can win without the heart. It's probably what she's counting on—me getting rid of the one in her way. Icy flames break out across my hands, flashing up my arms until I'm engulfed in them. I don't fight it. I welcome the blast of winter it brings to me, cooling my rage to a white-hot intensity.

As my anger cools, I consider my options. I cannot allow her to have the heart. Her reign would be worse than my father's if she took its power. But I can't lose Lucas. That thought is too much to bear. I close my eyes, and there's only light.

Light.

Theocles, the guardian of the doorway to Hevell, once told me I hold the Kinsman's light, that my gifts hold the answers I seek. Fire might not touch her, but I know something that might. "I don't have to kill you," I tell her. In the blink of an eye, I'm back in my firebird form. I circle the Hulda and her souls like a whip, spiraling over and over, creating a funnel.

I *call* out to the Hulda, leaving her lost souls untouched, and yank her into the center of my self-made funnel. When I am low enough to touch the swamp water, it ices over, cracking as it spreads, instantly freezing the surface. *"Seal in this criminal guardian who does not do what she should, as the Kinsman requires. Do not let her leave. Do not let anyone find her."* I take my wing, which bears the Mortifer Blade, and etch the marks I'd learned from the outcasts on the solid sheet of ice in front of me. *"May you meet the Kinsman when it is time to face your judgment."*

A loud clap echoes as my words secure her fate. I'm thrown from the Betwixt back into the real world.

And then I'm falling, falling, falling.

I land with a splash of water in the swamp. Weeds and other things floating in its murky depths cling to my arms and legs, tangling and pulling, as if wanting to take me to the bottom. I open my mouth to scream, and rancid water rushes in. I choke on it.

With a thought, I'm back to my fish form. I dart about the water with ease, though it's like a meadow here, with particles and pieces of vegetation floating everywhere. The urge to get out grows, and I push to reach the surface. Finally, my head emerges from the creepy depths and I change, heaving to get rid of the disgusting fluids I'd ingested. I spit and spit, but the essence doesn't go away.

"Sovereign. Are you okay?" Terror laces Rekspire's voice in my mind. *"You were here and then you were gone. I feared the Hulda took you."*

I swim over to the low-hanging bridge and climb over the

ropes and onto the boards, my weapon still in my hand. "She did." I pant to catch my breath. "But I'm okay."

"Why are you looking at the water? Is there a threat we need to be aware of?" He hovers over me, the other dragons joining him.

"I—I stuck the Hulda in a frozen brinicle." I sheath my dagger and stand. "But it's not iced over here."

"The Betwixt is not of this world," Shellsea says, a you-should-know-that attitude to her tone. "Like the ocean is not land. They are different."

I ignore her remarks to focus on what I need to do. "She has Lucas here somewhere. He's still alive. We have to find him."

"Tambrynn?" Someone, a familiar female, calls out my name from afar.

It can't be!

35

My heart lifts in eager joy. "Arrin?" I yell back. "Where are you?"

The bridge shakes, and I grab hold to stay upright. I don't wish to fall into the water again.

"There ye are, my dear girl." She nudges the surly-looking nomad in front of her with her walking stick. No, it's not her walking stick, but one very similar to the Eye of Fate scepter. "See, ye blustering ninny, I told yeh we'd find her in time."

Nobbert frowns and shakes his head. "Yeah, but did we have to run the last few miles to do so? And what's all the dragons doing here?"

"Running? How'd you know we were here? And why are you not sheltering somewhere safe?" I let go of the rope and put my dagger back in the sheath.

"We saw ye flying, a'course. So, we raced after ye to give yeh a gift." She holds out the metal scepter, its gems gleaming in the light. It's smaller than the Eye of Fate, having silver, bronze, and gold bars making up the handle. They're woven and knotted in an intricate pattern leading to a spear-shaped head holding a misty white and blue stone. She holds it out, pride exuding from her. "Ye're dragon there told us about poor Audhild, Kinsman rest her soul. And I remembered when we were children, we used to make jewelry for the eldrin folk."

Nobbert grunts. "Before they stole our mountain away from us and kept all the gems to themselves."

"They what?" I ask, my mouth opened.

"That's right, they took our mountains from us and made them their Sanctuary." He spits out the last word like it's poison. "Started giving themselves titles and all."

"*Ach*. That was eons ago." She slaps his arm. "Legends state this stone came from the foundation of the Kinsman's palace, broken into pieces when the One World split. It's one of the few secrets we kept from them eldrin after they took over. It can help protect ye from yer enemies. If'n ye're still in need of protection, that is."

I stare at the stone. It hums with power and light. "Could it be true? Does that mean—"

"That we used to be the keepers of the holy objects? Yes." Nobbert crosses his arms over his chest defiantly. "When we was children."

Arrin leans in conspiratorially. "That's why he never learnt to read. Wasn't time for school after that." She brightens and gestures with the scepter. "Anyway, this is just a thank'ee for sending yer dragon there to help us. We'd've all been them deplorable beasts had he not helped us out."

I take it from her and examine it. "How does it work?" I ask her.

Nobbert grunts. "Point it. It protects you. That's how it works."

Arrin steps in front of him, her bare feet muddy and

tracking footprints on the boards. "It's all to do with harnessing the light energy around ye. It focuses yer abilities when ye're holding it and lessens the effects of other magic used against ye."

"Oh. Thank you so much for your gift. How did you make it so quickly?" It warms in my hand. Like the Eye of Fate, it feels like I was meant to have it.

"After we took our mountain back, them eldrin weren't using anyways. Our leadership agreed you should use it to face off with that mage." Nobbert pokes a finger at me. "Be forewarned. We're taking our property back. Even if'n you defeat that menace, we won't be moved again." He spins and heads back the way he came.

"What about your kin the eldrin captured?" I ask Arrin, concerned. I had been part of Colly's abduction, after all. And even though we freed some of the other nomads, I always kept the young girl in the back of my mind.

"They left most of the camps unattended after the death mage began hexing everyone. He left most of 'em to die in them cages as if unworthy of being touched by his magic or some such nonsense. Only a few didn't make it to safety a'fore being captured by a couple of them beasts." She shrugs and sniffs loudly.

A war rages inside me, wanting them to stay and help me while also wanting them to get out and back to safety. My wish for their safety wins. "Where are you going now?"

"Back to the mountain. We're preparing a feast for yer inevitable victory over the death mage. Be a dear and don't get yerself kilt." She waves and follows Nobbert, who is already out of sight.

I turn to my hoard, the scepter held tight in my hand. "Spread out and find Lucas. We'll meet back where we entered the swamp."

Rekspire peers at me with suspicion in his dark eyes after the others leave. "And what are you going to do?"

I take a deep breath. "I sensed something in the water when I fell in. So, I'm going back under to find out what it is."

"You think it's Lucas?" Rekspire turns serious. His hands clutch the edges of his cloak tightly.

"I don't know. It's not him I sense exactly. It was more of a presence or a will to drag me to the bottom." I rip a piece of cloth off the end of my shirt and cover the top of my head, which is now throbbing with a sunburn. Circe, I knew, would laugh at me if she were here.

Rekspire frowns. "I can't follow you there."

"Search this area for Lucas. Maybe the broken tree houses." I step over the rope and balance myself on the edge of the wooden planks.

I jump in feet first, still holding the scepter, and change to a fish as I go. Calling on my lizard sight, everything becomes brighter, there are more colors than before. Bits of wood and pieces of plants float in the water. Ahead of me, however, is a large animal crouched in the weeds along the swamp's bank. Recalling the nomad's warnings, I stay well away from it.

Pushing out my ability, I search for anything that could be an aura or a living being. I find and then go past several strange-looking shelled creatures and fish. A bird drops below the surface to capture its next meal, so I swim deeper. The water grows cooler as I descend, the surface temperature warmer than I expected.

Minutes go by and I grow used to the detritus, tree trunks, and roots that spread across the base of the murky pool. A pulse to my left prickles along my scales.

Magic.

There, among some rocks at the bottom of the lake, I glimpse a camouflaged area. The closer I get, the more the magic blares against my senses. When I am upon them and break through the illusion, there are several enormous trunks. They resemble ones I'd seen loaded onto cargo holds of ships on Tenebris. I swim over the first. It's full of odd-shaped items and small bones, which are covered with algae and lichen. They're rounded and arc-shaped.

Holding my breath, I change to pick one up and study it. The scepter glows brightly, illuminating the area. When I turn one piece a certain way, I realize it could be one of the merpeople's crowns. I dig through the top layer and find several similar items. They all hold a faint magical aura.

Without my swimsuit, I have to change back before I can do much more than that. I swim around the trunks, getting as good a look as I can. At the back of the grouping, I spot a gold radiance. I dash over to it and find a weapon akin to what the doorman in the Aversum Way held. It's more elaborate, with gems inlaid in a delicate pattern on the handle up to the tines. It is free from the sea fragments which grow on the other objects.

I change to a girl, holding my breath, and grab hold of the item. It flares, knocking me backward. My scepter glows, easing the pain. Before I can swallow swamp water or drown, I change back. Silt and grime cloud around me as I land on the marsh floor. In my hand is one piece to show the others. I swim hastily for the surface.

My head makes it above water and I change. I'm winded from swimming so hard. I climb up on the lowest portion of the walkway, dragging the scepter to rest beside me, and lay on the boards, panting.

A dragon shrieking overhead draws my attention. My hoard is in a battle with two other dragons and someone wielding magic spells from somewhere out of my sight.

My body is lit up, warning me of the danger too late.

"Chosen one." Shellsea's head bobs up from the swamp. "We are under attack." Her enormous eyes bulge. "What do you hold?" She pulls herself out of the water and faces me.

"I believe—"

She snatches the object from my hand. "Our crowns. Where did you find them?"

I'm taken aback by her tone and fierce expression. Her hands are white as she clenches the item to her chest. Her eyes grow watery, her face softening as she sobs over it. Compassion wrenches hold of me despite knowing how dangerous the fishkin can be when they are in full control of their powers. And how devious they are in twisting their bargains in their favor.

And because of that, I set most of the empathy I have for her and her kind aside. "This is the fulfillment of any agreement you might think I owe you. I claim your help in continuing my search for Lucas, if your help is warranted or necessary, and until such a time as I am satisfied. Are we agreed?"

She hisses but concedes. "Fine. Agreed. Where are our treasures?"

I point in the direction I swam. "In the center of the lake, in the deepest part. There are trunks full of them I cannot bring to the surface. I warn you of a weapon stuck in the mire that seems to guard something. Do not touch it if you value your life." I flex my hand, remembering the sting of the magic. Thankfully, I had the nomad's gift to keep me from being injured.

She dives back into the water, her entry smooth and leaving no ripple behind.

I turn back to the battle in the air. The Junta, its snakelike body whipping about in the air, attacks my Pearl.

If he's here, Lucas must be nearby. But how do I find him?

A ball of energy hits me, or my shield, and sizzles across it. Another one hits just after, and then another one. I seize the scepter and hold it tightly.

Between the blue haze of my protection sphere and the light from the scepter's stone, a dark figure lifts from the ground and floats to the boardwalk. "Daughter. You're just in time to watch me destroy this kingdom." His feet land heavily against the planks, rattling them, making me teeter before I catch my balance. His cloak whips behind him, the force of his magic snapping it like wind. Power rolls off him, blackening his already malevolent aura. "Where did you get that weapon?"

Anger boils inside my gut. "That is none of your concern." I grab the Mortifer Blade, though I don't use it threateningly. Yet. "Where is Lucas? What have you done with him?"

He smiles, danger glinting from eyes that whorl black and red, reminding me of the Hulda. He's no longer slim, his body bulges with the power he's stolen from dragons. "I could say that is none of your business, though it truly is. But no matter the weapons you bear, nothing you have can stop me now."

A screech from the air makes me cringe. Though I have several in my hoard, the hexed Junta is holding his own. I don't dare take my eyes off my father, so I stare at him instead of checking on the welfare of my hoard. I grip my blade and the scepter to keep me focused on the real threat.

My father snaps his fingers.

I narrow my eyes at him, waiting for whatever he is about to do or say. Nothing happens right away. A moment or two later, however, and the water beneath the bridge swells. Bubbles erupt, and with them comes the muted screams of fishkin. My heart races. Shellsea went down. Could it be the treasures came to the surface? If so, what is his game?

I don't wish to show my father any sign of weakness, but with the rise of the water, I'm forced backward and must grab hold of the rope for balance. It's enough to widen his grin. His gaze never leaves me, his face twisting with malicious delight.

"Sovereign, be careful. They are guarding a weapon of some kind." Rekspire's warning is stilted by his fighting. A couple of sluagh dragons I hadn't noticed before join in the fray. They fly around my group, their flight bumbling, but effective, in keeping my dragons from reaching me.

Light glows beneath the surface as something arises. I'm forced to stand, awaiting my father's next move.

A flicker of light in the corner of my eye startles me. It flies into my chest and is gone before I can verify it was there. I wish Lucas were here to be my eyes and ears. Emotions threaten to overtake me and I brace to fight them off. I can't think about him at this moment.

"You wish to have your Watcher back?" My father's voice deepens. The water parts to reveal a clear cage. It floats. What's inside is obscured because it's fogged over. Its glass surface holds etched, golden symbols carved into the smooth surface. The edges reflect the moonlight.

My sight switches to a lizard's, and the etchings glow with dark magic. I can also make out the shape of a person inside the casket-sized box. I can't sense what's inside, possibly because of the spells on the outside. They resemble the outcasts' marks, only these are beautiful, not scrawled like the ones on Finnian and Circe's bodies.

The box spins, tossing the contents of the box around. I catch sight of bones that clunk around like loose twigs. Then a hand as if a person is there as well and is trying to brace themselves.

"I tire of these games. Who is inside your lovely container?"

Another light flickers at the edges of my perception. I twist slightly to gain sight of what it is, but it's gone.

Pixies? I hadn't seen any since I'd returned to the swamp.

"It's not one who, but two. One is still alive, and one is long dead. Both of them are important to you." His laugh is forced. "Come, my pet. Let's see who she chooses." He flings his arm out, sending a flash into the trees.

A figure drops from the limbs, the body crashing to the walkway with a crunch. Worn, eldrin clothing hangs from the body. They turn their head toward me.

I stagger backward, recognizing Grandfather. Wounds cover the parts of his body I can see. They weep through his clothes. One of his arms is broken and bent at an awkward angle.

The familiar buzz of my abilities expands until my whole body vibrates with fury. Though I know my father to be cruel, and nothing should surprise me, seeing my grandfather treated so badly shocks me. My eyes burn, and ice accumulates in my veins.

"Get up," Thoron orders him.

Grandfather jerks at his order. He takes a minute to stand. I try to reach out with my mind, hoping I can connect with him, maybe free him somehow, before my father tries to use him any further against me.

"*Tut, tut.* None of that." Thoron flicks his fingers at me, and I squeal from pain that bursts against my temples. "No cheating, daughter dearest."

I blink away the moisture from my eyes as the pain recedes.

"You have a choice to make."

I glare hate at him. "What choice are you talking about?" I can't help the frustration that's reflected in my tone.

"An exchange. You give me the dragon's heart, which was rightfully mine before that idiot stole it from me. In return, I'll give you back either your grandfather." He waves at the sluagh who shrinks back from his attention. "The pathetic hoard you've gathered." He flings his arm upward where both our dragon armies battle. "Or your Watcher." He motions toward the glass case.

36

My heart stops beating. My mind goes blank. I have the odd sensation of standing outside of myself. Light from the scepter radiates down the handle and into my hands, clearing my mind. I close my eyes and absorb the calming effect before opening them again to take in what's going on.

I'm still unable to view inside the glass container, but though my father is evil, I don't sense a lie in his words. Lucas's long fingers splay again against the side of the glass. His fists hit it as if he's trying to get out. Probably panicking.

Something inside me snaps, and my vision becomes a haze. I don't recall his question now. The only thing that registers in my mind is that Lucas is being held in a glass coffin while still alive.

Without moving, I send out a blast of ice shards toward my father. "Release Lucas." I scream at him, my anger and the scepter expanding the frozen knives to the size of swords.

I catch him surprised, for he's hit in several spots before he rallies and knocks the rest aside. Blood oozes out of several cuts. He shrieks in fury. Any façade Thoron had of civility crumbles as he sends a dark, thunderous cloud my way. I swing my arms in front of me to hold my shield in place. The force of his blow strikes, but thanks to the nomad's gift, my protection remains intact.

I change to my firebird form and race toward him, swinging to bear my talons as I get close. I knock him backward, though he remains uninjured when I arc back around for another attack.

"So be it, Daughter. None will be saved from my wrath. Not even you." Thoron sends a throbbing pulse of magic toward the glass casket.

Before the magic can hit the container, it is yanked down and out of danger. With my lizard sight, I spot several fishkin dragging the box down, their crowns in place on their heads.

I don't have time to rejoice as Grandfather attacks me, his beastly hands at my throat.

My wings make me unable to grab or stop him—he's too close for them to be effective. I try to change, but I can't with him strangling me. *"Grandfather."* My mind pleads to him. *"I know you're in there still. Fight him. Please. I can't let him have the true dragon's heart."* I send images of him to his mind, beating against my father's connection. It's frayed and not nearly as strong as Nyle's had been. It burns in my grip, but I send ice and then heat into it, praying it will be enough to sever the hold Thoron has on him.

"You have to kill him." Grandfather's words are weak, but they're there. *"To release me, all of us, he has to die."*

"But, how? How do I kill him?"

"With. Your. Light." Grandfather's voice tapers off until it's gone.

What light? The scepter? Or the dragon's heart? Both of them are brilliant in their glow.

Grandfather's grip has slackened, so I change back to my

girl form. As soon as I do, I'm being strangled by him again. I dig my fingers in, cracking the bones at his wrists, hating myself as I do it.

To my joy and dismay, it works. I'm freed. Now broken, his hands fall from my neck. He staggers, moving sideways into the ropes. I reach for him, dropping the scepter, but cannot catch him before he topples into the water and away from me.

Another blast of dark magic hits me. This time I know the prick of its intent—death. I fall to the boards and reach for the scepter. "Kill me, and you never get this heart. I promise you that."

I'd die first.

And I'm hit with another spell from above, like a swarm of gnats I hadn't seen hovering over my head. Darkness descends on me, seeping past my shield. It breaks, and I'm left only with the scepter's shell-like safety. Pressure continues, and slowly, that shatters as well. The scepter throbs one last time, but it's no use. Evil surrounds me. I'm repulsed by the wickedness that creeps into my pores, but I can't move, can't fight back.

A searing ball of energy grabs me, wrapping around me. It rips at my soul, tearing me apart piece by harrowing piece. Stabs of pain turn into an explosion until it's all I feel.

Numbness replaces the pain, and I drop the dagger and the scepter from unfeeling hands. My lungs shrivel, and any air I get is like daggers raking across my chest. My gasp is torture, and I close my eyes against the agony.

In the darkness, there's a tether similar to the one Nyle had around him. It's not a rope, but more akin to shackles across my wrists and ankles. Black tendrils from them creep across my body. They're reaching for the light inside me. No, for the dragon's heart. It still beats, although my heart has stopped beating.

"No." I scream into the emptiness. But no sound comes out.

The first despicable coil touches my chest and the darkness shifts, sucking me in.

No, it's sucking my spirit from me. It's a different torment, an excruciating raw defilement of my soul.

Again and again, I scream nothingness into the void, silently praying for the Kinsman to help me—save me. But it keeps going. On and on, it goes.

The power severs my memories from my mind. He consumes the love I had for Lucas, Grandfather, Audhild, and Mother. He's destroying everything that I consider my true self completely. Every good thing I've ever known has left me. Only bleak and wretched things remain. My are eyes forever opened to the darkness that is my father's spirit. I witness all the bindings he has to everyone he's cursed. Waning light comes from the center of what I used to be—the power he's siphoning from me. New, stronger chains fall into place upon me and my dragon hoard. They're falling without me to support them.

My father is turning all of us into his beasts.

I've failed.

I glance at the water, where the glass coffin was, but there are only cords disappearing into the murky swamp.

Lucas.

I can't fail him too.

Radiant light hovers before my face.

It's Astralee, and she holds a luminous ball. *"You can do this, Granddaughter. The Kinsman doesn't make mistakes. He created you with the power to defeat your father."* She stuffs the ball down my throat. *"Use the gifts he gave you. Don't give in to Thoron's power."*

And as if my eyes were clouded over before, my sight clears. Then it hits me what I must do. To save us all, I have to give it all up. Everything.

Thoron screams at Astralee. He tries to capture her before her light winks out and disappears, making his hold on me waver. At that moment, I'm able to get free. I have little strength left, so I use the waning power of the scepter to fuel my change. Silver scaled feathers cover my body once more, and I'm flying directly at my father. From my gut, I dig out every ounce of energy, all the gifts I have left to defeat him.

I pick him up by the waist with my talons. He reaches out to grab me but gets my crown of feathers instead. Flames ignite and Thoron stiffens with the shock. He screams curses into the air, but as soon as they hit me, my ability freezes them and they fall away like chips off an ice block.

Our bodies spin, flames and ice mixed together in a whirlwind of hot and cold. I change back mid-flight and embrace my father, holding him face to face. Though I am in my girl form, my wings remain, holding us suspended between the earth and the sky. The light from the scepter and what remains of the dragon's heart in my chest glow around us in a dazzling flash. "Your reign is finished, Thoron. Death you wanted, and death you shall get."

I *call* on the essence of magic within Thoron, some of which is my own that he stole. Most of which is dark and tainted. He thrashes to no avail. His energy fills me, and as it does so, it becomes glorious instead of cursed. The noxious blend of death and hate spins around like the brinicle, changing, changing.

I'm overwhelmed with the reserves of magic my father held. How many dragons have fueled him, I don't know, but it's gorging, every particle humming with the energy. The brinicle around us grows until I'm not using my wings to hold us up. We've become part of the tempest. I drag every particle of my father's power that I can, changing it as it flows into me. When I'm finished, I breathe it back into my father.

The brilliance coming from me burns brighter and brighter, turning my crystalline frost into an inferno, but I'm not overtaken. I accept the choice I make to sacrifice myself and allow the regeneration to fully take me. In doing so, I let it take my father too.

Thoron's all-black eyes widen and he opens his mouth in a wordless scream. As the light flows into him, his eyes become clearer until they turn back to normal-looking eyes—a shade of light hazel. The shadows that had surrounded his aura wisp away and are gone. Soon, there is nothing left to send into him. I'm empty, depleted of everything.

But my father is filled.

Light silently explodes from him, separating us.

There is no darkness.

But there is nothingness.

———

I awaken to the ruby light of a sunset shining down on my face. I move to sit up and realize I'm covered with limbs and leaves. The air is heavy with the scent of marsh and bogs, muck and water.

"She's awake," a familiar voice yells out. I can't place who they are.

I rub my head and find stubble instead of hair. "What?"

A hand grabs my arm, holding it away from my bald head. I glance up. A handsome man is smiling down at me. "It will grow back more beautiful than it was before." He threads his fingers through mine, and though I'm unsure, I let him do it.

"Do you remember what happened?" Another voice, kind and older, speaks from behind the first, dark-haired man. He suddenly comes into view behind the first man. He isn't handsome. Cuts and wounds mar his face, and his skin is stretched tightly across his skull. His eyes are clear, but he's gaunt, as if he's been ill.

"No." It's all I can say. My head hurts, and I'm so disoriented. Thoughts flow like sludge through my mind. What is going on?

"Here it is. I found it in one of the treehouses. It's probably small, but hopefully will cover what needs covering." A green-skinned woman hands the first man a bundle of flowered fabric. I blink at the silvery-edged scales that cover her body. Bushy eyebrows pucker over her bulbous eyes. "Is she okay?"

I draw back. Who are all these strange people? I try to shift away, but the first man holds me in a firm grasp. "Shellsea, could you assist her?"

The green girl sighs loudly. "If I must, but it is beyond any deal we've made."

"Could you do it out of the goodness of your heart?" the second man asks, an unreadable expression on his face. "What's left of it, anyway?"

She clicks her tongue at him. "Since she saved us all."

The men turn and walk off toward a grouping of large trees. I watch them go, confused.

Shellsea takes my hand. Hers is cold and damp, and she lifts me to stand. Instead of clothes, I'm covered from my neck to my ankles with singed silver feathers. I brush at my arm, but they don't fall away, and they're not soft like feathers. They're tough like rough hide.

"What is this?" I ask.

"They're your feathers. Like my scales." She moves her strange, leaf-like hair back to show me her neck where greenish-gold scales reflect the sun. Shocked, I try to move away from her, but she jerks one of my legs up and puts it inside the flowered dress she carries. "Now put your other feathered leg in."

I almost topple over but end up putting a hand on her head to get my other leg inserted into the dress. Her hair is moist, the strands hanging down to her back. I wipe my palm down the dress after we get my arms through the armholes.

The fabric comes to mid-thigh and is tight. "Is this mine?"

She breathes out, exasperated. "No. Does it look your size? It's a nomad's dress."

I don't know what a nomad is, but she doesn't seem inclined to want to answer questions, so I don't ask. I just want to—I hesitate.

Do what? I'm not even sure what I want to do or where I want to go instead of being here. I rub my temples where a headache wants to bloom and cringe at the smoothness.

What happened to my hair? I run my hand over my skull, but there's not a shred of it anywhere. Did I not have any hair?

The men walk back over. Several others accompany them. All of them are haggard, their clothes ripped and torn. Some have open wounds and marks on them.

The first man smiles at me. "I know you have a lot of questions. Let me try something first." He takes my hand and then snatches a dagger from the ground. In a swift motion, he slices it through the air.

And we're not at the edge of the trees any longer. This place is eerie and full of shadows. I yank against his hand, wanting to flee, run, and hide. He doesn't let me go.

"Astralee?" he calls out.

A hooded ghost drifts over to us, her feet not touching the ground. She glows like the moon.

My heart pounds heavy in my chest. "What is that?" I glance around, but there's nowhere to hide. The man's hold is steady, and though I yank, I can't get free.

"I am your grandmother. Why have you entered the Betwixt?" she asks, though her voice is in my head, not my ears.

My grandmother? "Not possible." I don't mean to say it, but it comes out anyway. The air is heavy with the weight of the specter's gaze, though she's unseen behind a shroud of gray mist.

"Tambrynn used a phoenix regeneration to kill Thoron." He lifts my arm. "See her feathers? When we were on Benario Vale, the phoenix breathed fire on her, and she remembered herself. Is there anything you can do to bring her memories back?" He leads me closer to the figure, but I lean away.

"Possibly. Do you have something of hers I can use?"

He hands her the dagger.

My eyes bulge. What's she going to do to me with that? I struggle full-on against the man's hold, but he's strong and using both hands now. And I'm weak.

"A talisman? That should work. Tambrynn, this will not hurt," the woman says.

The instant the dagger touches my head, memories flood through me.

Lucas. My father. The kingdoms. The dragons. And the battle at the end.

I stop struggling against Lucas. "Lucas?" Joy bursts from my heart, and I'm sobbing in his arms. "How? How did you survive the glass coffin?"

He holds me tightly, patiently waiting out the onslaught of my weeping. "I wasn't alone. Your grandmother was there with me, in spirit, anyway. The glass box was what Thoron buried her in. When the Junta brought me to your father, he put me inside with her bones. I think he fully intended to let me die in there. But he didn't realize that after you removed the Hulda from her position, another would replace her. One that would rule the lost souls with the compassion they deserve."

I open my mouth wide in surprise and stare at the misty figure. "You?"

Astralee's light beams. "The Kinsman works in mysterious ways. I accepted his request when he came to retrieve the Hulda. I will not misuse my position like she did." Her form hovers over the steaming swamp waters. There are no skulls for her to walk upon and no ghostly army behind her. All is calm and peaceful in the Betwixt now.

"I'm glad," I tell her. I realize then that I wear a silver tunic and pants, the color of my feathers and fine as silk, though my feet are bare.

Astralee interrupts my thoughts with a light touch on my head. "What a shame to lose your lovely silver hair. But you cannot stay here long or you'll be forever a part of the Betwixt. I believe you remember, it's not for the living."

Sadness flickers to life inside me, both for losing my hair and for having to leave so soon. "Will I see you again?"

"If you battle another death mage, I'll be there to help in any way I can."

I catch the humor in her voice. It's a significant improvement from the sadness I'd experienced from her before. "Thank you for taking care of Lucas."

"He was lost. How could I not?" Her image wavers. "Goodbye, dearest ones. May the Kinsman bless your paths."

And then she is gone, and we are back in Anavrin.

Eager faces await our return. More faces than I recognize. None of the sluaghs remain. They've all returned to their former selves. They mingle with my hoard and the fishkin.

I take Lucas's hand in mine. "I can't believe he's gone. What happened to my father's body?"

Rekspire steps up to answer. "He perished in your fire. You both were there in a violent, swirling storm. Then there came a flashing light, and when it was gone, only you, resplendent in your silver feathers, remained."

I swipe at the dampness gathering in my eyes.

Grandfather squeezes my shoulder.

I gape at him. "Your wrists. You're alive."

He chuckles.

"How?" Though his face is battered, his ears, nose, and mouth are no longer monster-ish. And his wrists aren't broken or bound. "You're healed?"

"We all were once you destroyed Thoron. It's all thanks to you, Granddaughter. Light unto darkness and all that. I'm very proud of you." His smile creases his normal, handsome face.

My thoughts turn to my father. A strange desolation hits me. "I know it had to end that way. I don't know why I'm so sad that it did."

Lucas hugs me. "Because you're not evil. You have the heart of a true dragon."

EPILOGUE—TWO YEARS LATER

A watery sun allows for dim light to shine upon where I stand in Taborfield's town square. Before me is a series of wooden stocks where indentured servants are bought and sold. I'm disguised as the Head Housekeeper of Lowborn Manor—a place built in honor of the treehouse city that my father destroyed. A dozen women and children are bound to posts as they await their fate. Far too many people for my liking gather around to bid on them.

After the battle in the swamp, we tore apart the eldrin hierarchy. As I'd done with the clans on Benario Vale, we replaced it with a Common Council where each race gets a seat and a voice. Even Nobbert liked the plan. Now, I vow to do the same here on Tenebris. But first I need to upend their system of indentureship—one servant at a time.

The gavel rings out, another person purchased. I grin. Nellie, now ten years old, is unshackled and handed over to a seemingly normal-looking land agent. Short and stout, with excess sideburns, my husband's disguise is so good that I have to look twice to be sure he is indeed Lucas. It took us months to find her, and a few shenanigans to get her tossed out of her last employment so we could buy her freedom. Hopefully, she will understand when I tell her what we did.

I make two more bids. First for twin sisters who look scared out of their minds, and, of course, want to stay together. I also bid on an aging woman who shouldn't have to work at this stage in her life. I wonder what she did to earn her indentureship and realize it's probably because of debts instead of crimes. No matter the cause, she'll find a home with us.

Arrin, of course, led the call for freed nomads to come to Tenebris. She is our real Head Housekeeper with Nobbert as the Farm Manager. I was surprised by how well the nomads took to the non-magical atmosphere of Tenebris. Not only they, but the trellers as well, have found a home among Tenebris's surly residents. We now have contacts in lumber, shipping, and manufactories on this kingdom. It is only a matter of time to change the way things are done and bring a better, more fair system into play.

We agreed to let a couple of the more fit servants slip through to other bidders—we don't want to arouse any suspicion until our plan plays out. My only consolation is that eventually there won't be any more indentured anything. In the meantime, the nomads and trellers have built a "grand palace" as they call our sprawling manor, along with a school to teach the children. Lucas, of course, will teach them as Madrigal had taught him.

The land came cheap since resources are abundant on Anavrin and Benario Vale, where we trade now. Labor there is cheaper since we reopened the Zoe Tree on Anavrin. It's open for regulated travel, something Grandfather instituted with a system of rotating missions. Anyone can apply. The only stipulation is that they work as they learn and earn a degree.

When they achieve their degree, they are free to own property on Anavrin relevant to their participation.

The bidding done, I sign the official papers, hand over the money, and lead my ragtag group over to where Areli's sleigh awaits us, disguised as a coach and two leads. The way the deer stags impatiently stomp only helps the illusion of a fine set of horses.

"How'd the bidding go?" she asks from her seat at the head of the sleigh.

"Better than I hoped." I drop a set of stairs Zenek had created for the nomads to enter the tall sled. I found he is a master carpenter. It is by his hand we filled our small village's furnishings and traded with fine gems out of Anavrin's mountains.

I help the old woman inside and pray silently that her heart will hold up for the trip. She sits opposite the twins, who huddle together in a corner of the bench seat. I settle in next to the woman, maintaining my disguise. Areli slaps the reins, and the sled takes off, startling the others with the speed. I almost smile, but I remember my first ride in this contraption and the sheer terror I experienced.

"Hold on," I tell them as I grab hold of the seat, knowing that though Areli is fond of keeping her passengers on their toes, she would let no harm come to them. I'm grateful when I notice the old woman is not as uncomfortable as I thought she would be. She holds on tightly and shows no sign of alarm.

We speed to meet Lucas beside the Fountain of Wishes on the other side of the square. There, Lucas and his group enter the sleigh, filling it up. I toss several coins into the fountain, recalling the monies he stole for us during the Spaw Ball.

He and I wait for the others to get settled and signal to Areli to leave, then we change to common blackbirds where no one can witness us and follow along behind.

The trip to Lowborn takes longer than two days, and we guard our passengers when Areli stops along the way to let them stretch and take care of their personal needs. None of them are aware of what's happening, nor do they suspect anything.

At the last stop of the journey, Lucas and I join them back inside the sleigh. We don't wear disguises, and no one questions our sudden appearance. It's not surprising. I've found people see much of what they're trained to and ignore the rest. And servants on Anavrin are trained not to notice or say anything that would lead to trouble. Even the youngest twin girls don't so much as look at us.

We round the hill toward Lowborn's small village with its barns and freshly tilled acres. Honey robinia trees line the driveway. They were a gift from Persimony and Zenek brought from Benario Vale. Anavrinian flowers grow unhindered along the fence milled by the trellers. A fountain splashes at the center of the yard that Neldrick maintains. He, a former Far Starlian thief turned plumber, is well on his way to earning a farming degree. Debbert, Nobbert's brother, works at clearing out stones along a ditch at the edge of the forest Mother and I used to pick mushrooms in.

The sight is one I've always longed to see—people living in harmony with one another. My greatest achievement to date.

I stand and clear my throat. "Your attention, please. I am Tambrynn, and this is my husband, Lucas. We have arrived at Lowborn Manor."

The group finally looks up to view the grand expanse. Pride in what we've accomplished makes me smile at their astonished expressions. It is a departure from what they're used to—from what anyone on Tenebris is used to.

"Tambrynn?" Nellie says, disbelief making her voice quiver. "From Broodmoor Estate? I thought you dead." Her eyes are wide and her hands shake as she clutches her small, beatup carpetbag.

"You're not seeing ghosts, Nellie. I'm very much alive. And this is not your new employment— Lowborn is your new home." I spread my arms wide. "As of this day, you're free."

ABOUT THE AUTHOR

Winner of the 2016 ACFW Genesis Award and finalist in the 2018 Grace Award and the 2020 Great Expectations Contest, Dawn has been recognized for her published and non-published works. Her flash fiction stories have been published in *Havok* magazine under both her real name and pen name, Jo Wonderly. Her debut novel, *Knee-high Lies*, was published in 2017.

As a child, Dawn often had her head in the clouds creating scenes and stories for anything and everything she came across. She believed there was magic everywhere, a sentiment she has never outgrown. Nature inspires her, and her love for the underdog and the unlikely hero colors much of what she writes.

Dawn adores anything Steampunk, is often distracted by

shiny, pretty things, and her obsession with purses and shoes borders on hoarding. Dawn lives in Iowa and helps her husband run their foodservice and catering business out of Omaha, Nebraska. When not reading, writing, or catering, Dawn loves babysitting her grandchildren, is parent to Snickers the Wonder Beagle, and can usually be caught daydreaming.

The Girl with Stars in Her Eyes

Firebird Series—Book One

Eighteen-year-old servant girl Tambrynn is haunted by more than her unusual silver hair and the star-shaped pupils in her eyes. Her uncontrollable ability to call objects leads the wolves who savagely murdered her mother right to her door.

When she's fired and outcast during a snowstorm, her carriage wrecks and she's forced to find refuge in an abandoned cottage. There, her life is upended when the magpie who's stalked her for ten years transforms into a man, Lucas. He's her Watcher and they're from a different kingdom. His job is to keep her safe from her father, an evil mage, who wants to steal her abilities, turn her into one of his undead beasts, and become immortal himself.

Can they make it to the magical passageway and get to their home kingdom in time for Tambrynn to thwart her father's malicious plans? Or will Tambrynn's unique magic doom them all?

Get your copy here:

https://scrivenings.link/thegirlwithstarsinhereyes

———

The Girl with Fire in Her Veins

Firebird Series—Book Two

Former servant girl Tambrynn struggles with her new firebird abilities, especially the internal fire she cannot control. So, she, along with her Watcher Lucas and her grandfather Bennett, journey to a hidden mountain keep to find the answers she seeks before she sets the kingdom aflame.

But there's a new dragon who's targeting Tambrynn, a mergirl who wishes to manipulate her, and the froggen king, Siltworth, who hasn't forgotten that Tambrynn destroyed his watery reign. When her father, the evil mage Thoron, attacks someone she loves,

Tambrynn's group is separated and she has to face another powerful foe alone.

Is she strong enough to withstand the deluge? Or will she drown in the fire and the flood?

Get your copy here:

https://scrivenings.link/thegirlwithfireinherveins

ALSO BY DAWN FORD

Woodencloak by Dawn Ford

The Band of Unlikely Heroes - Book One

Thirteen-year-old troll princess Horra Fyd's life changes forever after an unexpected visit from the fairy queen and her two daughters. Tales of fairies gave Horra nightmares as a young troll. Before evening falls, however, a real nightmare unfolds. Horra's father, King Fyd, goes missing. Her woodgoblin instructor is poisoned and uses his magic to revert to a seed. And a mysterious, gaunt man wearing a cape and playing a panflute joins the fairies in trying to capture her.

Horra flees but is instantly lost in a world she's never had to travel alone. A letter hidden in her knapsack from her late instructor informs her that a power hungry Erlking seeks revenge against her kingdom and their allies for a two-generation old war. She is tasked with getting his seed to the Weald, a magical forest. There it can regenerate into a druid, the only creature with the power to hold the balance between good and evil, and who is able to defeat the Erlking.

However, the Erlking is always one step behind her. Horra must fight to protect herself, but she has no magic. She accepts a gift from a dead druid spirit of a charmed woodencloak to disguise her. But magic failed her mother, how can she possibly trust it?

Can Horra have faith and courage enough to trust a power she can't see, and become a warrior heroine her foremothers can be proud of? Or will she allow fear to rule over her and lose everything that matters—including her life?

Get your copy here:

https://scrivenings.link/woodencloak

———

Mossycoat by Dawn Ford

The Band of Unlikely Heroes - Book Two

Troll Princess Horra Fyd may have succeeded in getting the druid seed to the magical Weald forest in time to sprout, but she's finding that getting her kingdom back in order is not as easy as she hoped. Oddar's subjects are rebelling and trolls are mysteriously disappearing without a trace. Horra and her father King Divitri are at a loss on what's happening, but they know who's behind it all.

When Horra's summoned back to the Weald to meet Rowan, the new druid warrior, she finds the woodgoblin a know-it-all stick in the mud. Rowan's not impressed with the troll princess, either. However, after a suspicious magical fire destroys the Weald, they're forced to rely on each other to venture out in a kingdom that's becoming more dangerous by the day.

Will Horra and Rowan be able to set their differences aside to become a strong team? Or will they fall into the Erlking's traps, stopping their mission before it even gets started?

Available July 9, 2024

https://scrivenings.link/mossycoat